The Dancing Ghosts

The Flintlock Sagas

Book 3

THE DANCING GHOSTS

WRITTEN BY

ALAN W. HARRIS

~ ~ ~ † ~ ~ ~

Fruitful Tree Publishing
Luray, Virginia 22835

This book is published by:

Fruitful Tree Publishing

321 Camelot Court

Luray, Virginia 22835

www.StoriesChangeHearts.com

This book is lovingly dedicated to all those individuals and families who appreciate a story that exalts Jesus Christ.

May His name be exalted in this one!

CONTENTS

PREFACE

Can you imagine life without good stories? I can't. The gift of being able to tell a good story I believe comes from God. The reason I believe that is because God and His Son Jesus use stories so often in the Bible. An interesting tale well told can change a person's life and soften a hard heart. I've heard it said that the person who tells the best stories changes the culture. If that's true then we in this country are in desperate need for some really good ones. For a number of years I have been asking God to direct me to write adventures that would draw people's hearts to Him. I have been faithful to record what I believe He has given me. It is up to my readers to decide their benefit.

Writing this third story in the Flintlock Sagas Series has been enjoyable, because it afforded me the opportunity to renew some old friendships from the first two books. It was especially satisfying to discover what happened to Susanna, Rebecca and Ember. I am always amazed at God's faithfulness and love even when we don't deserve it. It's important to note that as you read this book it is clear that our bad attitudes and actions don't determine how God feels about you. The scripture says that when we were at our very worst Christ died for our sins (Romans 5:8). God also says that

He is not willing that any should perish but that all should come to repentance (2 Peter3:9).

One of the important lessons that I hope my readers draw from this story is that it doesn't matter how hopeless your situation may seem, Jesus is always available for you and in Him there is always hope.

As in all of my books, each chapter has opportunities for parents and teachers to use the chapter questions in Appendix A to teach important scriptural and character lessons to your listeners and readers. I hope you will avail yourself of this resource since lessons taught while using an exciting story are lessons that go straight into long-term memory. You can read a lot more detail about this very exciting teaching principle at *StoriesChangeHearts.com*.

And don't worry, I've tried to include enough, fun, excitement, and adventure to keep you turning pages.

Before I end, I want to thank my wonderful wife, Valerie for all of her help with editing and suggestions, without which the book would not be readable.

May God's richest blessings be to each of you!

Alan W. Harris
Luray, Virginia,
September 21, 2021

Chapter One

UNEXPECTED DANGERS

Leaves crunched underfoot as three figures strode through the ancient Kentucky forest. A warning hissed, and all froze in place. With eyes searching, each ear strained to detect any unnatural sound.

The warm sunlight on the early summer day filtered through the green canopy, and with the light breeze wafting past the trunks of the giant trees, it made for pleasant hiking. Looking westward, the land dropped down to the banks of a wide green river that snaked its slow way to the south. To the east, between huge trunks of oaks and hickories, were glimpses of a verdant meadow.

Suddenly a deer sprang from a nearby thicket and bounded away. Each traveler breathed a collective sigh of relief. Two young women looked at the scout who had sounded the caution. His nod gave permission to resume the march.

As they continued their trek, the silence was broken by one of the women. "I really appreciate both of you coming with me." The speaker was Remember Warren, a dark-haired, brown-eyed, nineteen-year-old young woman. She wore a long buckskin shirt that came almost to her knees, and pants made of the same material covered her legs. Her shirt was belted around her narrow waist, and a sheath and hunting knife hung from the belt on her right hip. An interesting accompaniment to her wardrobe was a long, woven, leather sling tied around her waist. A deer skin pouch suspended from a strap around the girl's neck bounced against her left hip, and she carried a woven grass basket in her right hand.

"It's a beautiful day, Ember, and Asa and I are happy to join you," Katherine Middlebrook returned with a slight nervousness in her voice, "but I had no idea we would be traveling so far from Larkinboro." Nineteen-year-old Katherine wore a faded yellow work dress that came to her ankles, and she also carried a basket.

"We haven't walked *that* far, have we?" Ember, as her friends called her, asked off-handedly.

"You've led us north of the fort for almost two hours," Asa Whitlock answered from behind the girls. The twenty-year-old scout wore buckskins with a knife on his right hip and a steel-headed tomahawk in his belt. He carried a long-barreled Kentucky rifle with a powder horn, and an ammunition pouch was slung around his neck and hanging at his left side.

"Has it really been two hours?" Ember asked with surprise as she turned and look at the scout, who nodded his answer.

"Can you get us back home, Asa?" Katherine asked.

"Oh sure, I can get us back to Larkinboro, but I don't think it would be wise to travel much further north."

"Okay," Ember agreed. "I came this far because I couldn't find the plants that I need closer to the fort."

"Tell me again what we're looking for?" Katherine asked as she cautiously searched the forest around them.

"Spiked blazing star and goldenseal," Ember answered. "I've had to treat so many with sickness recently that I'm about to run out."

"We've really been blessed to have you at Larkinboro," Katherine said sincerely as Asa eagerly nodded his agreement. "You know so much about healing and caring for sicknesses and injuries."

"When I was a slave to the Shawnee, my mistress was the finest medicine woman in the tribe," Ember returned with a slight smile. "Jesus had me in a place where I could learn from the best.

"Okay, here's what let's do," Ember announced to her friends. "Katherine and I will walk to that meadow that we can see to the east. That's a great place to look for spiked blazing star plants. Asa, do you know what goldenseal looks like?"

"Not really," the scout returned honestly.

"All right," Ember returned, "forget the goldenseal. You go west, down the hill to the river bank, and look for blue clay. I need that for poultices."

"But how will I recognize it?"

At this statement both girls turned and stared at each other. Finally Katherine gave a sigh and said, "Asa...it's blue."

After a thoughtful pause the young scout grinned sheepishly and gave a nod. He started to turn toward the river but was stopped by Ember's voice. "If Kate and I find the herbs in the meadow, then we will slowly head through the woods towards the river searching for goldenseal. We'll meet you there when we're ready to head back home."

"Okay," Asa agreed reluctantly, "but if you need me, call loudly."

It only took Ember and Katherine a few minutes to walk to the open grassland. As soon as they stepped into the sunlight, the medicine girl gave a gasp of happy surprise. "Look, Kate! All those tall purple flowers are spiked blazing stars!"

"There sure are a lot of them," Katherine answered. "You should be able to get all you want here."

Ember whipped out her knife and began to dig up a plant. As soon as the roots were in her hands, the young healer cut off the top of the plant and dropped the roots into her basket. "It's really just the roots that I need," she said, looking at Kate.

With a nod her friend set down her carrier and, from the bottom, lifted out a long knife that she used to dig up the spiked blazing stars around her. Once acquired, the coveted roots were added to her collection. In less than an hour, the girls had both baskets half full.

"That should be enough," Ember announced as she studied the gathered roots. "Now let's head toward the river and see if we can find goldenseal."

The maidens had nearly reached the place where they had separated from Asa when a nearby scratching noise made them both freeze in their tracks. They looked around, trying to find the source of the sound, when suddenly a loud, terrifying squawking began, which caused both girls to jump. It was coming from above. Scanning the tree tops, they spotted the source of the racket. A large cougar had climbed an oak and was attacking an owl it had found in the hollow of the tree.

"That's a big cat!" Kate whispered nervously to her friend.

"You're right," Ember returned in a low voice. "Let's back quietly away from here and let it have its lunch."

Mercifully the cougar killed the mother owl quickly, and the battle noise stopped. Just then Katherine stepped on a dead limb that broke with a loud crack. Instantly the cat's head turned and spotted the two intruders.

"Oh no!" gasped Kate.

"RUN!" Ember hissed urgently, and both ladies dropped their baskets and sprinted away. Katherine ran downhill toward the river. Ember ran south through the woods.

Angered at the interruption of its meal, the big cat sprang from the tree and raced after Katherine. Ember glanced over her shoulder and saw the cat pursuing her friend. She immediately turned around and ran after them, screaming as she went, attempting to distract the predator. The young medicine woman clawed frantically to untie the sling around her waist.

When Katherine saw that the beast had chosen her for his next meal, she began yelling for Asa. Katherine was a fast runner, but she was no match for the bounding cougar. Taking another look back, the maiden saw that the hungry beast was rapidly overtaking her. "LORD JESUS, HELP ME!" she cried out her prayer as she suddenly tripped and fell.

Just then a rifle blasted nearby, and the cougar screamed painfully and crashed into the leaves and brush as it summersaulted down the hill.

Asa, still carrying his smoking rifle, ran to Katherine's prostrate form and knelt beside her. "Kate, are you hurt?"

"I skinned my hands when I fell," she said through clenched teeth as she pushed herself into a sitting position. "I'm just glad you got here when you did!"

"Me too," Asa agreed. "That could have been..."

At that moment both of them heard angry growling coming from nearby. Looking to where the cougar fell, they saw the now furious cat raising itself painfully from the leaves and brush where it had landed. With its rage-filled eyes locked on the two young people, the beast began limping towards them, blood streaming from a bullet hole in its shoulder.

"Oh no!" Asa gasped. "I only wounded it!"

"It's coming for us!" Kate cried as she saw murderous intent in those savage eyes.

Asa tried to quickly reload his rifle, but his shaky fingers dropped the bullet. The vicious cat was closing quickly, and both of them knew that Asa would not get his rifle loaded in time. Jerking out his tomahawk and knife, he stepped determinedly between Katherine and the approaching cougar.

Suddenly a hard object slammed powerfully into the side of the cat's head. The beast gave a sharp cry, tumbled into the brush, and lay still.

Looking up the hill, Asa and Katherine saw Ember running towards them, her empty sling in hand. "Is everyone okay?" Ember called.

"We are—thanks to you!" Asa said. "I don't know if I could have stopped that angry cat with just my hand weapons!"

"O Ember!" Katherine added with feeling. "I am so glad that you're good with that sling of yours."

"Excuse me a moment, ladies," Asa said as he walked toward the unmoving cougar, "but I need to be sure the cat's dead."

As Asa went to check on the fallen beast, Ember turned and began walking back up the hill.

"Ember," the still shaken Katherine called anxiously after her retreating friend, "where are you going?"

"To look for goldenseal," Ember calmly returned. "I haven't found any yet."

Katherine gave a deep sigh to calm her racing heart and hurried after her companion. "Well, you've convinced me!"

"Of what?" Ember asked over her shoulder.

"You know that class you and Rebecca keep saying you're going to conduct to teach the girls at Larkinboro how to use a sling? You've just convinced me that I need to be a part of it."

When they drew near to the tree where they first spotted the cougar, Ember gave a small cheer. Growing out of a mossy patch was a healthy cluster of goldenseal. Ember showed Kate what the leaves looked like, and she quickly found another bunch.

After several minutes they saw Asa trudging up the hill with his rifle under one arm, carrying a double handful of blue clay. Ember made room for the clay in her basket. The healer then handed the young scout a leaf and started him searching for goldenseal. Whenever a plant was found, they dug it up, roots and all, and put it in one of the baskets.

At the base of the tree where the large cat had been, Ember found what was left of the dead mother owl. As she examined the carcass, a movement in the leaves nearby startled her. Gaining courage, the girl cautiously looked for the source of the noise and discovered a baby owlet in full plumage. As she carefully studied the small bird, she noticed that one of its eyes was injured.

"Look what I found!" Ember called to her friends. She carefully picked up the frightened creature and held it gently in her hands so the others could see.

"It's a baby owl!" Katherine exclaimed. "It's so cute!"

"The cougar must have knocked it out of the nest when it attacked the mother," Asa speculated.

"Should we try to put it back?" Kate asked as she looked at the hollow in the tree quite a ways over their heads.

"With the mother dead, I don't think it's old enough to survive on its own," Asa announced.

"The little fellow also has an injured eye," Ember informed them. "He either hurt it in the fall, or one of the cat's claws may have torn it."

"So what are you going to do with it?" Kate asked.

"I'm a healer," the young medicine woman declared. "I'll take him back and do what I can for him." She found a comfortable spot in her basket for the injured bird, and removing her neck scarf, she covered the top of the basket.

"Are you about ready to head home?" Asa asked Ember as he glanced up at the position of the sun.

"I see two more goldenseal plants over by those rocks," Ember answered. "Let's dig those, which will make fifteen plants; then I will be ready to go."

Asa decided to lead them back along the forested hill overlooking the river that was now on their right. They had walked for over an hour when suddenly a rhythmic, drumming cadence was heard just ahead of them. Asa stopped and put his finger to his lips. Using hand motions, the young woodsman made it clear that he wanted them to stay where they were while he went forward to scout the source of the noise.

As he advanced, both young ladies were impressed at how quietly the young man traveled through the brush. When he reached a spot nearly fifty yards from the girls, Asa leaned against a large tree and peered around it and down the slope leading to the river.

What he saw made the hairs on the back of his neck stand on end. His heart pounded as he studied the situation below. Then remembering the girls, Asa forced himself to pull away from the chilling sight and hurry back to his friends. "Follow me," he whispered urgently, "an' be quieter than you've ever been in your life."

Chapter Two

A CLOSE CALL

"What's wrong?" Katherine asked with a confused look.

"Shhhh!" Asa hissed. "It's a bunch of Indians near the bank of the river doing some crazy dance."

"INDIANS?" Kate hissed urgently. "What are Indians doing so close to Larkinboro?"

"Well, you can bet it's nothing good!" Asa shot back as he led them forward along the top of the ridge. He knew the men at the fort would be asking him questions about the warriors, so he wanted to get one more look at them as they moved past.

"We don't dare make a sound, but we've got to slip by 'em an' get home as fast as we can! We need to let our friends know that trouble is near!

The overlook is right here, so keep low, keep moving, and be...”

The words hadn't left his lips when his foot caught on a root, causing him to fall hard on his face and slide a short distance down the slope. A number of dislodged rocks started tumbling straight toward the Indians below.

Both girls were quickly at Asa's side, pulling him back to his feet. Hearing the screams from below, the three of them were mesmerized at what they saw. The band of eleven Indians had stopped their dance and were gesticulating angrily at the intruders at the top of the hill.

“THEY'RE AS WHITE AS GHOSTS!” Katherine gasped as she stared at the angry warriors charging up the slope towards them.

“WHO CARES WHAT COLOR THEY ARE?” Asa shot back as he snatched up his rifle. “RUN!” He raced towards the southeast with the girls dashing behind him. He felt badly about being in front, but he was the only one who knew the way back.

The young scout constantly looked behind him as he sprinted through the forest. He wanted to make sure that he wasn't leaving the girls behind. Fortunately for all of them, both girls were strong and good runners.

“Run as fast as you can, ladies!” he huffed as he raced along. “Those Indians will be up that slope any minute, an' we've got to put as much distance between them an' us as we can before they get to the top!"

The war cries in the distance behind them made it clear the exact moment their fierce pursuers reached the crest of the hill. Asa took another quick look back before announcing his judgment: "We don't have as big a lead as I was hoping, but they've got to be tired after climbing up that hill. Keep running hard, ladies, an' maybe we can pull away from 'em."

For the next half hour they ran as fast as they could, rushing toward Larkinboro and the safety of its log walls. Asa took another look back to judge how close their enemies were. "I think they're gaining on us," he observed.

Katherine took that moment to glance behind and immediately tripped on a limb, crashing hard into the ground with a cry of pain.

"GET UP, KATE!" Asa cried as he slid to a stop and rushed to the fallen girl's side. "GET UP!"

"My knee!" she gasped in pain as she grabbed the bleeding gash on her right leg.

"Kate," Ember urged, "I know you're hurt, but the Indians are coming, and you've *got* to get up!"

"I don't know if I can!" the injured girl grunted through clenched teeth. On hearing these words, Asa hefted his rifle and turned to face the on-coming Indians.

"Ember," Asa said with cold determination, "get Kate back on her feet, and you two keep going. I will hold them as long as I can."

When Katherine Middlebrook realized that her friend was going to sacrifice himself to give them a chance to get a way, she resolved to not let that happen. Gritting her teeth and with a cry of pain, she forced herself to her feet. "ASA, HELP ME!" she demanded as she extended her arm toward the scout.

Lowering his rifle, Asa quickly slipped under her arm to support the injured girl. Kate turned to Ember and extended her other arm to her. Ember snatched up Kate's dropped basket and hurriedly provided support from the other side.

"NOW LET'S GO!" Kate ordered, holding up her bleeding leg and hopping on her good one. They rushed along in this manner for several more minutes.

"How close are they?" Katherine grunted to Asa.

"It doesn't matter," Asa shot back, "just keep going! We're almost to the fort!

It was obvious to all three of them that the war cries of the Indians were getting louder and that they would soon catch them. Just then the three broke through the brush and found themselves in a large pasture. A couple of hundred yards ahead of them rose the wooden palisade of Larkinboro.

"THERE'S THE FORT!" Ember called as they rushed into the clearing.

"But it's too far away!" Katherine moaned. "They'll catch us before we reach the gate!"

"We definitely need some help," Asa huffed as he cocked his rifle, raised the barrel into the air, and fired.

Eight seconds later a small crowd of screaming white warriors burst out of the woods and raced to capture their victims. Just then rifles began to spit flame from the top of the fort walls, and slugs began to zip past the ears of the Indians. At the same moment fifteen rifle-carrying frontiersmen charged out of the gates and with determined yells rushed to confront the charging Indians.

Asa heard a shout from behind and, when he looked back, saw that the white, ghost-like figures were hurrying back into the forest.

"Could you tell what tribe they were from, Asa?"

"I couldn't tell anything," Asa Whitlock returned with frustration in his voice, "except that they were Indians! I counted eleven of them, an' when we first saw them, they were doing some kind of dance!"

Asa stood in the front of the log meeting house in the town of Larkinboro. With him were the village scouts, Jack Cobb, Dirt Gurley, Jim Hart, and William Hackett. Also present were several other leading men of the settlement.

"I've never heard of Indians painting themselves white like that!" Asa said in amazement. "Have any of you heard of that before?"

"All of us at the fort didn't get a good look at 'em since they was so far away," said an older scout named Dirt Gurley. "You sure it weren't just the sunlight making 'em look like that? I've had the evenin' sun play tricks on my eyes afore."

"No!" Asa answered firmly. "It was nothing like that! These fellows, from head to toe, were as white as ghosts."

"Well, maybe they was outcasts from their tribe after they all caught some skin disease...like leep-rosy," Dirt suggested.

"Leep-rosy?" Asa asked with a confused look on his face.

"Yeah, you know...leep-rosy," the older scout insisted, "like in the Bible."

"I believe you mean *leprosy,* my good man," corrected Mr. Spebbington, the school teacher and minister of the settlement.

"Whatever!" Dirt Gurley snapped back. "Maybe they had that there disease, turned all white, got theirselves banished, an' then, when they was spotted gyratin' around in nothin' but their pantyloons, expressed their displeasure by chasin' our folks off."

Everyone sat there in stunned silence for a moment. Finally Mr. Spebbington responded. "Mr. Gurley, your reasoning capacity is truly an enigma."

"Why, thank'ee thar, Perfesser," Dirt responded with obvious pride.

"They didn't have a skin disease!" Asa returned. "We were close enough to see. They were painted white from head to foot. One of them pounded on a small drum and sang while the rest danced. Except for the drummer, they all carried lances that were a little taller than they were. They whirled them around their heads and stabbed the air in time with the drum beat. It looked like some kind of war dance."

"What do you make of it, Jack?" asked Mr. Middlebrook, Katherine's father and one of the settlement's leaders. Jack Cobb was viewed as an authority on everything related to the woods and Indians.

The scout sat in silence for almost a minute. Finally, after shaking his head slowly, Jack spoke his thoughts. "I've seen war dances, but I ain't never heard of Indians of any tribe paintin' theirselves white.

"How about you, Will?" Jack asked, turning to the young scout who was only a year older than

Asa. "Those years you were a captive of the Miami Indians, did you ever see anything like that?"

William Hackett just shook his head thoughtfully, then turned to his Miami friend Grey Fox, who was standing nearby. "Do you know any Indians who do that?"

"White paint on face mean *peace, purity,* or *light,*" their Indian friend informed them. "White used as war paint mean *mourning* or *death*. Paint on whole body sound more like war paint than peace. I have not seen dancers painted white. It not a Miami custom."

A lot of questions were asked by those in the group, for which no one knew the answers.

Finally Jack Cobb spoke up. "Whatever Asa saw, it don't sound good, an' I'm thinkin' we need to look into it." This statement was met with a unanimous nodding of heads. "Alright then," Jack continued, "Asa, how about you showin' Dirt, Will Hackett, and Grey Fox exactly where you saw these dancin' ghosts, an' let's see if they leave tracks."

"Ain't you an' Jim comin' with us, Jack?" Dirt Gurley asked.

"I'll admit I'm curious," Cobb returned.

"So am I," Jim Hart agreed, "but Jack asked me to escort a party of men haulin' a barrel of our gunpowder to Logan's Station."

"One of us scouts needs to stay here," Jack Cobb explained. "Besides, Captain Parks is due to come back through soon, an' I need to find out from him what General Clark's plans are."

"So, Ember," Katherine Middlebrook's seven-year-old brother Seth asked as he and Katherine's younger sister, Grace, stood by the basket looking at the baby owl, "what are you gonna name him?"

"Well, I hadn't thought about it. I didn't really want to keep him," Ember answered. "But with only one good eye, he'll never be able to catch mice to feed himself."

"Why not?" Seth asked.

"Because with only one eye, you can't tell how close you are to something," Ember returned as she dropped a leaf from one of the goldenseal plants on the floor. "Try it. Close one eye, Seth, and try to pick up that leaf."

The boy covered one of his eyes and stepped toward the leaf. Everybody laughed as he made several attempts to pick it up but closed his fingers before he got to it. Eventually the giggling boy was able to achieve his goal.

"See?" Ember said with a smile. "It's not that easy."

"But I did get it," the boy said proudly, holding up the leaf.

"Yes, but it took you several tries. The owl would eventually catch the mouse if he could make multiple attempts, but he will most likely get only one chance with each mouse he finds."

"That's right," Grace said. "The poor little fellow will starve to death."

"That's what I figure," Ember returned. "My plan is to feed him till he's bigger and see if he will be able to take care of himself."

"What will you feed him?" Grace asked.

"I've got some bits of warmed meat that I'm giving him, and he seems to eat it fine." As Ember said this, she held up a small strip of deer steak, and the small owl immediately opened his mouth to receive the morsel. "Every once in a while I will need to feed him a mouse, but I don't know how I will catch one."

"Oh, that's no problem," Seth spoke up. "I can catch all you want out in the corn crib. Me an' Lij Nelson catch 'em all the time."

"Oh, really? What do you do with them?" Ember asked curiously.

"Usually we climb up on top of the meeting house and drop them in the girls' hair when they come out from school."

"You *don't* do that!" Katherine exclaimed with a shocked expression.

"Sure we do," Seth answered his older sister sincerely. "It's lots of fun! The girls start screamin' an' run all over the place! You should try it with us, Katie!"

"In the future, Seth," Ember cut in before the boy's red-faced older sister had a chance to express her thoughts, "I think it would be better if you brought the mice you catch here for our little owl friend. Don't you agree?"

"Yeah, okay," the boy acknowledged, a little disappointed. "Since he needs 'em to grow up, we'll catch the mice and bring them to him, but it won't be near as fun. I'll go get Lij an' see if we can catch him one now."

As the lad ran out the door, Ember cut her eyes over to Katherine and smiled.

Katherine struggled to find the right words to express her disgust. Finally she blurted out, "BOYS!"

The Dancing Ghosts

Chapter Three

TRACKING GHOSTS

"You sure this here's the place, Asa?" The question was asked by Dirt Gurley as the four scouts stood on a wooded ridge looking down on the banks of the rolling river.

"Positive," the young woodsman returned. "Look! Right there's where I tripped. It's only been two days, but you can still see the leaves and ground I disturbed trying to climb back up the hill."

Cautiously Asa led the way down the wooded slope toward the river until Will Hackett called to his friend. Stopping just above the wide, flat bank, Asa Whitlock turned to face the others. "What's wrong?"

"Before we all go down there and walk over the tracks," Will began, "I think we should send one to study the undisturbed footprints."

"Good idear, Will," Dirt agreed. "Our best tracker should go first."

"That be Grey Fox," the Miami said confidently and pushed forward.

Both Dirt and Will gave an annoyed snort at Grey Fox as he moved past them, but neither objected. Dirt was a great tracker. Will was even better, but they both acknowledged that their friend Grey Fox was the best. It was just aggravating to them that he knew it.

They watched in fascinated interest as the Indian moved carefully around the flat area beside the river bank, pausing frequently to stare at the ground. After several minutes he walked over and put his hand on the trunk of a large beech tree growing nearby and waved to his friends to join him.

"Asa right," the Miami announced. "Lots of moccasin tracks."

"Can you tell what tribe they're from?" Dirt asked, looking carefully at a set of footprints near him.

"Not Miami, not Cherokee, not Shawnee, not Osage," Grey Fox answered. "Stitching on moccasin prints not like Indians around here."

"Which way did they go?" Asa asked, looking around.

"Tracks lead north, along river," the Miami returned. "But look here." As he said this, the Indian pointed to the trunk of the tree.

A number of strange symbols were painted onto the bark with white paint. The four friends stared at the markings in silence for several minutes. Finally Asa spoke up. "Do any of you know what those signs mean?"

"I ain't never seen nothing like it," Dirt admitted.

"Neither have I," agreed Will. "Have you ever seen markings like those, Grey Fox?"

"This one," he said, pointing to a set of curves, "could be *ghost, spirit,* or *Great Spirit.* Don't know others."

"So what do you think, Dirt?" Asa asked.

"Well, the good news is that them painted heatherns is headed away from Larkinboro. The easiest thing to do is to jus' head on home an' let sleepin' dogs lie, so to speak. But this whole deal ain't sittin' well with me."

"What do you mean?" Asa asked.

"Well, think about it. A band of strange Injuns in a place where they ain't supposed to be, paintin' strange marks on trees, doin' war dances, an' attackin' our people when you weren't doin' nothin' but lookin' at 'em, is not somethin' I think we need to ignore. We should find out who these reperbates are an' what they're up to.

"Grey Fox," the older scout announced, "let's track 'em."

With a nod the Miami set off to the north along the bank of the river, following the tracks until the sun set. When it got too dark to see, the friends made a meal of jerked deer meat and pulled leaves together for beds. They made no fire so as not to give away their presence and took turns keeping watch through the night. The next morning, as soon as it was light enough to see, they followed the trail again.

Late in the afternoon a faint smell of smoke in the breeze alerted them to the presence of a nearby village. Fully aware of the nearness of danger, the four scouts crept silently through the woods as they approached the enemy encampment.

"Ghost Warrior tracks lead here," Grey Fox whispered to the others as they viewed the Iroquois village through the brush from several hundred yards away.

"So do you think the ones we're following are Iroquois?" Asa questioned.

"There ain't no way to know," Dirt whispered back, "unless we can get closer to that village."

"How are we supposed to do that?" the young scout hissed.

"Grey Fox get close," the Miami announced confidently.

"Let me go, Grey Fox," Will returned, trying to protect his friend from danger.

"You could, Kajika," the Indian returned smugly, using William's Miami name, "but you have to make yourself look Indian. Grey Fox look Indian better than you." Not a leaf stirred as the stealthy Miami warrior crept away.

For the next three hours, the three friends took turns keeping watch and taking naps as they waited for their friend to return. When Grey Fox did reappear, he was so silent that it startled Asa, who was on watch, as he suddenly realized the Miami was standing beside him.

"What'd you learn?" Dirt asked eagerly, as they all gathered to hear Grey Fox's report.

"Ghost Warriors in village," the Miami announced. "They from tribe far to the West."

"From the West?" Asa questioned. "I'm surprised the Iroquois didn't scalp them!"

"Iroquois scared of Ghost Warriors," Grey Fox declared. "One white one claims to be shaman...man of magic."

"Do you speak Iroquois?" Dirt asked.

"No," the Miami answered, "but neither do Ghost Warriors. They speak in sign language, so Grey Fox know what they say. Almost everyone in Iroquois village got sick two days ago. White shaman say sickness come from spirits, and he will make village well if Iroquois accept him as chief."

"Are they going to do it?" William asked.

"The shaman say last night he told spirit of death to let people get well," the Miami explained. "All of village better today."

"How can he do that?" Asa asked incredulously.

"Don't know," Grey Fox returned, "but most Iroquois believe he has power and are afraid of him and his Ghost Warriors."

"So how is everybody doing with their braiding?" Ember asked as she and her friend Rebecca Norris walked around the group of girls and young ladies who had assembled for the special class to learn how to use a sling. The sixteen students were busy twisting lengths of thin leather strips into two small ropes to be used as the long ends of the slings. One end of each of the braided ropes was to be attached to each end of a woven leather pad that would hold a throwing rock.

True to her word, Katherine Middlebrook had joined the class and was busy constructing her own weapon. Several had questions as to how long to make their slings, but by the end of the afternoon, all of the weapons were finished.

"So how do we use them?" an eager Gardenia Leavenworth asked as she held up hers so Ember could inspect her work. "I want to hit somethin' with a rock!"

"If everyone is ready," Ember returned with a smile, "bring your slings and follow Rebecca and me."

The small army of student slingers followed their instructors out of the meeting house and across the open area at the entrance to the west gate of the Larkinboro palisade. After Ember had a brief discussion with the guards, the gates were opened, and the ladies filed out. Their instructors led them to a place near the southwest corner of the wall where a large pile of small stones had been amassed.

"That heap of rocks represents a lot of work," Katherine said to Ember and Rebecca. Kate saw both girls look at each other and start giggling.

"All it took was one plate of cookies," Rebecca answered, still chuckling.

"We hired a bunch of the boys to do it for us," Ember laughed.

"Really?" Katherine returned with a smile.

"Yep," Rebecca shot back. "Warm cookies are like gold to little boys!"

Ember had also had the boys set up three small logs a short distance away to use as targets. The ladies were patiently instructed on how to hold and load their slings. When everyone felt comfortable with the procedure, Ember and

Rebecca showed them how to sling the stones while all of them stood to the side.

"In order to hit your target," Ember explained as Rebecca stood beside her, sling at the ready, "you must keep your eyes locked on what you want to hit. You will then swing the rock in a circle once and release one end of the sling. The trick is to release the rock at the right time to allow it to fly forward and hit your target." She nodded at Rebecca, who in one swift move sent her stone flying into one of the logs. As the missile struck with a loud *smack*, Rebecca's success was met with cheers from their students.

Each one in the class was eager to start slinging, but Ember and Rebecca understood the difficulties of learning the skill. They knew that the first few stones each one threw could go anywhere, so only one was allowed to sling at a time, and the rest moved a safe distance away.

It took some time and a lot of rocks, but by late afternoon most of the stones were flying near the targets, and a few were hitting the marks. Finally Ember called everyone together. "As each of you can now see, slinging stones accurately is not easy. To be able to consistently hit your target, you must practice, practice, practice. Rebecca and I always keep our slings with us, both for practice and for protection. You should too. Your lives and the lives of those you love could depend on how good you become with the sling."

As they dispersed and headed back toward the gate, there was much excited chattering among the class about their new skill. Katherine joined Ember and Rebecca as they encouraged the others who were leaving.

"Which one of you came up with the idea of using a sling?" Kate asked after everyone else had gone. In response, both Ember and Rebecca pointed at each other and then laughed.

"After we escaped from the Shawnee," Rebecca began, "we thought we had gotten away, but they suddenly showed up and managed to recapture my sister. There was nothing we could do for Susanna, but the Lord helped Ember and me to slip away without our pursuers even knowing we were close by."

"We knew they would eventually track us down," Remember said, taking up the story, "but neither of us wanted to give up without a fight. We were valuable as slaves, so we didn't think they would shoot us. But somehow, we needed a way to keep them from getting close enough to recapture us, so we prayed about it."

"Did the Lord speak to you like He's done before and tell you to make slings?" Katherine asked Ember eagerly.

"Actually He spoke to Rebecca."

"The Lord speaks to you too, Rebecca?" Kate asked with surprise.

"I believe He speaks to all of us, Kate," the younger girl returned. "We just don't always recognize it. At the time I didn't realize He was speaking to me. After we prayed and asked Him to show us how to defend ourselves, the stories of David in the Bible kept coming to me. I just thought my mind was wandering. It was Ember who realized that Jesus was answering our prayer."

"When we realized what the Lord wanted us to do," Ember added, "we tore a wide strip off the bottoms of our skirts to make slings and started trying to figure out how to use them."

"So how long did it take both of you to become so good with your slings?" Kate asked curiously.

"Not long," Rebecca answered.

"Most of two days," Ember clarified.

"That quickly?"

"Well," Rebecca giggled, "as we traveled through the woods to escape the Shawnee, we really didn't have anything else to do but throw rocks."

"Our shoulders got pretty sore," Ember said as she looked at Rebecca, and both of them laughed again.

"I know you must miss your sister, Becca," Katherine finally said.

"Susanna and I were never close," Rebecca answered thoughtfully. "To be honest, she was a difficult person to be around, but I do think of her often, and I am sorry that she was captured. Ember and I have committed to pray for her daily."

The Dancing Ghosts

Chapter Four

THE CAPTIVE

"Ember," Rebecca Norris asked as the three girls walked back to the fort from slinging class, "do you think my sister, Susanna, is still alive? I mean, it's been nine months since we escaped from the Shawnee."

"I'm like you, Becca," the young healer returned. "I don't miss her sharp tongue and bad attitude, but I do think about her a lot. The Shawnee are not nice to their slaves, but they do prefer to keep them alive. If Susanna was able to control her tongue and submit to their demands, she should still be alive. I pray for her, and I haven't sensed the Lord telling me that I should stop."

"I know the three of you were captives together and that you two escaped," Katherine Middlebrook said, "but I've never heard what actually happened. How come your sister got recaptured and you didn't?"

"Rayford, the renegade trapper who enslaved us, came back to the cabin one day half drunk," Ember began. "Prisha, who was both our mistress and his squaw, knocked the liquor jug out of his hands and broke it. Rayford's anger was always terrible, but this time he tried to kill Prisha."

"He was a very evil man!" Rebecca agreed. "He was a murderer, and we were all terrified of him."

"To save Prisha," Ember explained, "I hit Rayford in the back of the head with an ax handle. Prisha knew he would kill us all when he woke up, so she gave us some supplies and told us to run. Prisha ran too."

"Where could she go?" Kate asked, fascinated by the story.

"She ran to live with one of her sisters in the nearby Shawnee village," Ember answered. "She said she would be safe there. Rayford was friends with the Shawnee, but Prisha was so highly honored as their medicine woman that she felt her tribe would protect her if Rayford came and demanded her back.

"I knew about a hidden cave near the cabin that I thought might lead us to the other side of the mountain, so we went there. Sure enough, the Lord led us through the cave."

"But you obviously didn't completely get away because they caught Becca's sister," Kate prompted. "How did that happen?"

Ember didn't answer the question at first. Instead she looked questioningly at Rebecca.

"Ember and I had gotten injured, and we were all tired," Rebecca said, taking up the tale, "so against Susanna's wishes, we decided to rest in the mouth of the cave for a few hours. While we were sleeping, Susanna stole our food supply, map, and compass and left us. When Ember and I woke up, we tried to find her. Eventually we heard her crying and found that Rayford and the Shawnee had caught her. She told them that, if they wouldn't hurt her, she would show them the cave where she thought we were still sleeping. Once they left to find us, Ember and I slipped away in the opposite direction."

"The Lord led us to William Hackett, Grey Fox, and Dirt Gurley, who were out scouting," Ember added. "They helped us, and when the Indians eventually caught up with us, with the scouts' rifles and our slings, we were able to fight them off."

"Oh, Becca," Katherine said with feeling, "I know you feel betrayed by your sister, but she must have been terrified! Who knows what any of us would have done in a situation like that?"

"It's okay, Kate," Rebecca returned. "In order for Jesus to forgive us, Ember and I knew that we had to forgive Susanna...and we have. I just feel sorry for her. Every time Ember tried to tell us how much Jesus loved us, Susanna would get angry. She wouldn't listen. Now she's in this terrible situation with no one to help her, and she doesn't have the Lord! All we can do now is to pray for her."

"God is faithful," Kate pronounced with a smile.

"Yes, He is!" both Ember and Rebecca returned enthusiastically.

A thick haze of smoke hung heavily over the large Shawnee village. The sun had not yet cleared the eastern horizon as the people began their early morning rituals. A few dogs barked at noises they heard in the surrounding woods, and murmuring sounded from behind the walls of the many mud-covered, stick houses.

An angry shout echoed from one hut near the southeastern edge of the village, followed by the sound of a sharp blow and a piercing cry of pain. More shouting occurred, the deer skin covering the hut doorway was thrown back, and a crying young woman was shoved out the door. As she slowly walked away from the shanty, more abusive words were hurled at her from a hard-looking squaw who stuck her head out the doorway.

At one time the slave's hair had been blond, but it was so dirty now that the color could not be determined. Her beautiful blue eyes looked out from swollen, puffy lids, and there was a fresh, bleeding bruise on her left cheek that burned as her tears flowed into it.

Susanna Norris hated her life as well as everyone and everything around her. She was the slave of a bitter and angry Shawnee widow whose husband, a chief, had died in a fight with Susanna's friends when she, Rebecca, and Ember had escaped from their Shawnee captivity the year before. Though the slave woman knew only a few words of the Shawnee language, it was clear that the squaw blamed Susanna for all of her misery and loss.

Susanna had selfishly turned her back on Ember and her injured sister, Rebecca. Her wickedness had been rewarded by being caught by the very Indians she was fleeing.

When the recaptured young woman had been brought to the Shawnee village, she had gotten so angry at her cruel mistress that Susanna refused to do the work that was expected of her. She got hit in the head with a piece of firewood for that. Shortly after, she had tried to run away but was quickly caught. The resulting beating she received left her back raw and bleeding.

Even though Susanna knew the Shawnee could not understand her words, she was afraid to express her true feelings out loud for fear her attitudes and emotions would reveal her true meaning. So she did the work she was forced to do, but in her heart she called her tormentors every vile name she could think of.

They lived in a cramped hut with her mistress's sister's family, each one of whom seemed to Susanna to be equally mean and angry. Because she hadn't jumped to her duties fast enough this morning, the slave had received a sharp blow to the cheek with a cooking spoon.

Stumbling in the cold morning air, Susanna carried a heavy clay pot to the creek for water. She needed to hurry, or she would get another beating when she returned. The beating was actually expected regardless, so she didn't push herself.

As she watched the water flowing into the pot, the desperate woman once again went over all of the obstacles to a successful escape. By the time her water jar was full, she had reached the same conclusion as always...there was no escape! A deep, black sense of hopelessness filled her heart once again. Her anger returned, and she vented it at every person she could blame for her predicament.

"Why did you have to die?" she raged at her parents. "Couldn't you have stayed alive and killed those Indians who attacked us? Dying was the easy way out...the cowards' way! Look at what you've done to me! If you had really loved me, you would have found a way to protect me! But no...you left me! You left me to *this*!"

In her uncontrolled anger, the bitter young woman shook her fists at the trees on the other side of the creek. "I hate you!" she continued. "I hate you both!

"And where is that *wonderful God* you were always talking about? What did all your ridiculous prayers get you? They got you killed! And look at where they got me!"

Suddenly she let out a shrill scream of pure anger. An instant later she slapped her hand over her mouth, terrified that she might have been heard. She held completely still for several long moments until she was sure no one was coming to investigate. Finally she gave one last vent to her rage. "I hate you all!" she whispered passionately. "I hate you, Mother and Father! I hate these Indians! I hate God! And I hate, hate, hate my life!"

She gave a deep sigh at the end of her exhausting emotional release and took another careful look around to be sure no one had been attracted by her cry. Satisfied that she was alone, Susanna hoisted the heavy pot onto her shoulder for the dreaded trip back to the hut.

As she pushed her way through the skin-covered doorway carrying her load, she almost ran into the sister's young boy, who was hurrying to leave. The lad, angry at having run into the slave, yelled furiously at Susanna and kicked her hard in the shin. With a cry of pain, the slave dropped the water jar and grabbed her injured leg. The clay jar shattered, splashing water over everyone. With cries of rage, each person in the hut rushed upon the young woman.

Susanna was hit so many times she lost count. She stumbled backwards and fell hard onto the ground outside the hut, but the blows continued. In her foggy, pain-filled mind, she had only one thought: *They'll kill me this time.* But there was no fear...only pain.

Just as she began to lose consciousness, Susanna heard yelling in the distance. Suddenly the attack ended, and there was more loud shouting. Her eyes were too swollen to see what was happening, but to Susanna the most important thing was that the beating had finally stopped. She gratefully embraced the warm blackness that slowly crept over her as her mind drifted into nothingness.

Chapter Five

THE SHAMAN'S MAGIC

An hour before daylight Grey Fox had once again crept down the wooded slope to spy on the Iroquois camp. As dawn began to break through the eastern woods, William, Asa, and Dirt were surprised to see their Miami friend hurrying back to their camp. "Ghost Warriors leaving," Grey Fox reported.

"Well, don't jus' stand there like we can read that Injun mind o' yors," Dirt snapped. "Where're they goin'?"

"Grey Fox not think he had to say," the Miami returned smugly, "since Dirt Gurley know everything."

"You orn'ry rascal!" the older scout shot back. "HEY! What are you smilin' at?"

"Dirt still mad he lost hat to Grey Fox in bet," the Indian announced with a big grin.

"It weren't no fair bet! I tol' you I was jus' teasin', but would you give a friend the beneefit of the doubt? Oh, no...you insisted I give you my hat...AND THEN you jumped in the river with it on AND LOST IT!"

"If Grey Fox had left hat on bank, Dirt Gurley would have stolen it."

"But it was MY HAT!" exclaimed the red-faced older scout.

"Dirt Gurley no have hat," the Miami returned calmly. "You lose in bet."

"Ain't you got the least bit of compassion for an ol' man havin' to run around for months with a neked head because of you?" Dirt whined with a pitiful look on his face.

Grey Fox snorted and smiled again. "You only *old man* when you want something."

"Why you scum-suckin' mole rat!"

"GUYS!" Will hissed. "Can we please just get back to scouting?"

Dirt Gurley gave the Miami a snort of disgust, which Grey Fox returned with an annoying grin.

"So, Grey Fox," William asked, turning to his friend, "which direction did the Ghost Warriors go?"

"They go north."

"Now was that so hard?" a still irritated Dirt shot back. "With the time you wasted with all your gum-flappin, we've probably lost 'em!"

"Huh, huh, huh," Grey Fox chuckled. *"Dirt still mad about hat."*

Suddenly the older scout's face flashed red as he glared at the Miami. Just then William's hand dropped onto Dirt's shoulder, and he said, "Grey Fox, would you track the Ghost Warriors, please?"

Still smiling, the Miami turned and led the way to the north.

Grey Fox was such an accomplished tracker that he did not have to keep in sight of their quarry. The exposed, damp side of a pebble that had been rolled or a small piece of moss that had been torn free from a patch on a rock by a careless foot were two of the many signs the Miami used to identify the path taken. By hanging back in this way, the scouts were able to avoid discovery while following the warriors. As the afternoon drew to a close, Grey Fox hurried forward alone to see if the Indians would stop to make camp. When they did, the Miami quickly returned to his friends to warn them before they got too close. In this manner the scouts trailed the warriors for two days without being detected.

Late morning on the third day, Grey Fox suddenly froze and held up his hand. The other three immediately stopped in their tracks. A moment later the Miami turned and sent a message to his friends in Indian sign language.

"What's he saying?" Asa whispered to the older scout just in front of him.

"He says them reperbates we's a trackin' stopped jus' ahead of us, an' we needs to be quiet...so *shush!*"

Asa had lots of questions, but he knew that now was not the time to ask them. They hid in silence for almost half an hour. Finally Grey Fox indicated that they should move further back into the woods. Hardly a leaf stirred as the four experienced scouts retraced their steps. When the Miami called a halt to their retreat, each of them drew near to find out what was happening.

"Shawnee village just ahead," Grey Fox said in a low voice. "Ghost Warriors hiding in brush watching village. After a while they talk and send out two scouts. Now they wait till scouts return. We wait too, but not so close."

"You fellas rest here," Will Hackett announced. "I'll slip closer and keep an eye out for the two scouts they sent. We need to know what they're up to."

It was almost two hours later when Will quietly rejoined his friends.

"Scouts come back?" Grey Fox asked.

"Yes," Hackett answered, "and as soon as they did, things began to happen. After they gave their report, the tall one, who's obviously their leader, said something to the others, then pulled out a cloth bag, and left with one of their scouts, heading west. The others stayed behind.

"I'm going to follow them. Grey Fox, I need you to slip back up and watch the rest of them until I get back."

With an understanding nod the Miami disappeared into the woods to the north.

"What do *we* do, Will?" Asa asked, a little frustrated.

"Just stay put for now. Grey Fox and I will join you as soon as we figure out their plans."

Without waiting for a response, the young frontiersman hurried through the brush to the northwest. Asa was amazed as he watched William leave. The Miami Indians called him Kajika which means *Walks Without Sound. That name sure fits,* Asa thought as he observed his friend hurrying noiselessly through the woods. William leaned forward and moved faster than someone would normally walk, but hardly a leaf or a branch moved as he passed. He had perfected a unique way of rolling his body from side to side to avoid contact with limbs and brush while at the same time rapidly spotting the next place to put his foot. Somehow, as William did all this, he was also completely aware of what was going on in the woods around him. To Asa it was uncanny, and it always amazed him when he watched Will do it.

William made good time in his silent rush through the forest, and when he crossed the trail of the two Ghost Warriors, he immediately recognized it. It wasn't long before he had the two in sight. Hanging back so as not to give away his position, he carefully trailed them until they were on the west side of the village. Suddenly they stopped, and the white-painted scout pointed and said something to his tall leader. They both moved ahead, and William crept closer to watch them.

The young frontiersman heard the babbling waters of the creek before he saw it. He watched as the white leader stepped down into the shallow waters, dipped his cloth bag in the creek, and began to pound it with a rock. This went on for several minutes until the leader seemed satisfied, then he left the sack in the creek, and the two of them began to retrace their steps.

William quickly dropped behind a moss-covered log and remained motionless as the two warriors passed. When he was sure that they were far enough away, the young scout rose and hurried to the creek. He couldn't actually see the sack that was dropped, but he could tell where it was. In a deeper part of the creek, a yellowish cloud rolled up from the pool and was carried toward the Shawnee village.

William quickly retrieved the sack and studied its contents. The wet pouch contained a bunch of plants, but because they had been crushed so thoroughly, he was unable to recognize them. He tossed the bag behind a tree and hurried after his quarry.

"You got any idear what that no-good swamp rat put in the water?" The question was asked by Dirt Gurley after Will and Grey Fox had reported back.

"I'm not completely sure," Will returned. "The leader beat the contents of the bag into mush. But whatever it was, he put it in a place where the whole village would eventually drink it."

"You got rid of it, didn't you, Will?" Asa Whitlock asked with concern.

"Sure I did, Whit," Will answered. "These fellas are clearly up to no good. Unfortunately I couldn't stop it all. A lot of juice from the crushed plants was already flowing toward the village. It made the water all cloudy at first, but the further down the creek it flowed, the harder it was to see."

"What do you think it is, Will?" Asa asked.

"Well, like I said, I don't really know, but I think I'm beginning to understand how our shaman works his magic."

"Do you think he was casting some kind of a spell on the village?"

"No, Whit," William returned with a smile. "I think that by crushing up those plants and putting the juice into their water, he's going to make whoever drinks it sick just long enough for him to show up and take credit for getting them well."

"Yessiree Bob!" Dirt agreed. "That's exactly what happened at the Iroquois village, and you can bet your granny's garters that them worthless pole cats is gonna do it again here!"

Chapter Six

TRAGEDY

"Have you named your owl yet, Ember?" Elijah Nelson asked when he and Seth Middlebrook walked in with another mouse. Remember Warren was busy making a large birdcage home for her tiny patient by tying bent willow wisps together with thin strands of dried tree bark.

"Oh, hello, Lij," the young healer said pleasantly. "Did you and Seth catch another mouse?"

"We sure did!" Seth chimed in, holding up the small wiggling creature to show her, "and he should be perfect. That last one was way too big for him to swallow, but this here one should be just about owlet-size."

"Well, let's see," Ember answered and turned to a covered basket sitting on her reading table. Lifting the woven lid, the tiny owl blinked its large, uninjured eye in the bright light. As soon as the baby saw Ember, he opened his mouth wide in eager anticipation of his next meal. "Okay, Seth, hold the mouse close to his mouth."

At first the owl drew back from the thrashing rodent, but then hunger conquered his reticence, and he quickly snatched the offered morsel.

"WOW!" Lij exclaimed. "Did you see that?"

"He may be small," Seth laughed, "but he knows what to do with a mouse."

The two boys and Ember watched in fascination as the young bird relished its meal.

"It's good that he has an appetite," Ember explained to the boys. "It shows that he's feeling better."

"Do you think his eye will ever get better?" Seth asked with concern.

"Unfortunately his eye injury was too severe to heal properly," Ember returned. "He'll only have one good eye from now on."

"So he'll look like a pirate!" Lij announced excitedly. "You should name him *Blackbeard*...or maybe *Blackbeak* would be better."

"Nah, Lij," Seth said, joining the discussion. "That ain't no fit name for such a fine owl as this."

"That *isn't*," Ember corrected.

"See, Ember agrees with me too," Seth added proudly. "An owl like him needs a grand name...a name to be proud of...a name like... *George Washington!*"

"Oh, yeah!" Lij's eyes grew wide as he quickly agreed. "He's that great general back east who's fightin' the British! That'd be a great name, Ember!"

"Yeah, Ember," Seth pushed. "How about George Washington?"

"Well-l-l..." Ember said thoughtfully, "it's an awfully big name for such a small bird."

"Aw, he'll grow into it," Seth returned confidently. "Let's call him George Washington!"

"Really, Ember? You're actually going to call that little owl George Washington?" This question was asked by Rebecca Norris as she and Ember led the girls and young ladies in their class out of the fort to practice slinging rocks again.

"Well, I just thought I'd call him George," the young healer smiled back.

"But of all the names you could choose, why would you pick that one?"

"You know, Rebecca, it really didn't matter to me, but it seemed to mean a lot to those two boys. I'll tell you what, if it bothers you to call him George, then call him General Washington."

"That's so formal," Rebecca giggled. "I could call him G.W., but that seems kind of disrespectful to the real General Washington. Okay, George it is."

"Well, here we are, ladies," Ember announced when they arrived at the place where the targets were set up.

"I see we have a nice new pile of rocks to throw," Katherine Middlebrook said with a smile.

"And all it cost was another plate of cookies," Rebecca returned proudly.

"I'll never understand economics," Kate laughed.

By the end of their session of target practice, both Ember and Rebecca were pleased with the results. Most of their students were hitting the mark consistently, and those who weren't were placing their stones very close to the intended target.

"You are all doing remarkably well!" Ember said with pride as she called them all together. "Any enemies who come after you are in trouble!"

"Excuse me," Gardenia Leavenworth said, raising her hand. "Throwing stones at logs is easy, but if I were supposed to hit another person with a rock, I don't know if I could do it. I mean, even if we were being attacked by enemies, I really wouldn't want to kill anybody."

"You wouldn't want them killing you or any of your family would you?" another girl asked.

"Well, no, but..."

"Gardenia," Ember said, taking back the discussion, "I think I have a solution for you. Rebecca and I have had that same conversation, and here's what we came up with." The young healer reached into a pouch at her side and drew out a clay ball about the size of a small hen's egg. She held it up between two of her fingers so everyone could see it clearly. "Rebecca and I call these *clay bullets.* If you hit somebody in the head with one of these, it will definitely stop them, but it is unlikely to kill them.

"We take a smooth stone about the size of a rifle ball and coat it with clay mud. We try to make them as round as we can. Then, after they dry, we bury them in the coals of a fire for a quarter of an hour. We only want the outside to glaze, so we pull them out before the whole thing hardens. If you sling one of these, the clay breaks apart when it hits, so it doesn't do as much damage as if you were slinging a rock. But believe me, these clay bullets carry enough weight that they will put the person or beast you hit with them out of commission for a while."

"But why glaze them at all?" another girl asked.

"Because if you don't, they will crumble into dust in your carrying pouch," Rebecca answered. "Believe me...we know."

"My pouch has two compartments in it," Ember admitted. "I carry my clay bullets in the front part and rocks in the back."

"Why even use rocks?" the same girl asked.

"I can tell you why," Katherine cut in, smiling at Ember. "Because sometimes your friends are about to be killed by a wounded cougar, and you need your throw to be lethal!"

When Susanna returned to consciousness, she still couldn't see. An attempt to move caused pain to shoot through her body, and she emitted an involuntary groan. She could hear Shawnee words being spoken to her, but she had no idea what they meant. Just then a hand gently lifted her head, and she felt the edge of a bowl touch her lips. The severely injured young woman took several swallows of the warm liquid before her head was laid down. A warm, wet piece of cloth was placed onto her swollen eyes. It had a strong smell that she couldn't recognize.

"Who...who are you?" Susanna managed to say. The answer was more unintelligible words.

The last thing she remembered was being beaten as she lay on the ground. She was not on the ground now. There was some padding under her that was covered by soft fur...a buffalo robe, she guessed. There was a fire nearby. She could smell it and feel its warmth. The conclusion that came to her was that she was in a hut, but it must be some place new because no one in her old hut would show her this much compassion.

The injured woman became aware that the intense pain was lessening. She was also becoming very drowsy. *Must be the tea,* was the last thought that came to her before she drifted off into a restful sleep.

To Susanna it seemed that she had only dozed for a few minutes, but barking dogs awakened her. When she opened her eyes, she found that she could see. Whatever was in the cloth had caused most of the swelling to disappear.

As the young woman studied her surroundings, she realized that she was in a strange hut. She lay on furs against one of the walls, and a cooking fire burned from a pit in the center of the hut, the smoke of which drifted out a small hole in the roof. Two women squatted beside the fire. One was an older woman who was cooking bread on a flat stone. The other had her back to Susanna and was stirring a steaming pot.

"Where am I?" Susanna asked, "and who are you?"

The woman cooking the bread looked at the injured woman and gave her a toothless grin. The one stirring the pot turned also, and Susanna was surprised when she saw who was returning her gaze.

"YOU!" she exclaimed. "I know you! I was your slave with my sister and Ember!"

"Emba," the squaw said with a smile and a nod. Her nurse picked up a small clay bowl, dipped some of the simmering soup from the cooking pot, and brought it to the slave girl. Lifting her head again, the squaw helped her drink the savory pottage. As hungry as Susanna was, the soup tasted wonderful. When she finished the entire bowl, the squaw quickly got her another.

The slave looked hard into the eyes of the squaw, trying to remember back to the short time she had known her. "What was it that Ember called you? Presee?"

"Prisha," the squaw answered as she patted her own chest. "You Su-ah-na."

By now the bread was done, and the older squaw tottered over to their patient and handed her a warm piece. When Susanna tried to reach up to take it, she painfully discovered that her right arm wouldn't work. Two lengths of straight tree branches had been tied firmly against her arm to immobilize it. Wincing in pain, the girl carefully laid her arm back onto her bed.

Prisha said some Shawnee words to her, brought both of her fists together like she was holding a stick, and pretended to break it to show the girl what had happened to her arm. Prisha then gently touched Susanna's leg and made the same motion. Letting her eyes follow the medicine woman's touch, the young woman saw another splint tied to her right leg.

They really were going to kill me this time, the injured woman groaned to herself. *It's a pity they didn't.* "I don't get it!" Susanna barked angrily. "Why did you save me? I never liked you, and I caused you as much trouble as I could. Why? Why did you do all this?" She used her good arm to try to communicate what she meant.

Prisha thought for a long moment, trying to recall the English words she had picked up from her long talks with Ember. Finally she looked the angry young woman in the eyes and said, "For Chief Jesu."

The Dancing Ghosts

Chapter Seven

THE DEATH MARSH

"Kajika, You and Dirt Gurley were right," Grey Fox reported, "Ghost Warriors try same trick with Shawnee. Shaman tell them people sick because spirits angry with them."

"So some of them did get sick?" William asked.

"Yes," the Miami answered, "but only a few. You got poison out of water in time to keep most of village from sickness, but that no stop shaman. He convinced them that he magic man and have great power. He say spirits tell him to come and heal their people."

"Don't tell me," Dirt Gurley said disgustingly, "they believed that bucket o' muck."

"Yes," Grey Fox returned. "Shaman's speech, plus seeing sick get better when Shaman said they would, make his muck bucket ver' believable to Shawnee."

"Okay, we found out what they're doing," Asa said, "so what do we do about it?"

"We know what they're a'doin'," the older scout answered, "but we don't know why they're a'doin' it."

"Shaman bring whole village together so he can speak to them," Grey Fox announced. "That what I come to tell you."

"Alrightee then," Dirt announced, "let's all slip closer up to the village, an' maybe we can find out what this is all about."

The Miami led them forward until they came to a thick clump of brush very near the village with a clear view of the fire ring in the center. *We close as can get without being seen*, Grey Fox signed to the others.

We close enough to read his signs when he speaks, William signed back.

Suddenly the young frontiersman felt a tap on his shoulder. Turning, he saw Asa lifting his hands and giving him a questioning look. To answer, William touched one finger to his own lips, used two fingers to point at his eyes, then pointed both fingers toward the Shawnee village.

Got it, Asa thought to himself. *Be quiet and watch. This whole sign language thing would be easy if they just used signs people could understand.*

When the Shawnee village had assembled, the shaman pulled out a small drum and beat a cadence while singing a wordless tune. In response, the other ten Ghost Warriors formed a circle around their leader and began a very animated dance. They crouched and stomped as they waved their arms out from their bodies, while slowly and rhythmically twirling in a circle. As they danced, the warriors stabbed the air with their lances.

William touched Grey Fox to get his attention. *Do you know this dance?* he signed. The Miami just shook his head *no.*

Both the Shawnee and the hidden scouts were mesmerized by the performance. After several long minutes of the hypnotic movement, the dance came to a sudden end. When it did so, all eyes turned to the shaman.

The spirits have sent you healing, the white-painted magic man began, *but they are not pleased with you. For too long the Shawnee have lived only for themselves. It is time for all Indians to unite as one tribe and to drive out the devils from the east who pollute our land. The spirits have sent us to lead you in this great war.*

Just then there was a commotion in the back of the crowd. The people parted and allowed two men to walk to the front. One was a tall frontiersman wearing a wide-brimmed hat and carrying a long rifle. The other was stunning in his spotless red coat and white trousers.

Asa didn't need anyone to tell him that he was looking at two British agents. The settlers had experienced the work of these men before. As the war continued in the East, the British used agents to stir up the war-like tribes against the American settlers, even giving the Indians guns, powder, and ammunition to accomplish their murderous work.

The Shawnee village seemed to be familiar with these two and acted receptive. The friends watched as the Shawnee chief and elders introduced the British officer and his interpreter to the shaman. The interpreter signed a message to the Ghost Warriors, but the friends were unable to see it clearly because the red-coated officer stood in the way.

Suddenly the shaman's arm shot straight into the air, and in an instant his ten warriors surrounded the two newcomers. He beat his drum again, and once more the strange dance began. It went on for half a minute before the shaman gave a scream. Instantly ten lances shot forward, and the two agents fell dead.

The attack took all of them by surprise, but Asa let out an involuntary, "WHAT?" Immediately he slapped his hand over his mouth.

Just then a rifle shot was fired from the edge of the village closest to the scouts, the ball ripping through the leaves of their hiding place.

"RUN!" the Miami yelled. "THEY SEE US!"

Instantly all four scouts leaped to their feet and sprinted back through the woods. More rifles fired. Asa felt burning pain as one of the balls tore through the sleeve of his hunting shirt, creasing his shoulder. At the same time he heard a grunt of agony and looked back in time to see Grey Fox crash to the ground with a bullet in his back.

Will was quickly at Grey Fox's side.

"Leave me!" the Indian grunted to his friend.

"You wouldn't leave me," the young frontiersman shot back.

"ASA, HELP!" Will yelled as he tossed Grey Fox's dropped rifle to Dirt and grabbed the Miami under his right shoulder. Asa knelt quickly at the Indian's left side. With a mighty heave the two lifted their groaning friend to his feet. Will and Asa drew Grey Fox's arms over their shoulders to support his weight.

"Lean on us!" Will exclaimed.

"Come on!" Dirt barked as he fired one of the rifles at the oncoming warriors. "We gots to go!"

As Will and Asa hurried through the woods with Grey Fox, Dirt Gurley followed to cover their retreat. He was pleased to see that his last shot had slowed the Shawnees' pursuit.

It encouraged William when he realized that his injured friend was actually running with him and Asa. "You doin' okay?" he asked as they ran.

"Grey Fox...been better," the Miami grunted back. "Strength be gone soon. Best we go...to Death Marsh."

"I've already decided that," Will returned. "We've been running east since you were shot."

"The Death Marsh doesn't sound very inviting," Asa called from the other side.

"Grey Fox and I discovered it last year when we were scouting up here in Shawnee country. We needed a safe place to hide, and the marsh turned out to be the perfect spot."

"How far is it from here?" Asa huffed as they rushed through the woods.

"A lot farther than Grey Fox can run, I'm afraid," Will said, glancing down at his injured friend.

"Grey Fox...will make it," their friend grunted as he trudged between them.

William smiled at his determined companion, but he could tell that the Miami was getting weaker. Just then he heard Dirt's rifle bark behind them.

"I winged one of 'em!" the older scout informed them. "Some of 'em will have to tend to him, an' the rest'll be a mite more cautious.

"How ya doin' there, Grey Fox?"

"Grey Fox...jus' fine...'cept for bullet in back."

"Well, I'm sorry, friend," Dirt returned with compassion. "I wish we could let you rest, but we gots to put some distance between us an' them reperbates. Can you keep goin'?"

"Grey Fox...can run Dirt Gurley...into ground...even *with* bullet in back."

"Why, you pompous windbag!" the older scout snapped. "I almost wish them polecats had shot me too, so's I could outrun you!"

Will glanced down at his injured companion and saw that the Miami was smiling at this exchange.

On they plodded to the east as fast as the weakening Grey Fox could travel. Although they were forced to slow down on the wooded hillsides, they were not too steep for them to climb. Amazingly Grey Fox was able to keep going for almost four miles before all of his weight dropped onto his friends' shoulders.

"Grey Fox!" Will called as he felt his friend collapse. "Lay him down, Asa!"

The young frontiersman looked with concern into the face of his injured companion.

"Strength gone," Grey Fox said weakly. "Can go no further...must leave me."

"We gotta keep movin', fellers!" Dirt called out from behind. "Them Shawnee is still on our tails!"

"How much further is it, Will?" Asa asked urgently.

"It's still about a mile from here to the edge of the marsh, and then it's a ways in," Will answered.

"It's not much further, Grey Fox," Asa pleaded, "can't you go a little bit more?" But there was no response.

"He's passed out," Will announced. "I need both of you to help me get him up on my shoulders! Once I've got him, Asa, you'll have to carry my rifle."

A minute later the muscular youth was rushing through the woods with his unconscious friend on his back. In less than a quarter of an hour, the ground around them began to grow damp, and standing black water could be seen through the woods on their left.

"We made it," Asa called out, "but it's all muck and nastiness! How can we possibly get in there?"

"We need to skirt the south edge of it to find the way in," Will answered as he took the lead with his heavy load.

"You sure 'bout this, Will?" Dirt questioned suspiciously with his nose wrinkled up. "This place looks terrible!"

"Well, we didn't name it the Death Marsh for nothing," Hackett called over his shoulder. "Grey Fox and I have had to stay here several times. We scouted it for most of three days before we found a way into the middle. Just stay with me."

William led them onward for another twenty minutes. He was breathing hard when he came to a giant beech tree. "This is where we go in," Will announced as he leaned against the gnarly trunk of the ancient tree, "but I need to catch my breath."

"Do you need to lay Grey Fox down?" Asa asked.

"If I do, I'm afraid that I won't be able to get him back up."

"I hate to push you," Dirt said as he came trotting up from where he had been scouting their back trail, "but I can hear them bloodthirsty heatherns comin' after us!"

"Okay, okay" William huffed, "I can keep going. Both of you stay right behind me and step where I step."

William moved behind the large tree and lifted his arm until he was pointing at another exceptionally large pin oak growing from the wooded marsh. With his eyes locked on the oak, Will walked along the soggy ground for fifty steps, then he suddenly stopped. He looked to his right and, in the distance, spotted a large rock rising out of the muck. Turning toward it, he carried his friend along this new line until he reached the mark. Through the trees to the left, he sighted on a pair of white oaks growing against each other. On and on, the young frontiersman led his friends deeper and deeper into the deadly marsh.

"Well, how about that?" Dirt spoke up after several minutes of marching. "I figured this was jus' a big ol' stagnant swamp, but there's a current of water flowing in that channel to our left."

"There's actually a freshwater spring in the middle," William answered back. "That's where we're going. The water doesn't taste too good, but it will give us something to drink."

"How much further, Will?" Asa asked a few minutes later.

"We're almost there," he huffed back.

William was breathing hard and walking slower when he led them into a small clearing with a mud-covered hut resting in its center. "Help me put him down," Will grunted as he dropped to his knees. Asa and Dirt quickly grabbed the Miami and laid him on the ground. Slowly and with a groan, William rose to his feet.

They rolled Grey Fox onto his stomach, and Dirt quickly knelt beside him. With his knife the older scout cut through the Miami's blood-soaked hunting shirt to expose the wound. "The bleedin' has slowed way down," he announced, "but the bullet is in there purdy deep. There ain't no way I'm gonna get it out with my huntin' knife."

"Can you make a bandage for him?" Will asked.

"I should be able to wrap up his wound by cuttin' strips off the bottoms of our huntin' shirts," the older scout returned. "But Will, he's too weak to travel back to Larkinboro."

"And if we try to carry him back," Asa added, "the Shawnee will have no trouble catching and killing us."

"Come on, Whit," Will announced and started back into the marsh.

"Where're we going?" Asa wanted to know.

"You and I are going to collect some tree branches to make beds for Grey Fox and Dirt, then you and I are headed back to the fort to get help."

Thirty minutes later they returned with enough branches. As soon as the first bed was made, the friends very gently moved their injured companion onto it. Fortunately for Grey Fox, he remained unconscious and felt no pain as they moved him.

"Whit, we'll leave Dirt all of our jerky for them to eat on till we get back."

"That's a pitiful small amount of grub for the two of us," Dirt said as he observed the collection of jerked meat. "What happens to us if you two get delayed gettin' back here? If I try to shoot a swamp rabbit or some other critter, my rifle shot will give away our position to the Shawnee."

"Hanging on the back wall of the hut is a bow and a quiver of arrows," William informed the scout. "Like I said, Grey Fox and I have had to hole up here several times. Just pay attention if you leave the clearing. Make sure you can find your way back. Also, the spring I mentioned earlier is right behind the hut, so you should have plenty of water."

"You know how far away from home we are," Dirt said grimly. "You ain't gonna be makin' no quick trip."

"We'll travel as fast as we can, Dirt," Will Hackett answered, looking squarely into the older scout's eyes. "Just keep him alive till we get back." As the young frontiersman said this, his eyes dropped to the prostrate form of his unconscious friend.

The grizzled older scout gave a determined nod; then Will turned and led Asa back along the secret trail that led out of the Death Marsh.

When they reached the big beech tree at the southern edge, Will paused to listen for enemies. Asa knew that danger could be all around them.

He also knew that if anyone could detect enemies nearby, it was William. The two remained motionless in the brush for almost ten minutes. Finally William raised his hand and motioned to his friend to remain in place. The young frontiersman silently disappeared into the surrounding thicket.

After three quarters of an hour and still no sign of William, Asa began to get nervous. He was trying to remember how to find his way back to Larkinboro if Will didn't return. Asa was certain that he could eventually get home, but finding the way back to this swamp was a different matter. Just then his missing companion silently appeared at his elbow, which so startled Asa that he jumped, causing William to smile.

"I hate it when you do that!" Asa growled in a low voice.

"You just need to be more alert," Will returned, still smiling.

"Nobody can be *that* alert!"

"Are you ready to head home?" Will questioned.

"Is it safe?" Asa asked with concern.

"The Shawnee lost us in the marsh. They're hunting for us east of here."

"So we go southwest, right?" Asa asked.

"Good for you, Whit!" Will returned with a note of pride in his voice. "We did a lot of wandering around to get here, but you kept your sense of direction. We'll make a top notch scout out of you yet."

William took one more careful look around, then turned back to his friend. "Stay right behind me, Whit. We'll move slowly at first. Try not to leave any marks that will show the Shawnee the way into the marsh."

Chapter Eight

STEPS OF FAITH

The two friends crept slowly through the brush and tall grass, hiding their movements from spying eyes that might be watching for them. Once they were well into the woods bordering the marsh where they had left their companions, Will Hackett halted and turned to face Asa. "I haven't sensed any sign of enemies since we left the marsh, Whit, so let's put some miles behind us."

"I'm ready," Asa agreed. "Grey Fox is counting on us."

Will led them through the woods in a long distance lope. It was far short of a sprint but faster than a jog. Most woodsmen and Indians could maintain this pace for hours. William's personal preference was to run at a more rapid rate, but Asa, being unaccustomed to it, would tire more quickly.

Just as well, Will said to himself as he contemplated these thoughts. *After carrying Grey Fox, I'm in no shape to go faster.*

It was the middle of the afternoon when they left the marsh. Four hours later the sun had set, and twilight was on them. William halted beside a creek, which allowed them to rest and get a drink. "The moon's coming up," William announced as he looked through the forest to the east. "It's almost full, so we should be able to see. Can you keep going?"

"Give me a couple more minutes," Asa returned, still breathing hard.

Ten minutes later, they were off again. Will used the moon to keep their course true. With the night coming on, the young frontiersman slowed their pace as they made their way through the shadowy woods.

Over an hour later they burst out of the forest into a moon-lit prairie. Without a word William increased their speed over the sea of grass. The heads of deer nesting in the grass occasionally popped up, and they viewed the strange creatures racing past them in the silvery light with startled curiosity.

It was past midnight when the two tired friends came upon thick woods. William again called a halt at the edge of the forest. "We'll rest here for a few hours, Whit. The moon's going down, and we won't be able to see the stars in this dense forest."

"That's suits me," Asa wheezed. "I'm beat!"

Both scouts stepped inside the edge of the tree line and pulled up a pile of leaves to use as a bed. Collapsing on their respective leaf mounds, they pushed more on top of themselves to insulate against the cool night air.

"Lord," Asa prayed out loud, "please keep Grey Fox alive till we get back. Thanks for bringing us this far safely. We're gonna need you to watch over us tonight, Lord, 'cause Will an' I are too worn out to guard ourselves."

"Amen," muttered William. With their hands gripping their rifles, both scouts were asleep in moments.

"The sun's coming up, Whit."

Asa thought it was part of his dream until a firm grip on his shoulder forced him to wakefulness. "It can't be morning!" Asa groaned. "We just lay down!"

"Come on," William coaxed. "We need to get moving. Grey Fox's life is at stake."

Painfully Asa dragged his cold, stiff, and sore body out of his pile of leaves and hurried dutifully after his friend.

Like Asa, Ember Warren had also been sleeping deeply. She was dreaming about having a conversation with Prisha, the Shawnee medicine woman who had been her mistress when Ember had been a slave. Over time Ember had led the squaw to become a follower of Jesus, and they had become good friends. It was a happy dream because Ember was glad to see her mentor again. A bright light began to shine behind Prisha, and as Ember watched, the light grew brighter and brighter until the squaw disappeared in the intense radiance. Then out of the center of the light walked a man in a shining white robe.

"Is that you, Lord?" Ember asked as she shielded her eyes with her hand.

"Get ready, dear one," a voice spoke to her from the intense brilliance. "You are needed."

Instantly Ember's eyes opened, and she was awake. She lay in the large feather bed that she shared with Katherine Middlebrook. Kate's steady breathing told Ember that she was asleep. Ember knew that she had been dreaming, but the voice had been very vivid.

She had received two other visions of Jesus when she was a slave of the Shawnee. They had been wonderful, and she thought about them constantly. On several other occasions the young woman had also heard the Lord speak to her. Since

Ember knew His voice, she could not dismiss the dream.

Quietly, so as not to awaken Kate, Ember climbed out of bed. Lifting an unlit candle from a nearby table, Ember walked out of their bedroom and across the main room of the house to the large fireplace. With the iron poker Ember carefully raked the ashes off the coals where Mr. Middlebrook had banked the fire the night before. She rolled one of the red coals onto the hearth, and touching the wick of the candle to it, she began to blow at the coal. With each breath it glowed brighter and brighter. Suddenly a flame popped up from the smoldering wick. Placing it in a brass candle stick, she returned to her room with the light and positioned it on a chair beside the trunk where she kept her few possessions.

As the roosters outside began to crow, Katherine Middlebrook was awakened by a sound of movement in her room. She sat up in bed and was surprised to see Ember seated at their table. She was dressed in her buckskins and was going through her medicine bag.

"Ember," Kate said groggily, "what are you doing? Why are you dressed like that?"

"The Lord spoke to me," the healer answered without looking up. "He told me to get ready because someone needed me."

"Who needs you?"

"I don't know," Ember returned. "He hasn't told me yet."

"Well...," Katherine questioned, "don't you think you should wait until you know what you're supposed to do before you go to all that trouble?"

"I know enough to obey Him," her friend answered confidently. "That's my responsibility right now. If I am faithful in the little things, then He will trust me with more later."

Ember went through her entire medicine bag, making sure that all of her equipment was in good shape and that all of her bags and pouches of medicinal herbs were full. From some clean cloth rags that Mrs. Middlebrook and a few of the other ladies had given her, the young healer made several additional wrappings and pads to use for bandages.

When all of her medical supplies had been thoroughly inventoried, Ember turned her attention to her sling and ammunition pouch. Her leather sling was not worn and seemed strong and usable. Her pouch also appeared to be in good repair. At this point she emptied the contents and counted the throwing rocks and clay bullets. Concerned that only four bullets rolled out, she remembered that a week ago she had emptied the bag she stored them in. Immediately she grabbed the storage sack from the trunk and rushed out the door.

The sun was well above the eastern horizon, and people were stirring. Ember needed to walk to the nearby river to collect the rightsized stones, but she knew that she would not be allowed to go alone. Scanning the lookouts milling around the front gate, she noticed one who was just getting off guard duty.

Wallace Murch was a young man a few years older than Ember who had taken several opportunities to talk to her since she had arrived at the fort. She knew he liked her, but she was not interested in him and had actually tried to avoid him. She felt guilty asking Wallace to go with her to the river, but she knew he would eagerly do it, and she was desperate to get the rocks. "Hello, Wally," she said with a smile, trying hard not to sound flirty.

"Oh...uh...Hullo, Miss Ember," the wide-eyed, smiling young settler gushed. If Dirt Gurley had been standing there at the time, he would have said that the boy was grinnin' like a mule eatin' briers. "Ya' know, Miss Ember, I wuz hopin' I might run into ya...ah shore wuz! An' glory be, Ah did!"

Ember cut him off before he could say any more: "Wally, I know you must be tired after standing guard, but I wanted to ask you a favor."

"Oh, anythin' Miss Ember, ma'am! Anythin' atall! You jus' name it, an' ol' Wally'll take care of it fer ya! If you can think of 'er, Ah can do 'er! Why

Ah was actually hopin' that Ah could do somethin' fer you jus' so's Ah could show you what a useful feller Ah can be. You know Miss Ember, many a night..."

"WALLACE!" Ember exclaimed to stop his speech and to get his attention. A wave of remorse was beginning to roll over her. "I need you to escort me to the river to look for rocks." As soon as the words left her mouth, she regretted that she had used the word *escort.*

"*Huh, huh, huh.* Why, Miss Ember," Murch leaned forward to answer, his huge grin growing even bigger, "Ah'd escort *you* to the moon!"

"The river will be far enough, thank you," the young healer returned curtly, then turned and strode purposefully for the gate.

Finding stones of the right size and shape was not the problem. Ember was able to collect a sack full in less than an hour. The problem was getting rid of Wallace Murch after they had returned to the fort. He stayed right with her all the way back to the Middlebrooks' house, regaling her with stories of his unique abilities.

"...an, ya' know Miss Ember, besides bein' able to whistle through my nose, Ah'm about the fastest runner in Larkinboro...o'course Ah gots to run barefooted to get my speed up. Ah reckon my speed comes from my long toes."

Ember didn't want to be rude, but she was getting desperate. Finally, when Murch took a breath, she blurted out, "Thanks, Wally, but I've got to take care of some girl business!" She darted into the house, quickly closing the door behind her.

The rest of the day she spent crafting more clay bullets. So that she wouldn't have to go outside again and risk another encounter with Murch, Ember begged Katherine's sister, Grace, to get her a bucket of wet clay from beside the well.

Ember took her small, rounded stones, covered them with wet clay, and rolled them in her hands until they were round and about the size of a walnut without its husk. When they were ready, she slowly baked them in the coals of the fire, removing them before the clay hardened all the way through. When they were cool, she put ten of them in her ammunition pouch, along with a few throwing rocks, and deposited the rest of the bullets in the storage bag she kept in her chest. Making them had taken her most of the day, but she was satisfied with the results. She had just decided that everything was as ready as she could make it when she heard a cry from outside.

"RUNNERS COMIN' IN!"

The Dancing Ghosts

Chapter Nine

THE NOBLE QUEST

Just as the sun was setting, Will Hackett and Asa Whitlock ran through the open gates of Larkinboro. A small crowd of guards and settlers surrounded them, listening as the two scouts, still breathing hard, related their news.

"Is he hurt bad?" Jack Cobb asked with concern after he heard the report.

"Bad enough, I'm afraid," young Hackett returned. "Dirt wasn't able to get the bullet out."

"He was able to stop most of the bleeding," Asa added, "but Grey Fox was pretty weak when we left."

"Why don't you two get some food and rest a few hours," Jack directed. "I'll have an army of men ready by midnight for you to lead us back to get 'em."

"I don't think that will work, Jack," Will returned thoughtfully. "It's right in the middle of Shawnee country. If we take an army in there, they'll know it right off, and we'll have a terrible fight on our hands. Plus, if Grey Fox survives this, it's going to be over a week before he can travel. I think the best thing is for Asa and me to take Ember Warren back with us so that only a few of us have to sneak in there. I'm pretty sure I can get the three of us to Dirt and Grey Fox without alerting the Shawnee. Then, when Grey Fox is better, we'll sneak back out."

Jack thought on the scout's words before he spoke. "Well, I don't like it, but I see your point, an' I cain't think of a better plan. So I reckon we'll do it your way."

"I'll go tell Ember that we need her," Asa volunteered and immediately left for the Middlebrook house.

"We got something else to discuss," Will said, looking Jack in the eye.

"I'm all ears," the older scout returned.

Will carefully related all of their experiences with the Ghost Warriors. When he finished, Jack remained in thoughtful silence for several long moments. Finally he said, "Since they murdered the two agents, it's clear that the shaman and his followers ain't workin' for the British. An' from what the Miami reported to you, it sounds like this whitewashed magic man is determined to unite all the tribes for a great big war against ever'body who ain't one of them."

"That's the way it looks to me too, Jack," Will agreed, "and the real scary part is that he seems to be doing it. That trick he pulls by poisoning their water and then claiming to heal them when they get better is convincing. It worked with the Iroquois, the Shawnee, and who knows who else before we found them."

"If the white shaman is able to unite *all* the tribes," Jack Cobb concluded, "then...we're done for."

"Ember?" It was Mrs. Middlebrook. "Asa Whitlock is here to see you."

Hearing the call, the young healer closed the lid on her trunk, walked into the large family room of the house, and saw Asa standing by the front door, his hat in his hands.

"Hello, Asa," Ember said with a smile.

"Hello, Ember."

"Mr. Whitlock, would you care to sit down?" Mrs. Middlebrook asked politely.

"Oh...uh...no, ma'am," the young scout returned nervously. "I have an important message for Miss Ember, an' then I need to get home.

"I'm sorry to spring this on you so suddenly, Ember, but..."

"Someone's hurt badly, and you need my help," the young healer announced, cutting Asa off. "When do we leave?"

Asa stood there with a shocked expression on his face. "How..."

"Jesus told me early this morning," she answered his unasked question. "I've been spending the day getting ready.

"So when do we leave?"

"Will and I are going to get something to eat and rest a few hours. You should do the same. We'll leave at midnight."

"Where will you be going?" Mrs. Middlebrook asked with concern.

"Grey Fox was shot in the back. He and Dirt Gurley are hiding at least a two days' journey north and west of here."

"Oh my!" she exclaimed. "That's Indian country! Will you be safe?"

"No, Mama Middlebrook, we won't be safe," Ember answered, "but it will be fine. It's the right thing to do, and the Lord made it clear to me that He wants me to make this trip. My faith response is to go. Your faith response is to send me."

The concerned lady turned and gave Ember a mother's hug. Wiping away a tear, she said, "Following Jesus isn't always an easy thing, is it? I'll fix you an early supper so you can go straight to bed and get as much sleep as you can before midnight.

"Mr. Whitlock, you should hurry home. I know your mother's going to want to do the same for you."

Asa and William were exhausted and fell asleep almost immediately. Ember, on the other hand, was excited about the coming adventure and had trouble drifting off. It seemed to her that she had only just closed her eyes when Mrs. Middlebrook's hand on her shoulder woke her up.

Ember had slept in her buckskins, so when she rolled groggily out of bed, all she had to do was pull on her high-top moccasins, tie her sling around her waist, and throw the straps of her medicine bag and ammunition pouch over her neck.

Asa and Will were standing in the family room when she walked out. The whole Middlebrook family gave her hugs as she left.

"Here's some warm bread I made for you," Katherine said, handing her friend a loaf wrapped in a cloth napkin. Ember thanked her and stuffed the bread into her medicine bag.

"I asked Seth if he and Elijah Nelson would make sure to feed George and to keep his cage clean," the young healer said to Katherine. "Could you be sure they do?"

"Sure," Kate returned and gave her friend another hug.

"We need to go, Ember," Will Hackett said. "Grey Fox needs you."

"I'm ready," she said with a smile.

"Be careful!" Katherine said, addressing all of them but looking into William's eyes.

"We will," the young frontiersman said with a smile.

They hurried to the front gate where Jack and several of the men were waiting for them.

"We scouted the surrounding woods," Jack announced, "and discovered no sign of the enemy. The moon's up, so you should have light to travel by for a while, but that also means the enemy has light to see you as well. I don't need to tell you to be careful, but...be careful."

"Don't expect us back soon," Will returned. "If he survives, it's going to be a number of days before Grey Fox can travel."

"Mr. Spebbington had a bunch of folks in the meetin' house earlier this evenin' prayin' for Grey Fox an' your trip," Jack added.

"Good!" Asa responded. "Please tell the folks to keep praying. All of us are gonna need God's grace *and* favor."

"Alright," Will announced as he scanned the meadow outside the gate in the rising moonlight, "let's go."

William had traveled through the forest with Ember before and knew she was strong, but he wasn't sure how far and how fast she could travel. He set the pace at an easy trot. After they crossed the meadow and found the trail that led north, Will called back over his shoulder, "Are you doing okay, Ember?"

The young healer understood what he wanted to know. "I think I can handle a faster pace," she called back. Both William, who was leading, and Asa, who was in the rear, smiled at Ember's pluck and toughness.

Without a word Hackett increased their speed to something closer to a long distance run. Every fifteen to twenty minutes William would again check on Ember. After the third time, the young healer huffed back a response, "I'm doing fine, Will. I'll tell you when I need to rest." Again, a smile crossed the two scouts' lips.

From then on William stopped checking on her. It was almost three hours later before Ember called for a breather. "Can you rest on your feet?" Will questioned. "It would be helpful if we could keep walking."

As the three of them continued, Ember reached into her medicine bag and pulled out the fresh loaf of bread Katherine had given her. She tore off a piece and handed the remainder to her companions. They also pulled some off and passed the rest back to Ember.

After a quarter of an hour of steady walking, Ember reported that she was ready, and Will picked up their pace. At midday they stopped beside a creek. Eating a meal of the remainder of the bread and some deer jerky, they all took long drinks from the clear, cold water, then started off again. They continued through the afternoon with only occasional breaks. When the sun set, darkness came on quickly.

"We won't be able to see much until the moon comes up a few hours from now," Will announced. "Let's try to get some sleep until then. I'm sorry, Ember, but we can't chance a fire."

"I'll be fine," she returned as she reached into her bag, pulled out a shawl, and wrapped it around her shoulders. In the dimness she saw her two companions sitting on the ground, dragging leaves around themselves. "Oh, I'm sorry, fellas. I only brought one shawl."

"Well...um...I'm okay with sharing," Asa said hopefully.

"Nice try," Ember returned flatly and lay down with the shawl tightly wrapped around her.

"'I'm okay with sharing,'" Will said, imitating his embarrassed friend, and punched Asa in the shoulder.

Will Hackett had them up and moving through the forest by the time the moon was high enough to light their way. A few hours later the first rosy glow of dawn illuminated the eastern sky. They walked along single file, chewing on strips of jerky until there was enough light; then William broke into a long distance run. Traveling in this way with intermittent rests, they were able to cover a lot of ground through the next day and part of that night.

The morning of the second day was uneventful as they raced along the track Will had chosen. After stopping for a brief rest and a lunch of more deer meat, the rapid procession began again. About three hours into the afternoon run, Hackett suddenly stopped, holding up a hand that immediately put the others on guard.

Ember, who was directly behind him, started to ask what he had noticed, but as she did so, the scout put his finger to his lips. They crouched in place for several long minutes, trying to remain as quiet as possible.

Suddenly William pointed to his right, and a moment later Ember heard a faint rustling of leaves. As they watched, two Shawnee warriors stepped into view. They were walking one behind the other about twenty yards away, headed back the way the three friends had come.

After they had passed, Will moved closer to his two companions. "We're getting close to the marsh," he whispered. "Those are two of their scouts looking for us. If those warriors continue in the same direction, they'll cross our trail in a few minutes."

"Do you think they'll spot it?" Ember asked.

"They'd be pretty poor trackers if they don't," Will answered. "We can't use our guns, Asa, or we'll call the whole tribe down on us."

"What do we do?" his friend asked as he saw William lay his rifle and his ammunition pouch and powder horn on the ground.

"You and Ember stay here and be as quiet as you can. When they find our trail and head back this way, I'll get behind them. If they come close to where you are here, try to drop the one in the lead with your sling, Ember.

"If she misses, Whit, you'll have to take care of him with your tomahawk and knife. I should be able to handle of the other one. And both of you...pray!"

On hearing this, Asa turned and looked at Ember, whose lips were already moving in a silent petition to God. When Asa turned back to his friend, William had disappeared. Once again Asa shook his head at how swiftly and silently Will Hackett could move through the woods.

Laying down his rifle, powder horn, and ammunition pouch, Asa slowly drew the steel-headed tomahawk and knife from his belt. Still praying, Ember unwound the sling at her waist. Reaching into the pouch at her side, she carefully loaded a clay bullet.

They watched as the heads of the Shawnee warriors could be seen in the distance moving through the forest. Suddenly the lead Indian stopped, and the other moved up beside him.

"They must have found our trail," Asa whispered. "Get ready!"

The truth of Asa's words was confirmed when they saw the Shawnee turn and begin moving cautiously towards them. So silently and carefully did the warriors move that it seemed to them as if the Indians slowly floated toward their victims. They were twenty-five yards away...then twenty...now fifteen! Suddenly there was a faint sound just to the west, and both warriors turned to face it.

"Now!" hissed Asa, and Ember stood up, whipped her sling around once, and launched her missile.

The swishing noise of the whirling sling caused both Indians to jerk back around. The lead Shawnee spotted Ember and raised his rifle to fire. At that instant the clay bullet smacked him in the forehead and exploded into a thousand pieces, dropping him unconscious to the earth.

Asa leaped past Ember and charged the last warrior. The alert Indian raised his rifle and aimed at Asa's chest. His finger had just come to rest on the trigger when stars exploded in his head, and he too dropped senseless to the ground.

When the warrior fell, Asa and Ember saw that, standing behind him, was Will Hackett, holding his tomahawk. He had hit the Indian in the head with the flat side of the blade.

Chapter Ten

SWAMP LIFE

"You cut that kinda' close, didn't you?" Asa snapped when he saw William smiling at him. Ember was on her knees making sure the two unconscious Shawnee were okay.

"Whit, you knew I would be there for you," Will returned, still grinning. "I saw how you charged right into the muzzle of that warrior's rifle. That was amazing! You know, it does you good to show how brave you are once in a while, especially when..." Instead of finishing his sentence, Will winked and nodded toward the still-kneeling Ember.

"Can't we just agree that on occasion, when I need to, I can do my duty?" Asa answered with the concerned look still on his face. Squinting his eyes together, Asa continued, "My nerves would be better served if friends like you didn't make so many demands on them."

"Are they okay?" William asked Ember when she stood.

"They're both going to have a couple of monster headaches when they wake up in an hour or so," she explained, "but they should be fine."

"Get some vines, Whit," Will directed. "We'll truss these two up so that it takes even longer before they can report us to their friends."

As Asa left, Will bent down and pulled the tomahawk from the nearest Shawnee's belt and stuck it in Ember's knife belt. "Hang onto that," the young frontiersman announced. "You may need it." He then took the other one's tomahawk and both of their knives and threw them as far as he could into the forest. He also collected their powder horns and shot pouches.

As Will finished, Asa returned with an armload of vines. William dragged both warriors to the base of a nearby ash tree, and the scouts bound the two unconscious warriors securely to it.

"We'll take their rifles with us," Will said as he tossed one of the weapons to Asa. "Now grab your stuff, and let's get out of here before they wake up or their friends come by."

William checked the position of the sun and struck out to the north. Within two hours the three friends reached the edge of the swamp.

"So who named it the Death Marsh?" Ember asked with raised eyebrows, looking at Asa.

"It wasn't *me*!" Asa shot back defensively.

"Hee, hee!" William chuckled. "Grey Fox and I decided to call it that."

"Couldn't you have named it something more pleasant?" Ember asked.

"We didn't want to name it something pleasant!"

"How about we call it Daffodil Lagoon?" said Asa as he gave Ember a big smile.

"Well, that's better than the Death Marsh," she agreed.

"Oh please!" Will groaned. "The next thing you're gonna want to do is start hanging up lace curtains in there.

"Come on; let's get moving."

William led them along the west edge of the marsh. They traveled slowly, stopping occasionally to let their leader scout ahead to look for enemies. It took them over an hour to travel a little more than a mile. Finally William came back with the report that the giant beech tree wasn't far away. When they reached it, once again the young frontiersman took time to scout their back trail before leading them into the swamp.

As soon as they walked into the camp, they heard an excited voice from nearby, "Praise the

Good Lord an' bless my neked head! You three is a sight fer sore eyes!"

"Dirt," Will called anxiously from across the clearing, "how's Grey Fox?

"Well, he's still with us, but he ain't doin' so good. He's weak and in a lot of pain. I'm sure glad you came, Miss Ember. Our Miami friend is in quite a fix."

"Take me to him, Mr. Dirt," the healer answered as she slipped the medicine bag off her shoulder.

As soon as Ember saw the injured warrior, she knew he was in trouble. "He's shivering with chills, but his skin is burning hot," she announced. A quick look at the wound in his back told her what she needed to know. "His wound is turning foul," she added. "The infection is going deep and will kill him if we can't stop it."

"It's all my fault!" Dirt Gurley bewailed. "I couldn't get that stinkin' bullet out of his back! I cleaned his wound twice a day, Miss Ember! Honest, I did!"

"It's not your fault," she assured him. "You did the best you could with what you have. What you've done has kept him alive so far, but we have a lot of work to do to save him."

Reaching into her bag, she pulled out a shallow, fired clay bowl wrapped in cloth. Handing the dish to the older scout, she said, "I need you to fill this with clean water and place it on that small fire I saw just outside the hut." Anxious to be of some use, Dirt grabbed the container and hurried to complete the task.

Pulling out her shawl, Ember spread it on the ground next to her patient and began laying out the herbs and materials that she was going to need. Satisfied that everything was near at hand, she grabbed three of the small leather pouches and went out to the fire.

"Is there anything we can do to help, Ember?" Will asked.

She looked up and saw three pairs of anxious eyes staring intently at her. "As soon as the water gets warm enough," she began, "I'm going to make a tea that should help with the infection and get his fever down. Then I'm going to give Grey Fox something to make him sleep so I can get the rifle ball out of his back and thoroughly clean that nasty wound. When I get to that part, I'll get Mr. Dirt to help me. As for you two, the most important thing you can do is pray."

"We've already started," William answered.

"Since we aren't needed here, Asa," he continued, "let's take the bow and arrows and see if we can find some game."

"I've seen several big swamp rabbits around the camp," Dirt informed them. "I even managed to shoot a couple with that bow of yours."

A few minutes after the young scouts left, Ember mixed dried herbs from her pouches into the now hot water to brew up her medicinal tea. Using the cloth the bowl had been wrapped in as a hot pad, she lifted the container off the fire to cool.

When it was ready, Ember had Dirt lift the Miami's head so he could drink the tea. "You must drink it all, Grey Fox," the healer told him when he opened his eyes. "It will help you."

It took several minutes, but she was able to get her patient to swallow the entire bowlful. When he finished, Grey Fox smacked his lips. "Ah, feverfew," he said weakly.

"Yes," Ember answered, "and a few other things. You should start feeling better as the herbs start to work."

Ember turned back to her medicine bag and pulled out another leather bag with markings on it. Reaching in, she pulled out a rhododendron leaf. Then she spent several long moments studying the Miami's size. Looking back to her leaf, she made a small mark on one of the edges with her fingernail. She then made herself guess her patient's size all over again. Once she had made her final decision, she made another nail mark on the leaf only slightly further down. Pulling out the knife at her waist, she carefully cut off a portion, using her second mark as the line of measure. Taking what remained of the leaf, she turned back to her patient.

"Grey Fox, I want you to chew on this. You are to swallow the juice, but do not swallow the leaf." The Miami nodded and opened his mouth to receive it.

Ember explained,"Chewing the leaf will make you very groggy. Once you are completely asleep and can feel no pain, I will remove the bullet from your back and clean your wound."

"It's gonna be alright, buddy," Dirt said tearfully as he patted the Miami's shoulder.

"Dirt Gurley afraid for Grey Fox?" the Indian asked weakly.

"Oh, I wuz before," Dirt answered as he turned to wipe away his tears, "but now that Miss Ember's here, you're gonna be fine."

"Dirt Gurley crying for Grey Fox," the Miami said with a weak smile.

"Burn yer hide, you ornery rascal!" Dirt snapped. "I'm tearin' up 'cause if'n you wuz to croak on me, there'd be no way I'd get you to replace my hat you stole!"

"You lose...hat...in..." But Grey Fox never finished his sentence. He was sound asleep.

It was almost sunset when Will and Asa came walking back into camp. They had a dead deer hanging on tree limbs that rested on their shoulders.

"That there's a purdy pathetic excuse fer a deer," Dirt called to them when he saw the small doe they carried.

"We had to take what came to us," Asa answered. "We decided to leave the marsh in hopes of finding bigger game than a rabbit. It turns out that whole area south of the swamp is crawlin' with Shawnee. We must have seen five different groups of 'em searchin' for us."

"We spent most of the day dodging enemies," William added. "I finally gave up and headed back to the beech tree. We were squatting near the tree making sure no Shawnee were watching when this small doe walked out of the brush right in front of us. We dropped her, grabbed more dry wood to carry her with, and came back to camp."

"Well, yer too late," Dirt shot back. "I done got some eels roastin' over the fire. We'll eat the deer meat tomorrow."

"Eels!" Will exclaimed, "Dirt, what are you thinking? Eating eels is fine for us, but you can't serve eels to a lady like Ember!"

"What chu talkin' about?" the older scout returned. "Miss Ember's the one who had me roast 'em up!"

As Dirt said this, Ember stepped out of the hut. "Hey, fellas," she said with a smile, giving the small deer an appraising look. "Hmmm, I guess you won't be mounting that one over the fireplace."

"Listen, with all the war parties after our hair, we were fortunate to get this little one," Will said defensively.

"Oh, we'll put it to good use," Ember returned. "It looks like we're going to be here for a while. Mr. Dirt and I were able to remove the bullet from Grey Fox's back, and he's resting comfortably for now, but with the infection in his wound, he's still in danger."

"I'm so glad you were able to get that bullet!" Asa added excitedly. "How was Grey Fox able to stand the pain of you digging it out?"

"Little Miss Healer here had Grey Fox chew on a rhododendron leaf, an' it knocked him out colder'n a crawdad!

"Just chewing on one leaf did that?" Asa asked with surprise.

"Only part of a leaf," she corrected quickly. "You have to know exactly how much to give, or it could kill him."

"*Hee, hee, hee!*" Dirt chuckled. "But Miss Ember, she knows pree-sactly what she's a'doin'! Yessiree bob! Right now she's got ol' Grey Fox catchin' up on his beauty sleep. But if he slept fer a week, it wouldn't help. *Hee, hee, hee!* Don't tell 'im I said that.

"Once the Miami does wake up, that rascal's probably gonna be as hungry as a bear! I didn't know if you fellers would find game or not, so when I spotted a nest of eels in the marsh behind the hut, I mentioned it to Miss Ember."

"When I was a captive of the Shawnee, we ate eels on special occasions," Ember informed them. "I actually really like eel. The squaw I served usually cooked them in a stew, but they're good roasted too." As she said this, she looked at the eels and licked her lips.

Leaning close to William, Asa sighed under his breath, "What a woman!"

Chapter Eleven

SPECIAL HELP

With her broken bones, Susanna was unable to do anything other than lay on her bed, not that she wanted to work. Her body was almost entirely covered in bruises, and even small movements caused her pain.

"You all broke," a young voice sounded in Susanna's ear as she lay sleeping early one morning. When the injured slave opened her eyes, she saw a plump Shawnee girl eating a piece of flat bread standing over her. "Good thing Auntie Prisha find you. She fix you good."

"Who are you?" Susanna said with a yawn, annoyed at being awakened.

"I am Tapakikisafeewee," the girl returned, "but you may use my Englich name, Waxing Moon."

"So Prisha is your aunt?" the slave asked.

Waxing Moon smiled and nodded proudly. "I live in hut beside this one," the girl volunteered. "My father is Yellow Bear, and my mother is Moon Beam. She is sister to Auntie Prisha, great medicine woman of the Macaju clan. One day, Tapakikisafeewee be great medicine woman like Auntie Prisha. I be so..."

"How did you learn to speak English?" Susanna asked, interrupting the monologue.

"Oh, I learn from Englichman school when tribe go to Canada for summer. Waxing Moon speak much good Englich."

Presenting more questions to the talkative girl, Susanna found out that the older squaw was Prisha's elderly mother and that she also had been a renowned medicine woman in her day, although, according to Waxing Moon, "She ver' old and kind of crazy now.

"Why Auntie Prisha keep you?" the plump girl asked abruptly. "You no good as slave. You broke. Better for her if she let you die."

"Well, I never!" the injured slave shot back. "What a terrible thing to..."

"Even if you not broke, you still no good," the girl continued. "You skin white like the color of a fish belly. An' you hair not pretty and black like Tapakikisafeewee's. You hair look like yellow clay.

An' you eyes all messed up! Not pretty and brown...they jus'...jus' sickly color."

"They're blue!" Susanna growled, growing very tired of this conversation. "I'll have you know..."

Hee, hee, hee! The girl giggled as pieces of bread tumbled out of her mouth and fell on Susanna's chest. "You blue eyes funny! Look like you ate poison mushrooms! *Hee, hee, hee!* Bet you have sickly name too."

"My name is Susanna, and..."

"Tapakikisafeewee thought so!" the girl interrupted. "You name no good. But you no worry, I give you better name."

Susanna was angry now. "I'll give you a better..."

"I know," Waxing Moon said, cutting the slave off. "Since you look sickly like you eat poison mushrooms, I call you Mushroom Girl!"

"OH, NO, YOU WO..."

"Yes," Waxing Moon said, very pleased with herself. "Mushroom Girl is good name for you." She turned away from the injured slave, who was red-faced and trembling with anger. *Hee, hee, hee*! the girl giggled to herself as she turned to walk out of the hut, still eating her bread. "Mushroom Girl." *Hee, hee, hee*!

Between Prisha and her mother, they kept a pot of feverfew tea brewing constantly for Susanna to help reduce her pain. Several times a day Prisha took a large deerskin bag and left. Occasionally she would have just returned when someone would arrive at their door and take her away again. Susanna remembered that Prisha was the primary medicine woman in the tribe, and she expected that all of the healer's comings and goings were part of her duties.

During the times when it was just Susanna and the mother, the older squaw would shuffle around the hut straightening and cleaning, sometimes cleaning the same objects over and over. When she tired of this activity, the squaw would sit by the fire and sing while rocking back and forth. All of this made Susanna a little nervous, but she had to admit that the toothless old woman was always kind and gentle to her.

The injured slave was stunned at how attentive her two care-givers were to her needs. These were Shawnee women...her enemies, and yet they were constantly giving her tea to ease her pain, feeding her, changing her bandages, and doing all the things she couldn't do for herself. The bitter young woman was speechless when she experienced the two squaws doing the most degrading and lowliest of tasks to make sure their patient was properly cared for. Susanna spent a lot of time thinking about all that Prisha and her mother were doing for her, and it just didn't make any sense. The more she thought about it, the more appropriate Waxing Moon's words became. With all of her injuries, she really wasn't worth all this effort.

"I wouldn't do what they're doing, even for my own sister," she muttered after they had finished changing her bandages again. "Why are they doing it? I just don't get it."

It was two weeks before Prisha let Susanna get up from her bed. The squaw rolled a large clay pot into the hut and turned it upside down. Then she placed several layers of fur pelts on it. With a lot of help from the medicine woman and her mother, they were able to get the weak and hurting girl up on her good leg and seated on the make-shift stool.

"Now what?" snapped the injured woman in obvious discomfort.

"Need...be...up," Prisha returned, struggling to find the words. "Too long...bed."

Susanna was not able to grind the corn for the flat cakes with only one good arm, so Prisha did that. The squaw then poured the meal, some water, and melted deer fat into a bowl and set it in front of Susanna.

"What am I supposed to do with this?" the young woman barked with irritation as she stared at the bowl and its contents.

Pointing to Susanna's good arm, the squaw used signs to make it clear that the girl was to knead the dough. When Susanna started to argue, Prisha gave her a stern look and pointed at the bowl. Still growling, the injured woman stuck her good hand in and began mixing the dough. After twenty minutes Susanna called out, "Okay, it's done!" and shoved the bowl away.

Prisha, who was stirring a pot of stew by the fire, called out something that Susanna didn't understand. When there was no response from the girl, the squaw stood up, snatched a small amount of dough from the bowl, dropped it onto the table, and smashed it flat with her hand. She then pointed to the bowl and said, "Make cakes."

Once again the self-centered young woman began to argue, but another hard look from Prisha motivated the girl to form the flat bread cakes.

From then on the medicine woman made sure Susanna did regular chores. While she had never liked work of any kind, Susanna had to admit that it gave her something to do and made the time go by faster.

A few weeks later, when the bones in her arm had healed, her work load increased. Soon the splint was removed from her leg as well, but when

Susanna tried to stand on it, sharp pain shot through it, and she had to sit back down. Prisha spent several minutes feeling the leg bones and concluded that the break had not healed. In addition to replacing the splint, Prisha began cooking up special herbal teas that she required Susanna to drink.

During this time, the injured woman used a long stick to support herself as she hobbled around the hut. A few weeks later, the splint was again removed, and while there was a little pain in the leg when she stood on it, Prisha felt it was healed enough for her patient to walk on. Susanna tried to use the leg for four days, but finally the pain increased, and the medicine woman reapplied the splint, concluding that the break had still not fully healed.

When Susanna looked down and saw the hated splint on for a third time, her frustration exploded. "YOU CRUMMY LEG, WHY WON'T YOU HEAL? I've got to get away from these Indians, but I can't escape if my leg doesn't heal!"

Just then she remembered a conversation she had with Ember when they were slaves together a year ago. "Why don't you try praying to God?" she had said to the angry girl.

"Why don't I try praying to God?" Susanna repeated the remembered words to herself.

"Alright!" she snapped in pent up anger. "I'll pray to God!

"Dear God...WHY HAVE YOU DONE THIS TO ME? MY LIFE IS TERRIBLE, AND YOU HAVEN'T DONE ANYTHING TO HELP ME! WHAT KIND OF A GOD ARE YOU ANYWAY?" At this point the young woman broke down, sobbing in anger and frustration.

In a few moments she raised her head and saw the older squaw had stopped her mindless singing and was staring at her. When she saw Susanna returning her gaze, the old woman gave the captive a large toothless grin and nodded contentedly. The injured slave gave a deep frustrated sigh and shook her head in hopeless resignation.

In spite of the captive girl's bitterness and anger, the medicine woman would not give up on her injured leg. She brewed teas for Susanna to drink, sometimes five times a day. Prisha also took mixtures of dried herbs in animal fat or marrow and used them as poultices that she applied on the break. Susanna noticed that after several minutes, the herbs began to heat up her leg even to the point of making her perspire.

Sleeping was the only way Susanna could escape the misery of her existence, so as soon as the evening meal was eaten and she had completed her chores, the injured captive hobbled over to her bed of furs and fell asleep. One night she had only been in bed an hour when an ache in her leg woke her up. As she opened her eyes, she saw the medicine woman and her mother kneeling beside her and speaking unintelligible words in low voices. They were looking up so they did not notice that Susanna was watching them.

They're casting spells! she thought to herself. *The Shawnee witches are trying to work some kind of magic on me!* The young woman gripped the sides of her bed and tensed, preparing for an attack by demons. She glanced anxiously around the hut, searching for a nearby weapon. Just then both squaws stopped talking and looked down at her. The older woman's face brightened into her wide, homely grin, and even Prisha's hard face seemed to soften with a hint of a smile.

The medicine woman pointed upward and said, "Chief Jesu...He help." She then reached down and very gently touched the captive's broken leg and said again, "He help."

The poultices continued for four more weeks, and several more times Susanna caught the two women praying over her. The praying made the injured woman uncomfortable, but as desperate as she was for her leg to heal, she tolerated it.

At the end of the fourth week, Prisha decided that it was time to recheck the leg. After she removed the bandage and splint, the medicine woman spent a long time gently massaging the injured leg and carefully feeling the bones. Susanna studied the squaw's face for any sign of her judgment. Finally the healer gave a satisfied nod and motioned for the captive to stand. Prisha and her mother assisted the young woman as she carefully rose to her feet.

Putting full weight on her leg, she discovered that there was no pain. Her leg actually felt strong enough to support her. Her confidence grew as she took several tentative steps. The more she walked it became clear that the break had finally healed, and a smile of relief slowly began to spread across her face.

When she looked up, she saw that the older squaw was grinning bigger than Susanna had ever seen, while at the same time she was clapping and hopping up and down. Prisha also gave the young woman a happy smile.

I don't get it! the injured captive thought to herself. *They are two Shawnee women...I've done nothing but cause them grief and trouble, and they are both genuinely happy for me. I just don't get it.*

As Susanna looked into the face of the Shawnee medicine woman who had done so much for her, she saw the squaw point upward and say with a knowing nod, "Chief Jesu, He help!"

Chapter Twelve

AN UNPLANNED EXIT

Over the next ten days, as they waited for Grey Fox to regain his strength, the friends developed a routine. The men took turns standing guard and tending their small fire through the night. During the morning, while the last one to stand guard rested, Ember tended her patient, and the other two hunted for anything edible.

Grey Fox was recovering nicely. The infection in the wound had given Ember the most trouble, but persistent washings with herbal teas had finally cleared the diseased tissue.

"Ya know, Miss Ember," Dirt Gurley had said with a grin as he looked over her shoulder while she treated her patient, "if'n ya ain't quite certain all the nastiness is gone, I'd be happy to heat up my knife blade an' stick it in there...jus' ta be sure. *Hee, hee, hee!*"

"Dirt Gurley keep his stinking knife away from Grey Fox's back," the Miami quickly returned, "or he be missing more than just his hat!"

"Yep," Dirt giggled over his shoulder as he left, "he has just about returned to his orn'ry ol' self."

With each passing day the Miami grew stronger. He got bored with sitting against the wall of the hut, so he started walking around the edge of the camp looking for pieces of firewood.

On a day when Will and Dirt were away hunting for food, Asa, who had been left to guard the camp, was splitting wood next to the fire with his tomahawk and talking to Ember as she warmed a tea of herbs to apply to Grey Fox's wound. The Miami himself walked over, carrying an arm-load of limbs, and set them near Asa. The Indian then dropped onto the ground beside Ember.

"Have you heard words from Chief Jesus?" the Miami asked. "Grey Fox like to hear what He say."

"I like hearing from Him too," Ember answered with a smile, "but it doesn't happen very often. Most of the time I hear from Him just like you do, Grey Fox, by reading His word, praying, and waiting for His Spirit to give me understanding."

"Yes," the Indian agreed, "Grey Fox can read Holy Book since happy fat man taught me."

"I had heard that Mr. Spebbington was teaching you to read," Ember returned, trying to hide the smile that wanted to creep across her face. "I've spent time talking with him as well, and he really loves Jesus.

"So what have you been reading in the Bible?"

"Grey Fox has read stories Chief Jesus told His followers. Many teach about king-dom."

"Do you know what *the kingdom* is?" Asa asked, looking up from his chopping.

"Yes," the Miami answered with confidence. "The happy fat man tell Grey Fox that a king is a great chief and king-dom is place great chief rules. When Chief Jesus tell stories about king-dom, He teach about place He rules."

"You mean like heaven?" Asa asked off-handedly.

"Chief Jesus's king-dom much more than heaven place," Grey Fox shot back. "Chief Jesus rule in heaven, but He also rule here...in my heart...in your heart too. King-dom is here!" As the Indian said this, he pounded his chest.

"So, Grey Fox," Ember asked, curious to know how much the Miami had learned, "how does a person know if they are in God's kingdom or not?"

"Oh, that easy," Grey Fox answered confidently.

Asa stopped chopping and looked at his friend, eager to hear his answer.

"Since king-dom is place King rules, person must ask self, 'If King tells me to do something, will I do it?' If he will, then King rules over his heart, and he is in king-dom. If there something King Jesus wants and person is not willing to give, then King not rule over his heart, and they not in king-dom. Anywhere King rules *is* king-dom."

Just then Dirt Gurley came stomping into camp, mad as a wet rooster. The older scout threw his fishing spear onto the ground beside Asa. With a yell the younger scout jumped away as a terrifying creature as big as his leg and with a long mouth full of razor sharp teeth thrashed beside him.

"WHAT IS THAT?" Ember yelled.

"That right there," Dirt returned with disgust, "is frustration in the flesh. I spotted me an ab-so-tively beautimus sunfish in that black pool 'bout a stone's throw to the west of here. I spent most of an hour tryin' to get close enough to the thing to spear 'im. An' when I did, no sooner had I pulled it to the surface than this nasty varmint leaps up out of the water and grabs it...fish, spear, an' all!"

"But what IS it?" Asa asked again, staring at the strange, ferocious creature still snapping and thrashing and trying to free itself from the spear.

"It's a stinkin' ol' gar," Dirt answered. "Some folks calls 'em alligator gars 'cause their hide looks like a gator's."

"Can you eat them?" Asa asked as he kept his distance.

"Let me tell you a story," the older scout returned. "A few years back, me an' Jack Cobb was trappin' with Ranse Boudreaux down on the Arkansas. Ol' Ranse wound up catchin' a gar almost as big as that one. Ranse wasn't sure what to do with 'im at first, but he finally decided that he was hungry enough to eat 'im. It took Ranse a' entire day to clean that thing, but all he got was two strips of nasty-lookin' meat that tasted like mud. *Hee, hee, hee!* Ol' Ranse looked like he'd been in a war when he finished. He lost more meat than he got outta that fish. So, to answer your question, if you're a bonehead like Ranse Boudreaux, yes, you can eat a gar."

"Why bring to camp if you no eat it?" Grey Fox asked.

"Because I don't want to lose my next fish to that vicious varment, AND," Dirt added, "I don't want to lose none of my fingers tryin' to get my spear out of his mouth while he's still alive and snappin'!"

Dear one, a voice sounded in Ember's mind. To the young woman that familiar voice was the sweetest she had ever heard.

Lord, is that you? The healer prayed in her heart.

You and your friends are in danger. You must leave this place.

"We must go!" Ember suddenly said out loud. As she spoke, the three men turned to look at her. She was staring into the woods to the west of their camp.

"What's wrong, Ember?" Asa asked with concern.

"Chief Jesus speak to you?" Grey Fox asked.

"Yes, I think He did," Ember returned. "Something is not right, and we must go now!"

"We cain't leave now, missy," Dirt said condescendingly. "Will ain't back from huntin', an' Grey Fox ain't rightly healed up yet. Maybe in a few days..."

Ember turned anxiously to Asa. "We have to go now!"

Asa, who had learned to trust her insights, nodded and gave Grey Fox a questioning look.

"Grey Fox strong enough," the Miami said, responding to the unasked question. "If medicine girl say *we go*, then we go!"

"Now be reasonable!" Dirt started to argue, but just at that moment a rifle shot was heard in the distance.

"We've got to go NOW!" Ember said again, jumping to her feet and sprinting to the hut to gather her things.

"Alrightee then," Dirt exclaimed, suddenly convinced, "let's break camp!"

"Get our stuff together!" Asa yelled over his shoulder to Dirt and Grey Fox. "I'll watch for Will!"

Shoving his tomahawk into his belt and snatching up his rifle, Asa stood at the western edge of their marsh island, straining to catch a glimpse of their returning companion. He didn't have long to wait.

"Here he comes!" Asa shouted to the others when he spotted Will Hackett leaping from log to solid place as he rushed through the swamp. Behind him rifles fired and screaming yells were heard.

When William reached Asa, he was pleased to see everyone waiting for him and ready to travel.

"What happened?" Asa asked as his friend arrived.

"I traveled to the western edge of the marsh looking for game and ran into a scouting party of Shawnee. Fortunately they can't travel through the swamp any faster than I can."

Dirt stepped up and handed Will his rifle, ammunition, and powder horn. As soon as the young scout received them, Dirt handed over

William's pack. Sliding the pack straps onto his shoulder he said, "Alright, let's go!"

"Wait!" Ember called out. Everyone turned to face her.

"We can't go south."

"But...that's the way out of the marsh," Will argued.

"There's danger that way," Ember explained.

"Chief Jesus talking to her," Grey Fox announced.

"Did He give you another way out of here?" Will asked urgently. Just then a rifle fired from the west, and the bullet zipped through the leaves near them.

"No," Ember shot back. "All I know is that there is danger to the south!"

"An' there's danger to the west a'plenty!" Dirt added as another Shawnee bullet struck the mud-covered wall of the hut.

"Follow me!" William said decisively. "And stay close!" As he finished speaking, young Hackett hurried to the other side of their camp and entered the marsh heading northeast.

"Do you know where you're going?" Asa asked from the rear of their small column. At that moment more rifles fired in their direction.

"Away from them!" he heard his friend yell back.

William led his friends through the thick, boggy woods by jumping from one patch of raised ground to another. After several minute they came to a very large beech tree that had been blown over in the past. Climbing up on the massive log, Will reached down and helped Ember up beside him.

"Keep going!" William said urgently and sent the girl down the length of the fallen trunk. He then helped Grey Fox, who assisted Asa and Dirt Gurley as William hurried after Ember.

They rushed along the length of the dead tree for almost a hundred feet before they came to the shattered top. Will stepped off the tree onto a damp, moss-covered island. Just then another rifle fired from the distance, and small limb exploded beside Asa's head.

"Here they come!" Dirt shouted as he jumped off the log beside Will and the girl.

"Let's slow them down!" Will ordered and raised his rifle as Grey Fox joined them.

As soon as Asa landed beside his friends, he whipped around and saw several of the Shawnee warriors climbing onto the log they had used. William's rifle cracked, and the first enemy fighter fell into the black water. Dirt and Asa fired, and the rest of the Indians threw themselves back the way they had come. Unable to aim properly due to his injury, Grey Fox held his rifle level with his hip and fired into the woods in the distance.

"Keep them off the log for a few minutes," Will said to Dirt and Asa. "That'll give me a chance to scout ahead.

"Any ideas?" Will asked Ember as he stepped past her.

"No, but I'm praying!" she quickly answered.

"Pray hard!" Hackett called over his shoulder as he hurried through the marsh to the northeast, searching desperately for a path to safety.

"Here! Load rifle!" the Miami said as he shoved his gun at Dirt.

"Load your own stinkin' rifle!" Dirt shot back.

"Wound in back still hurting," Grey Fox returned smiling. "Load rifle!"

Dirt snatched the weapon and growled, "You need me to wipe your nose too?"

"Here!" Asa snapped as he handed his own rifle to the Indian. "I'll load it!" The young scout took the gun from Dirt and began pouring gunpowder down the barrel. "All this over a hat?"

Chapter Thirteen

ALMOST DEFENSELESS

Will Hackett had been gone less than five minutes when he came rushing back. Ember saw him coming and warned the others, who were firing their rifles at any enemy they saw.

"I'm glad to see none of the Shawnee have made it across that log," Will said when he arrived.

"A few of 'em tried to wade through the marsh to get at us," Dirt reported, "but the water and the mud was too deep, and we was able to turn 'em back.

"But that ain't our problem. A passel of 'em took off to the north jus' after you left. I figure they're a'tryin' to out flank us. They'll probably do it too—if'n you ain't found us a way outta our pre-dickeement."

"I did," Will returned. "Let's go, and step right where I do."

They followed single file behind the young frontiersman as they went through knee-deep water to the northeast. After twelve paces Will stepped onto a small, weedy island of solid ground. From there he began hopping from one solid patch to another.

Suddenly they heard fierce screams and war cries behind them. They knew that the Shawnee had discovered their escape and were rushing across the long log after them.

"Should we try to slow them down again, Will?" Asa asked as he turned and searched the dense woods for signs of their pursuers.

"NO!" Will said emphatically. "No shooting! It's going to be hard for them to track us in this swamp, and we don't want to help them find us. Keep going, all of you. I think we're almost out."

Sure enough, in a few minutes they discovered that they had left the standing water behind them. The ground was soft and damp but definitely not marshy.

"Alright everyone, let's pick up the pace!" Will called and immediately began a long distance run. Hackett kept constantly looking behind. Not only was he watching for enemies, but he was anxious to know if Grey Fox had the strength to keep up.

The Miami noticed Will looking at him and understood his concern. "Kajika," Grey Fox called to his friend, "you run like turtle! We all lose our scalps if you no go faster!"

William smiled at the courage and gameness of his friend and dutifully increased his speed.

They emerged from the woods surrounding the marsh and raced across the rolling hills of a grassy meadow. They had not quite reached the forest on the other side when Shawnee war cries again were heard in the distance behind them. All of the fugitives took a quick glance behind.

"Well, we put a little distance betwixed us an' them feathered heatherns," Dirt observed.

"Not enough!" Asa added. "They're only about three hundred yards behind us! If we can't lose them, Will, they'll eventually catch us."

"I'm workin' on it, Whit!" William yelled back. "Keep running!"

When they reached the woods, the young scout saw that they had gained a little distance on their pursuers, so he turned south in the direction of Larkinboro. They maintained their steady pace for the next hour.

Eventually the escaping friends found themselves ascending a long, steep, wooded hill. All of them were blowing hard when they reached the top.

"I'll slow the pace a little as we go down the other side," Will announced. "That will help us catch our breaths."

When they reached the bottom of the hillside, William looked back and noticed Grey Fox starting to lag behind the others. Examining his friend's face, the young frontiersman saw the clear signs of fatigue.

"I cannot keep up," Grey Fox said clearly, stating the facts. "You must leave me."

"You're right," Will agreed, "but not here. Let's keep going. I think the river is close by."

On they pushed through the forest with their leader listening, sniffing the air, and carefully observing the land. Will noticed the ground tended to slope to the west, and he followed it. They actually heard the river before they saw it. The forest had thinned considerably, and another meadow opened before them as they reached the edge of the wide green waterway.

"Whit, you and Ember are staying with Grey Fox," William ordered. Before his young friend could protest, their leader continued. "I need you and Grey Fox to give Dirt and me your rifles."

"You're leaving us defenseless?" Asa gulped.

"It's the only way. Dirt and I have to convince the Shawnee that all of us are still ahead of them. While we're doing that, you three are going to get in the river and hide under the overhang of the bank. Once the Shawnee chase us, you'll be free to climb out and find your own way back to Larkinboro."

"But..." Asa started to protest.

"No time for *but*," Grey Fox said, shoving Asa and Ember toward the river. "Kajika right! We hide under bank. Waste no more time! Go! Go!"

Confident that the Miami would get Asa and Ember where they needed to be, William and Dirt, both carrying two rifles each, hurried across the small meadow to the south.

As Ember started to step off the bank, she held her medicine bag over her head. Grey Fox realized that she needed to keep its contents dry, so he took the bag from her and shoved it into a hollow log lying on the bank next to them. The three dropped into the slow-moving water and quickly pushed themselves under the overhanging bank.

William and Dirt Gurley reached the southern woods and climbed another forested hillside. About half way up, Will stopped and turned around to observe the meadow where their friends entered the river. Just as he did so, a band of almost thirty Indian warriors came charging out of the opposite woods. When they reached the place where Grey Fox and the others were hidden, the leader stopped and began searching the ground for signs.

"They've noticed their tracks!" hissed Dirt. "Those feathered rascals is gonna find 'em!"

"Let's give them something else to think about," the young frontiersman directed. "Shoot, but don't hit any of them. We don't want to leave any wounded behind. *All* of them must chase us!" As soon as he said this, the young scout raised his gun and fired first one and then the other at the enemies below. Dirt Gurley quickly did the same.

With so many rifles firing at them, the Shawnee were convinced that the entire party they had been chasing was just ahead. Several of their firearms were discharged up into the opposite wooded hillside, and with their war cries echoing through the woods, the chase was on again.

Will and Dirt paused just long enough to finish loading their rifles. "Our friends will head south to get back home," Will announced.

"You're right as rain," Dirt agreed, "so we need to make them screamin' heatherns chase us some other di-rection."

"Let's go east a ways and then swing back north," William said as he snatched up both of the rifles he carried and raced off.

With Dirt hot on his heels, the young frontiersman and the older scout sped through the trees, making plenty of noise and leaving lots of signs of their passing.

Reaching a steep, forested hillside with exposed rocks and boulders, they were panting hard when, after the steep climb, they arrived at the uppermost ledge. "Let's slow them down again while we catch our breath," Hackett suggested as he took aim at a rock near the lead Indian's head and fired.

"Now that right there is a peach of a' idear!" the older scout agreed as he too placed an accurately aimed shot near another one. "We'll hold 'em at bay till we get rested, then high tail it away from here. *Hee, hee, hee!* Once them side winders gets wind that we've hit the bush, they'll have to sprint up this here hill after us. An' when they finally hauls their worthless hides to the top, they'll be a'wheezin' like Preacher Mayfield's pipe organ! All the while me an' you will be gallupin' through the woods fresh as two daisies! *Hee, hee, hee!*"

They timed the firing of their rifles to make it look to their pursuers that more than two men were shooting. Will fired one of his guns, waited a few seconds, then fired the second, making sure that none of the Indians were hit. As he quickly reloaded his rifles, Dirt fired his in the same way. A few seconds after he finished, Will was ready to shoot again.

"I just saw a few of them sneaking off to the north, trying to flank us," William announced.

"I expected as much," Dirt returned. "Them rascals gets dangerous when they starts thinkin'."

"How are you feelin'?" Will asked. "Are you ready to run?"

"Ab-so-tively! Let's lead these swamp rats on a chase they'll never forget!"

With a smile and a wink, the young frontiersman jumped to his feet and sprinted northeast with the older scout racing after him.

"Do you think they're gone?" Asa whispered to Grey Fox as the three of them clung to the roots of a tree protruding through the bottom of the bank under which they hid. Only their heads were visible above the swirling green water that constantly pulled against them.

"We wait little longer," the Miami whispered back.

It was difficult to remain in the same spot. The water was too deep to stand up, and the roots they clung to were muddy and slick. Once Ember lost her grip, but Asa grabbed her before the current pulled her away.

After ten more minutes Grey Fox made eye contact with the other two and nodded. Using the protruding roots above their heads as handholds, he led them back to the place where they had first entered the water. Pausing and listening frequently, the cautious Miami made his way up the bank, then reached back and grabbed Ember's hand, helping her up the steep slope. When the three of them lay together in the grass of the meadow, Grey Fox handed Ember her medicine bag that he had retrieved on his way up.

"Which way do we go?" Ember asked as her eyes took in their surroundings.

"We follow river," Grey Fox returned. "It flows south, way we need to go."

"If we do that, we'll just run into those Shawnee again," Asa voiced his thoughts. Just then faint gun shots could be heard in the distance.

"No," the Miami said with confidence. "Kajika know we must go south, so he and Dirt Gurley lead our enemies east. We follow river."

"I don't like this," Asa said nervously. "I feel almost naked without my rifle. Except for our knives and tomahawks, we're practically defenseless."

"Oh, I wouldn't say that," Ember spoke up as she unwound her sling from her waist and loaded a stone.

"What comforts me," Asa announced when he saw Ember's weapon, "is not that you have it, but that you're so good at using it."

"You speak truth!" Grey Fox agreed. "When she use sling, medicine girl a warrior!" In response Ember gave them both a meek smile.

"Come! We go!" the Miami announced in a low voice and walked quickly along the bank of the river.

As soon as the three friends had disappeared into the woods, a wraithlike figure rose silently from the brush on the north edge of the meadow. His skin was a ghostly white, and beside him were two Shawnee warriors. Using Indian sign language, he sent one of the braves hurrying to find the others in their war party. Once the messenger was gone, the Ghost Warrior and his companion stealthily followed their prey.

Chapter Fourteen

TROUBLE

For the next hour Grey Fox led them south at a quick walk. He figured that, of the three of them, he was the weakest, so he used his own strength to decide when they needed to stop or if they could speed up. During their times of rest, Ember pulled pieces of dried deer or fish that she had grabbed as they left their marsh camp out of her medicine bag.

"I haven't heard any more gun fire," Asa observed during one of the rest periods.

"Kajika and Dirt Gurley have led Shawnee long ways off by now," the Miami answered.

Ember watched Grey Fox as she chewed on her dried venison. She was baffled by this brave Indian warrior who chose to make his home with them, and she had lots of questions.

"How far away is your tribe, Grey Fox?" Ember asked curiously.

"Many days' hard march to north and west," the Indian answered. "Hard to say for sure. Tribe move camp a lot...maybe north near French forts, or could be far west near great sea of grass."

"Do you miss them?" she asked again.

The Miami thought several long moments before he answered. "Grey Fox would like to see them again, but Kajika, Dirt Gurley, Jack Cobb...they are Grey Fox's tribe now."

"How did you and Will Hackett get to be such good friends?" Ember probed, her curiosity still not quenched.

"The Miami captured Kajika when he was young man and made him slave, but he not like any slave ever taken before. He not afraid. Even as captive he bore himself like warrior. He much eager to learn Miami language and ways. He great hunter, and even as slave he fought with us against our enemies. To thank him, the tribe adopted him and made him Miami. He given the name *Kajika,* which means *Walks Without Sound.* It clear to all in tribe that Great Spirit, our Father in Heaven, showed His favor to Kajika.

"At first I not like him," the Miami continued, "but after he saved my life, I saw his true heart, and he became my friend and brother."

"He saved your life?" Ember questioned with her eyebrows raised.

"Twice, counting this time," the Indian answered off-handedly. "Grey Fox save his life many times. But Kajika gave Grey Fox great gift...he taught me about Chief Jesus and how to follow Him.

"Before, Grey Fox lived for himself," the Miami continued. "In before life, I want be great warrior...want much honor and respect."

"Those are noble things," Asa said, joining the conversation.

"No!" Grey Fox shot back. "Those things not last. Once Grey Fox dies, friends may remember him, but when friends gone, no one remembers. But now Grey Fox serves Chief Jesus, so my life and all my deeds done because of faith in Jesus are forever. The honor Jesus gives His servants never ends! Happy fat man says that Grey Fox's life with Jesus has 'eternal purpose.' That sound pretty good! This new life much better than old life.

"Come! We walk some more."

As they continued along the river, the forest seemed to grow thicker. To their left the land began to rise, revealing occasional rocky outcroppings.

With their enemies hunkered behind rocks and logs at the bottom of the hill, Will Hackett and Dirt Gurley pushed themselves to cover as much ground as they could. They did not want to lose their pursuers just yet, but they did want to create a little more distance from them.

"I'd say we done out-foxed them Shawnee flankers they sent out," Dirt said as they ran. "Didn't you say they was circling us to the north?"

"Right," William called back over his shoulder. "So we'll keep heading east and maybe a little south, just to be sure we stay ahead of them."

"You don't think that we lost 'em, do you?" Dirt asked a couple of minutes later. As a reply, William suddenly stopped, turned back to the west, and fired one of his rifles into the woods behind them. A distant chorus of screaming war cries echoed through the woods.

"No," Will said with a smile as he quickly reloaded his rifle, "I'd say they're still on our trail." Dirt grinned back and fired first one, then the other of his rifles. Tossing one of the empty guns to his partner to load, they hurriedly recharged the firearms and raced east.

"Hee, hee, hee!" Dirt giggled. "They's gonna be hoppin' mad when they finds out that they're a'chasin' only two of us!"

"That's why we've got to stay far enough ahead of them that they can't tell it's just us," the young frontiersman added.

For the next two hours, the scouts raced on, stopping occasionally to fire their rifles in the direction of their pursuers.

"We got another climb ahead of us," Will called back to his partner. "Are you up for it?"

"What'cha see?" Dirt huffed back.

"Just ahead, through the trees, there's a ridge looming over us," Will answered. "Do you think you can make the climb, or do we need to turn south?"

"If'n we head south, we'll be leadin' them marsh eels back towards our friends!" Dirt exclaimed. "I ain't too excited about climbin' that ridge, but I figure we need to do it."

"I agree," Will answered. "Let's slow down to a quick walk and catch our breath before we start the climb."

It turned out to be more of a long, steep hill than a vertical climb, but even so, it was going to take both hands to do it. Borrowing a trick they had learned from Gray Fox, the scouts cut two straight limbs from nearby trees and ran the limbs through the trigger guards of both of the rifles they carried. Then they shoved the ends of the limbs under their belts behind their backs. The two scouts pulled a long, narrow strip of leather they each carried with them and took turns helping each other wrap the strip around the upper ends of the rifles, then tying the leather in front of their chests to keep the rifles pointed up as they climbed.

"You ready?" Will asked when he had Dirt's leather strip tied securely.

"Lead on!" the older scout returned.

Using saplings, rocks, and low hanging limbs for support, the two began the arduous ascent. They were almost two-thirds of the way up the slope when the distinct sound of their enemies could be heard through the thick woods and brush behind them.

"They found where we cut our saplings," Dirt announced in a low voice. "They know this is where we started up."

"Climb hard, Dirt!" Will hissed back. "We've got to reach the top before they catch up!"

After several more minutes William could see the top of the ridge. He looked over to his friend to encourage him and saw the older scout with a death-grip on a small tree, gasping for breath. Quickly working over to his friend, Hackett grabbed his companion's arm to help him.

"Sorry, Will..." Dirt gasped. "I'm all done in! Go on without me!"

"Stop talking and climb!" the young scout said firmly, using his powerful arms to pull his friend up the hill. With Dirt spending what little strength he had left, William got both of them to the top of the ridge.

As Dirt Gurley lay on his back wheezing, William untied the leather strap and yanked both of his rifles from his belt, looking down the steep slope for targets. No longer encouraging pursuit, the young frontiersman aimed and fired in earnest. He dropped two Shawnee and quickly retrieved Dirt's rifles as well. He had just fired one and was taking aim with the next when he suddenly cried, "OH NO!"

"What is it, Will?"

"How many were chasing us?" Will asked.

"You saw 'em," Dirt answered, getting back to his feet. "There was about thirty of 'em." Dirt leaned over the ridge to view their enemies.

"Well, there's only fifteen of them now!" Will returned.

"Do you think they're tryin' to flank us again?" Dirt asked as he searched the ridge top to their right and left.

"No, I don't!" Will answered urgently. "I think they figured out that they are only chasing two, and they sent half of their party back to find the others."

"When do ya think they figured *that* out?" the older scout asked urgently

"I don't know," William shot back, "but I think our friends are in trouble!"

"GREAT SMOKIN' POLE CATS!" Dirt exclaimed. "AND WE TOOK THEIR RIFLES! Will...we done stepped in the soup!"

The sun was lower in the sky by the time Gray Fox and the others had completed their third hour of hiking. "It'll be getting dark soon," Asa observed as he studied the sky. "We'll need to find a place to bed down."

Grey Fox grunted and nodded his agreement. Instinctively they all looked at the surrounding woods. To their right the river was still present, but it had changed dramatically as they traversed beside it. The deep, steady current had now become an angry cataract, rushing around large rocks and exploding over others.

"I guess we could gather some tree bows and bed down here beside the river," Asa suggested.

"Not here!" Ember said with concern. "I don't feel good about this place. Something is just not right here."

"Did Chief Jesus speak to you again?" the Miami asked.

"No...not with any words that I could hear," the healer answered, "but something just isn't..."

Suddenly a scream was heard from the north. Turning toward the war cry, the three friends saw the Ghost Warrior thirty yards away, pointing at them. From the east came the report of a rifle, and a ball zipped past, creating a red crease along Asa's neck. With a cry of pain, the young scout grabbed the injury and stumbled backward.

"They find us!" Grey Fox shouted. As he yelled this warning, twelve warriors leaped from the brush and from behind trees to their east and rush down the wooded hillside straight for them.

Ember, whose loaded sling was in her hand, sent one of her clay bullets rocketing into the face of the nearest charging Shawnee. She was just reaching for another bullet when two strong hands grabbed her by the shoulders and yanked her off her feet and into the surging river.

When her head broke the surface, she took a quick look around and saw Asa clinging tightly to one of her arms. Grey Fox's head bobbed in the swift current just behind them. She was also aware of rifle balls crashing into the water near them and others ricocheting off the passing rocks as they were swept away.

The Dancing Ghosts

Chapter Fifteen

A DEADLY PERIL

William Hackett took careful aim with the last loaded rifle as Dirt hastily recharged the others. The young frontiersman's weapon spat fire, and he quickly turned and assisted his companion in the reloading.

"We've got to find the others before it's too late!"

"That's a great idear, Will, but the problem is that we'll be leadin' these slobberin' weasels chasin' us right to 'em."

"I don't think so," the young scout returned. "I really don't believe they'll continue after us at all."

"How do you figure that?" Dirt asked with a confused look on his face.

"Because I've just wounded four of them...three in the legs. It's going to take almost all the rest just to get their hurt friends back to camp. They could send one or two after us, but with everyone else helping the injured, there wouldn't be enough warriors left to protect the rest."

"Well, ain't you just a smart cookie!" Dirt said with a grin.

"Maybe," Will answered, "but you never really know what the Shawnee will do. We better keep at least one eye on our back trail...just in case." He finished loading the last rifle as he spoke.

"Come on!" the young scout said firmly. "We need to find our friends! It may already be too late!" Turning to the south, he hurried along the wooded ridge.

When he felt that Dirt could handle it, Will increased their speed. They kept a fast pace for nearly half an hour. Satisfied that they were not being followed, Will turned west, and the two friends hurried down the steep, wooded hillside until they had descended to the base of the low mountain. Hackett checked the position of the sun, then struck out slightly south of west.

"Do you know where you're a'goin'?" Dirt questioned as he trailed his companion.

"We'll head back to the river and hope to cross our friends' trail," the answer was called back.

"Do you think we'll find 'em in time?" Dirt asked, dreading to hear the answer. There was a long pause before he heard his companion's voice.

"Don't know...just pray!" Nothing more was said for the next two hours as the scouts raced through the woods, anxious for their imperiled comrades.

William called a halt when he detected the faint smell of sour mud. Behind him he heard a long sniff from his older companion. "River's nearby," Dirt said in a low voice. "I smells it."

"Come on," Will hissed as he moved cautiously through the brush.

"Just take 'er easy-like," Dirt cautioned. "We don't know what might be waitin' for us."

Neither scout made a sound as they crept through the undergrowth. Soon they stood on the banks of the familiar river. They saw no one, so both scouts began searching the soft ground for any signs of tracks.

"Over here," Will called to his friend in a low voice. Dirt made his way further south along the bank where Will stood and examined the soft, damp earth in front of them.

"Yep," Dirt voiced his thoughts, "they're ahead of us, and it looks like somebody's tailin' 'em."

"I see where Shawnee moccasins walked over our friends' tracks," William said as he carefully studied the trail, "but there's another set of moccasin prints that I don't recognize. They're not Shawnee, Chickasaw, Cherokee, or Miami." He pointed as he spoke.

Dirt said as he also studied the prints, "You know, it could be one of them Ghost Warriors."

"Most likely you're right," Will agreed.

"But there ain't no big herd of them varments trailin' our bunch," Dirt Gurley concluded as he continued studying the footprints. "It only looks like two or three of 'em."

"I agree, Dirt. This small group found our people and probably sent word to the main war party. That's why half of the ones chasing us turned back."

"But where are they?" Dirt asked. "That group that left us should've got here before we did." Just at that moment gunfire was heard in the distance.

"They're ahead of us, springing an ambush!" Will snapped and sprinted south along the river bank.

Ember, Asa, and Grey Fox bounced rapidly down the river, pushed along by the fast-moving water. Without looking back, the three could tell that they were outpacing their bloodthirsty pursuers because the bullets fired at them were not landing as near as they had been.

The further the swift water carried the three friends, the faster and wilder the river became. A sudden wall of water rose up in front of Ember as a massive wave continuously blasted against a submerged boulder. When she hit the boiling hydraulic, the young woman shot from the water with a scream and crashed back into the turbulent river halfway between Asa and the Miami.

"EMBER!" Asa tried to shout as water splashed into his mouth and up his nose. He churned through the rolling waves to reach her. On arriving on top of the nearest crest, he searched frantically for the girl. Just as he started to panic, Ember's head popped from the water ten yards ahead. Swimming with all of his strength, he managed to catch up to her. She was coughing violently as the young scout grabbed her arm.

Clinging tightly to Asa, the terrified young woman fought to keep her head above the violent waters. The fear of death no longer came from the bullets of the Indians...it came from the river.

"SWIM RIGHT!" they heard Grey Fox yell from a short distance in front of them. "TO RIGHT!"

The roar of the water was deafening as Asa, holding tightly to Ember, swam with all of his strength toward the western bank. Large boulders ahead had narrowed the river considerably, and all the water rushed through a seven foot wide opening between walls of rock. Using both legs and only one arm, the young scout made slow progress against the powerful current.

"HELP ME SWIM, EMBER!" he called over the noise of the rapids. "WE AREN'T GOING TO MAKE IT!"

Jesus, help us! the young woman prayed. Her faith in the Lord reduced her fear, and she swam as hard as she could for the shore. Try as they might to reach the land, a powerful, invisible hand seemed to force them faster and faster down the river. They knew by the strong pull of the water that something terrible awaited them just ahead. When it seemed that there was no escaping the rapidly approaching doom, they abruptly reached a place where the powerful current began to lessen.

They both felt it, and Asa cried out, "SWIM! SWIM! WE'RE ALMOST FREE OF THE CURRENT!"

Their arms were aching and their chests felt like they would explode when the two friends finally reached the shelter of a large boulder lying near the bank. They found that they could touch bottom, and Asa helped his exhausted companion to wade to shore. Hearing splashing in front of them, they looked up to see Grey Fox hurrying to help. It was difficult to get their weary limbs to climb the rock-strewn bank, but when they reached the top, all three dropped to their knees to catch their breath.

A few moments later the Miami rose to his feet to view the river. "Good thing we get out!" he announced to the others. "Big waterfall...right here!"

"God was certainly with us!" Ember responded.

"Everyone okay?" Grey Fox asked as he looked at the other two.

"Asa's not!" Ember exclaimed as she saw the bleeding crease along the side of her companion's neck. The young scout reached up to touch the right side of his neck and brought back a hand covered in blood.

"Unfortunately," Ember began, "all my medicines and bandages are sopping wet, but it will have to do."

"At least the river cleaned it for me," Asa said with a smile.

Ember searched her bag for what she needed. She smeared a wet paste of ground cone flower seeds and feverfew directly onto the wound and gently covered it with a dripping bandage. When she finished, she surveyed her work.

"I'll do a better job when we get back to Larkinboro," the healer assured him.

"Do you think we lost the Shawnee, Grey Fox?" Asa asked as he felt his new dressing.

Before the Miami could answer, a bullet ricocheted off the boulder he leaned against. The friends leaped for cover as another rifle ball tore through Ember's medicine bag.

"We need to run before they can cross the river!" Ember yelled from where she crouched behind one of the large rocks.

Grey Fox took a quick look over the top of his boulder, and immediately two balls glanced off the stone beside him and one zipped past his ear. "Too much open space behind and too many rifles in front! We try run, they kill us!"

"So what do we do?" Asa asked urgently. "You and I both lost our hand weapons in the river."

"My sling is gone also!" Ember added.

Suddenly the roar of the river was drowned out by a terrifying war cry just above their heads. Grey Fox jumped to his feet just as the screaming Shawnee, tomahawk in hand, started to leap upon them. Asa snatched up a driftwood pole lying against the rocks to use as a weapon, but it was too late. The enemy warrior had already launched himself at Grey Fox. At that instant a fist-sized rock smashed hard into the forehead of the attacking Shawnee. The Miami shoved the unconscious warrior to the side as he flew past.

Both Asa and Grey Fox turned and gave Ember a look of surprise. The young woman shrugged her shoulders and said, "I only lost my sling...that doesn't mean I can't still throw a rock."

"You throw good!" the Miami declared with a nod. Just then more war cries sounded as several more enemy warriors prepared to leap across the boulders to reach them. "More come! You fight with rocks," he said to Ember. "We fight with sticks!

"Asa, toss me stick!"

The young scout flipped the pole he held to his friend and quickly grabbed another that lay nearby. The three turned to face the oncoming enemy fighters, but as they did so, more bullets flew near them.

"Stay down until they get here!" the Miami called out.

"THEY'RE HERE!" Asa yelled as he saw an enemy leap from the top of the boulder. Grey Fox clubbed the Indian in the side of the head as he landed. Another warrior followed the first, and Asa thrust his stick forcefully at the attacking Indian's chest. Alertly the Shawnee firmly grabbed Asa's pole. With a cry of triumph, the Indian drew back his tomahawk to finish his victim when a chunk of limestone bounced forcefully off his head, dropping him backward into the raging waters.

The young scout nodded a *thank you* to Ember and quickly readied himself for the next attack. It helped that the boulders above the falls were so narrow that only one warrior could make it across at a time, but the Shawnee were all lining up to charge them.

From behind the protection of their boulder, the three friends heard a rifle shot sound in the distance, then a scream and a splash. Suddenly there was another shot and another cry of pain. Stealing a glance over the edge of the rock, Grey Fox saw that the Shawnee were no longer interested in them. Something on the wooded hill to the east had them all upset. At that moment another shot rang out, then another, and two more of their number dropped. The Shawnee fired their rifles recklessly into the eastern woods, screaming in anger as they did so.

When they finished firing, there was silence for a moment as the Indians waited for the smoke to clear. They had begun to think that they had silenced the guns of their invisible enemy, but the deadly fire began again, and several more were hit. One of the warriors yelled something, and instantly the remaining braves broke and ran to the north.

Chapter Sixteen

BAD NEWS

Shortly after the attacking war party fled north, the three relieved friends saw William Hackett and Dirt Gurley appear out of the woods on the opposite shore. The two rescuers quickly climbed the boulders and prepared to leap the gap over the roaring water to join their friends. Will lifted one of the two rifles that he carried, and Grey Fox quickly scrambled up the rocks to receive the weapon as his friend tossed it across. When it was Dirt's time to jump, Asa caught the gun that the older scout tossed to him.

"Is everyone alright?" William asked when they were all together again.

"Asa was wounded in the neck," Ember answered, "but it's just a minor wound."

"Hey!" Asa shot back. "I resent that!"

"Hee, hee, hee!" Dirt giggled. "It don't feel minor to you, does it, Asa? *Hee, hee, hee!"*

"You're exactly right!" Asa agreed with a smile. "A minor wound is one that somebody else has."

"What I meant was," Ember continued, cutting off the foolishness, "that as long as it doesn't fester, it should heal fine. The only other casualty is my medicine bag. The poor thing's been gut shot." As she said this, she lifted the large pouch and poked her finger through the bullet hole.

"We all grateful to Chief Jesus that He send you in time," the Miami added, speaking to Will and Dirt.

"It were a' awful mistake, us takin' your rifles!" Dirt said sincerely.

"Yes, that's right," Will agreed. "I feel terrible leaving you unprotected, but I really thought we could trick them into chasing us."

"It was good plan," Grey Fox reassured them. "Shawnee just outsmart us."

"It actually worked for a while," Dirt added. "Me an' Will figures that one of them Ghost Warriors hung back when the rest came after us. He an' one or two of the Shawnee with him must have spotted you when you clumbed outta the river, an' they sent word to the war party. When we realized that we only had half a them varments chasin' us, we knew all of yous was in big trouble."

"We got rid of the ones after us; then we tried to get back to you as fast as we could," Will reassured them.

"We're just glad you did!" Ember agreed.

"Enough talk!" Grey Fox said firmly as he checked to be sure his rifle was loaded. "We need go before Shawnee come back. I lead...Kajika, you watch back trail." Without waiting for any debate, the Miami turned and marched quickly south along the west bank of the river.

For the first hour Asa, who was last in line, kept looking over his shoulder for William. He knew his friend was hanging back to be sure they weren't being trailed by enemies, but he thought he would have caught up with them by now. By the end of the second hour the young scout was getting concerned and said as much to Grey Fox when they stopped to rest.

The Miami thought for a moment, then asked, "Has Asa heard rifle shots?"

With a confused look on his face, the young scout answered, "No."

"Then Kajika fine," the Indian announced confidently. "If enemies about to capture Kajika, he would fire rifle to warn us that they come."

An hour and a half later, as they marched through the woods, Asa suddenly heard a voice speak beside him. "Did you miss me?"

In spite of himself, Asa jumped. "Will Hackett," the young scout snapped in anger, "if I didn't have to tell your mother, I'd put a rifle ball in you myself right now!"

"Come on, Whit!" young Hackett laughed. "I'm just trying to train your senses. It's what friends do."

Asa rolled his eyes and muttered, "I may not survive this friendship."

When they realized that William had returned, Grey Fox stopped the march.

"What's the report from the rear?" Dirt Gurley asked what they all wanted to know.

"I made sure the Shawnee weren't following, then I started back to you," the young frontiersman began. "About an hour ago I noticed a covey of quail flushed a ways to the west, so I slipped over to investigate. I saw a party of about thirty Cherokee warriors moving north."

"Cherokee?" Dirt asked with surprise. "Headed north? That's good news. Them rascals must be gonna fight the Shawnee."

"I don't think so," Will returned.

"Why not?" Grey Fox asked his young friend. "Cherokee enemy of Shawnee."

"I managed to get a good look at them," Will answered. "I saw that the leader of the Cherokee carried a peace belt."

"A PEACE BELT?" Dirt gasped. "GREAT SMOKIN' POLE CATS!"

"WHAT?" Asa asked anxiously. "What does that mean?"

"It mean they go to make peace with another tribe," Grey Fox answered.

"Who are they making peace with?" Asa asked again, still confused.

"What other tribe do you know of in these parts?" Dirt said as a hint.

"The Shawnee," Ember answered.

"Right!" Dirt shot back. "And that may be good for them, but that's terrible news for us!"

"But why would they do that?" Asa returned. "The Cherokee and the Shawnee hate each other! They fight all the time!"

"The real answer is that I don't know," Will Hackett said, "but I suspect the Ghost Warriors have something to do with it."

"Great land o' Goshen!" Dirt exclaimed. "If all the tribes start bandin' together, we're in a whole heap a trouble!"

"Grey Fox," Will said to his friend, "we need to get back to Larkinboro as quickly as we can."

The Miami nodded and started a long distance lope to the south.

It took almost two days for the five companions to reach the gates of Larkinboro.

Everyone was both excited and relieved to see them all back safely.

Ember found quite a list of sick and injured who were anxious for her to return. Though she realized the she would be very busy, Ember determined to make time to check on Grey Fox and Asa to be sure their wounds healed properly.

As soon as all the men of the settlement could, they assembled in the meeting house to hear the scouts tell what they had learned.

"You mean those Ghost Warriors are real?" Mr. Spebbington, the school master and preacher of the settlement asked.

"Oh, they's real alright, Perfesser," Dirt shot back, "an' as dangerous as a nest of rattlers!"

After the full story had been told, Jack Cobb voiced his thoughts, "Since you saw them kill the two British agents, it's clear that these Ghost Warriors ain't workin' for them. So what do you figure this is all about?"

"Grey Fox and I think they're trying to unite all the Indian tribes and wage a war of annihilation against everyone else," Will answered.

"How can they possibly do that?" Jack Hart, another of the settlement's scouts asked skeptically. "The Shawnee, the Chickasaw, the Cherokee, the Delaware, the Yuchi...they've been tryin' to kill each other for centuries."

"Leader of Ghost Warriors claim to be magic man...a shaman," Grey Fox answered. "They trick tribes into thinking he has great power."

"And it's working!" Will agreed.

"Yessiree Bob!" Dirt spoke up. "They's scared to death of 'im!"

"Scared enough to turn over control of their villages to him?" Jack Cobb asked.

"It appears so," William nodded. "I even saw a delegation of Cherokee with a peace belt heading for the Shawnee village where the Ghost Warriors were."

"That's bad!" Jack Hart said what everyone was thinking.

"All of this simply because they think this shaman character can heal people?" Mr. Leavenworth asked skeptically.

"The white ones dance," Grey Fox explained. "Shaman made signs to Shawnee and told them dance calls all spirit world to fight for dancers."

"Thinkin' that all their pagan spirits is fightin' for 'em," Dirt explained, "has got them heatherns to where they don't believe they can lose."

"I've never heard of anything like that," Jack Cobb, the most experienced and respected of the scouts, said with concern.

"If these Ghost Warriors are able to unite all of the Indian tribes, we'll be in big trouble!" John Hackett, William's father, said with deep concern.

"We really need General Clark and the army he promised to get here as soon as possible," Mr. Spebbington added. "Has anyone heard any news about when the general might be arriving?"

"Captain Parks is the only one who would know," Cobb answered. "He and his men have been coming by every couple of months to get our scouting reports. He's due to arrive back here anytime now."

"He and General Clark need to know about the work of the Ghost Warriors," John Hackett said emphatically, "and we need to make plans."

William's mother and several of the other ladies of the fort made a big fuss over Grey Fox being shot. They fed him wonderful meals, constantly checked on how he was feeling, fixed him plates of cookies, and baked him cakes.

"Is that *another* cake?" Dirt Gurley asked in amazement when the Miami walked into their cabin carrying a third cake in as many days.

Grey Fox just shrugged. "Ladies good to Grey Fox," he smiled back. "They think much cake and cookies good medicine for wounds. Grey Fox think so too."

"Well, I don't know about that," Dirt returned, "but I do know that if you keep eatin' all them sweets, you're gonna wind up fatter'n a hog on butcher day. Say, why don't you share some of them goodies with your ol' buddy Dirt?"

"You wounded?" Grey Fox asked.

"Well, uh...no, I ain't."

The Miami just snorted and shoved another fistful of cake in his mouth. "*Umm*," the Miami muttered contentedly as he made a great show of licking the icing off his fingers. "Maybe Grey Fox get shot again soon."

"Maybe I'll oblige you," the older scout growled.

The Dancing Ghosts

Chapter Seventeen

PRISHA'S SERMON

Susanna was grateful that her broken arm and leg had finally healed, but neither of them were completely straight. She was unable to fully extend her arm, but it was her leg that bothered her the most. With all that it had taken for her leg to mend, there was a definite bow in the bone that caused a noticeable limp when she walked. Waxing Moon summed up her evaluation of Susanna's situation in one phrase: "Mushroom Girl—you broke!"

The many daily chores were a distraction, but Susanna's constant obsessing over her disabilities produced depressing thoughts and a sense of hopelessness in her.

One morning she had just finished cleaning up after their meal when she heard Prisha call her name, "Su-ah-na."

When the captive turned, a large pile of dirty clothing was placed in her arms.

"We go...wash," the Indian woman said, proud of herself for remembering the English words she had learned from Ember a year before.

Prisha, assisting her mother, led the way to the creek. Susanna followed with the load of laundry. They arrived at a spot in the stream where the water was shallow and there were plenty of smooth stones on which to scrub the dirty clothes.

As a slave, Susanna expected to have to do all of it, but to her surprise, Prisha and her mother both took a third. They spread out along the creek, each woman finding a favorite spot.

It was a very pleasant day, and being outside in the fresh air and listening to the sweet songs of the running water should have lifted Susanna's spirits, but she could only think of her own misery. Taking an article of clothing, she would dunk it in the water, pull it out, and smack it hard on the large, round rock beside her to loosen the dirt in the garment. Every time she did so, she snarled, "I hate this!"

After venting her anger on the clothing several times, she then dunked it back into the water. The wet garment was slapped down once more onto the smooth rock and scrubbed repeatedly across the surface. "It's awful, it's awful, it's awful..." the girl chanted as she scrubbed.

Finally the clothing was dunked once more and tossed into a pile of clean items to hang up later.

Snatching another item, she began again. "What a disgustingly miserable, terrible, awful life!" she spat. "I cannot think of a worse life than this one!"

Suddenly a thick stick struck the young woman in the side of the head so hard that she saw stars. Susanna screamed in pain as she grabbed her head and fell into the creek. The injured girl heard yelling, and when she looked up, there was her old mistress, shrieking at her with hate-filled eyes. Down came the stick again and again. Susanna, still screaming in terror and with blood streaming down her face, tried to defend her head from the blows with her good arm. Injured in several places, she tried to stand up to flee, but every time another blow would drive her back down.

Just as Susanna saw the stick draw back to deliver another blow, a sopping wet tunic struck the irate woman in the face. Angrily the rage-filled squaw ripped the wet garment from her head and flung it to the ground. As she did so, Prisha's mother pushed against the woman and began yelling back at her. The sobbing Susanna tried to use the distraction to get to her feet, but she was hurting so badly and was so disoriented that she stumbled and fell onto the bank.

Furious at being interrupted, the fierce squaw pushed the old woman to the ground, yelling viciously at her. Just then Prisha charged into the angry squaw, knocking her to the ground. The medicine woman was quickly at her mother's side. Once she was sure the older woman was not injured, she helped her to her feet.

Seeing that her daughter was taking charge of their attacker, the old woman hobbled over to Susanna, sat beside her, and held the wet and injured young woman comfortingly in her arms as she applied pressure on the bleeding wound on the girl's head. The distraught captive welcomed the embrace and sobbed on the old one's shoulder.

The medicine woman turned to face the aggressor and began an angry speech, pointing first to the woman, then to her mother, and finally to Susanna.

At this point the mad woman began yelling loudly, stomping her foot, and shaking her stick at the captive.

Suddenly Prisha let out a powerful yell that scared them all. She snatched the stick out of the hand of the threatening squaw and broke it over her knee. Furious, Prisha shook the broken ends of the stick in the woman's face as she let out a string of Shawnee words that seemed to terrify the squaw. Still venting her anger and making her points, Prisha began moving toward the woman in slow, measured steps. As she did so, the other squaw began to slowly retreat.

By the sound of Prisha's voice, she seemed to be getting angrier and angrier as she moved threateningly forward. Finally the other squaw broke and ran. Prisha threw the pieces of broken stick after her retreating form and yelled a few parting words.

Susanna still clung desperately to the old woman as Prisha knelt beside her and began to stroke her head gently.

"PLEASE DON'T LET HER TAKE ME!" the terrified slave pleaded. "PLEASE DON'T LET HER HURT ME!"

"Be alright," the medicine woman said soothingly. "She no hurt you more. She say...you her slave. Come to take Su-ah-na. She much angry...very much...bad angry! She say you hers and must come! She say she hurt Prisha, mother, and Su-ah-na if you no come. Prisha say...uh...*no.* She no be back."

It was a long, slow trip back to the hut for the three of them. Both Prisha and her mother held onto the injured young woman to keep her from stumbling and falling again. When Prisha got Susanna in her bed and her mother sitting down, she put a pot of water on the fire and returned to the creek to gather all their laundry. Once back home, the medicine woman lost no time in adding selected herbs to the steaming water. After several minutes of steeping, Prisha poured a bowl for her mother and another for Susanna.

As the injured captive sipped her tea, the medicine woman began to clean and treat her new wounds. The worst one was the injury to the side of her head. The savage blow caused a three inch gash that had to be sewn closed.

Susanna cried quietly during this whole process. She had learned an important lesson this day that caused her to look at her situation differently. Her life could indeed be much worse than it was with Prisha and her mother, and a feeling of appreciation for these two women began to grow in her.

The next day a very sore Susanna got up from her bed without being called and began the chores. During their morning meal she took the opportunity to ask Prisha the question that had nagged her all night. She knew the squaw only understood a few English words, so the young woman phrased her question carefully, "Prisha."

The medicine woman stopped eating her flat bread and turned to look at the young captive.

"Why do you do this for me?"

The squaw nodded her understanding of the question but reflected for a moment before she answered. "I just like her," the squaw said as she pointed out the door. "Much angry...mean...you know, but Emba teach Prisha."

Thinking back, Susanna remembered from the year before when she and her sister had been captives with Ember. She remembered that long after she and her sister went to bed, Ember stayed up and talked with the medicine woman in Shawnee.

"Emba show Prisha better life," the squaw continued. "Happy life. Life with Jesu. Emba love Jesu, and she say Jesu love Prisha. I say, 'Mi ti, Jesu no love Prisha.' 'Hee nee!' Emba say. 'Jesu love Prisha much!'"

"What happened?" Susanna asked with interest.

"Prisha start see Jesu...in Emba. She change...much different...ho wa si...much good different. She say it Jesu in her. Prisha like Jesu in Emba. Want Jesu in Prisha. Emba say Prisha take Jesu as Chief. Come time Prisha take Jesu as Chief, and He take all bad from Prisha...now Prisha ho wa si...much good different. Prisha teach mother. She make Jesu Chief." As she said this, she looked lovingly at the older woman.

Susanna saw Prisha's mother brighten at the name of her Chief. She gave a big grin and said, "Jesu!"

"Jesu much care for you, Su-ah-na," the medicine woman began again. "We show you."

As poor as Prisha's English was, Susanna understood what she was saying, but it didn't make any sense to the selfish girl. She had experienced the medicine woman's hardness. She could almost still feel the whelps on her back from the beating Prisha had given her for hurting Ember and trying to running away when she had first been made a captive. But the squaw was so different now. *What could change cruel Shawnee squaws into these kind and compassionate women? Could this whole Jesus thing be true?*

Chapter Eighteen

FLIGHT SCHOOL

"I don't know, Ember, George Washington just ain't been hisself since you left." Seth Middlebrook reported with concern when Remember Warren first arrived back home.

"Hasn't been himself," the healer corrected.

"Yeah, that's what I said!" Seth replied. "The little hoot ain't takin' care of hisself; he's got no interest in Lij an' me tryin' to play with 'im, an' he's only et two mice since you been gone! We's worried about the poor little guy! He's gotta be sick with...I don't know...owl pox or...whatever owls get!"

"Well, he is an orphan, Seth, and he's very young," Ember tried to explain. "Maybe all of this has been too much for him. Let's go see how he's doing now."

Seth and his friend Elijah hurried ahead of Ember into the bedroom where the little bird was kept. He sat hunched over in the corner of the stick cage Ember had made for him, showing no response as the two boys rushed over and tried talking to him.

"You see, Ember," Seth moaned, "he just won't do nothin'!"

"I wonder if he's too cold," Ember said her thoughts out loud. "Maybe we should move his cage closer to the fire."

As soon as the little owl heard Ember's voice, he whipped around and began screeching and jumping against the side of the cage to get to her.

"JUMPIN' JACKRABBITS!" Elijah exclaimed. "Look at that!"

"He weren't sick atoll!" Seth laughed. "He was just missin' you, Ember!"

She opened the cage door, and George quickly hopped out and clawed his way up the arm of her leather shirt until he was on her shoulder. The anxious little owl then pressed against the young woman's neck, peeping continuously.

"Hee, hee!" Elijah giggled. "He thinks you're his mama, Ember."

"Well, I guess I'm the closest thing to a mama he's got," the healer agreed. "How long has it been since he ate?"

"It's been a few days," Seth admitted.

"How about you boys see if you can catch a mouse for him?" Ember asked.

"Oh, I got one right here in my pocket!" Seth answered eagerly. He reached into his pants and pulled out a squirming rodent.

The startled young woman pulled back as the boy held the wriggling creature just in front of her face. "SETH MIDDLEBROOK," she gasped, "YOU CARRY A LIVE MOUSE IN YOUR PANTS' POCKET?"

"Sure!" the boy returned pleasantly.

"WHATEVER FOR?" Ember asked in astonishment

"Well...you never know when you might need one."

She glanced over to Elijah who, with a serious face, gave rapid nods of agreement.

Ember found little time for rest after she returned. She was amazed at how much sickness and how many injuries were a part of daily life in the settlement.

"I can't believe how busy you are!" Rebecca Norris blurted out as they left one house and made their way to the next summons for Ember's help.

"I told you we would have a lot to do," the healer smiled back. "Thanks for coming with me,

Becca. It really helps to have someone carry the extra medicines and bandages."

"Oh, I'm glad to do it," the younger woman returned with a smile of her own. "Do you work like this every day?"

"Some days aren't as full as others," Ember answered, "but there seems to be no lack of injuries and sicknesses to deal with."

"I can't imagine what they did before you came," Becca added. After some thought the young woman asked, "Ember, do you think sickness is God's judgment on people?"

"Oh, it's clear in the Bible that God occasionally brings judgment on people because of their bad choices and rebellion against Him, but scripture also tells us in Genesis that sickness and death are things that came from us."

"From us?" Rebecca asked with a concern look on her face. "What do you mean?"

"Well," Ember answered, "when Adam and Eve sinned by eating the forbidden fruit, the consequences were death and sickness. God warned Adam that in the day they ate the fruit, they would die, and from the moment they did, they were dead to God spiritually and began to die physically. In the book of First Corinthians in the New Testament, Paul said that *in Adam all die, but in Christ all shall be made alive.*"

"Adam and Eve sure did mess us up!" Becca snorted. "Why did God put that tree in the garden anyway? Surely He knew they would eventually eat it."

"That used to bother me too, Becca, but since I've spent time with Jesus and I've seen how much He loves us, I understand it better. You see, God loves us so much that He longs for us to love Him back. When He made Adam and Eve, God's greatest joy was for them to love Him. But, Becca, love has to be a choice. You can't make someone love you. They have to *choose* to love you. That's the only way it's real love. By putting the tree of knowledge of good and evil in the garden and telling them not to eat of the fruit, God was giving them a choice to love Him or not."

"But they chose not to love Him," Rebecca said sadly.

"We all have," Ember returned. "We've all sinned and rejected God's love. Now, if someone rejected your love, what would you do?"

"I'd reject them," Rebecca shot back.

"The beautiful thing about God is that He's not like us," the healer responded. "Even though we reject Him and sin against Him, God's love for us is so amazing that, instead of rejecting us, He compassionately comes to us. It's like He eagerly says to us, 'I know your life is a mess right now, but if you'll let Me, I can fix it!' Do you remember Mr.

Spebbington's sermon Sunday? He preached from the book of Romans chapter five where it says *but God commended His love toward us, in that, while we were yet sinners, Christ died for us.*"

"So God gives people the choice to love Him or not, knowing that we're so messed up that we are going to choose not to love Him."

"Correct," Ember responded, "but that's not the end of His love. He keeps drawing our hearts to Himself, and when we decide to finally trust in the love He showed us through the sacrifice of His Son Jesus paying the price for our sins, then He redeems what we've broken."

"Redeems?" Becca asked.

"That's the most amazing part," the healer returned with a smile. "When we give our lives to the Lord, He takes our broken and useless lives and turns them into something beautiful and of great value to Him. It's what He loves to do, and it is absolutely wonderful!"

One day several weeks later, Ember walked out of the Middlebrooks' house wearing a thick leather glove on which was perched a large owl.

"GREAT HONK!" exclaimed Dirt Gurley when he spotted the bird. "Is that the baby owl you rescued a while back? Why...HE'S HUGE!"

"He did fill out," the young woman giggled.

"Hey, Asa!" Dirt called to the young scout just finishing his guard duty. "Look'a here at this little bity hooty owl Miss Ember done raised! The rascal's a whopper!"

"Yeah!" Asa chuckled as he walked up. "I've been watching him grow. As soon as we figured out he was a great horned owl, I knew he would be big."

"How in the name of Sam Hill do you keep 'im fed?" Dirt asked incredulously.

"Well, he does eat a lot," Ember answered. "It takes most of the boys in the fort to catch enough mice for him. He's a little over five months old now, and I think it's time for him to learn to fly. So I'm taking him out to see if I can teach him."

"That sounds interesting," Asa responded with a gleam in his eyes. "Mind if I go with you?"

"Come on," the girl answered as she continued toward the gate.

"So how do you teach an owl to fly?" Asa asked curiously as they stepped into the open area outside the gates.

"Well, he's going to have to teach himself," Ember answered. "What we're going to do is help him strengthen his wing muscles and discover what he can do with them."

As she spoke, she held out her gloved hand where the owl sat and slowly rotated her wrist forward. This caused the large bird to feel like he was going to fall forward, and in response he spread his wings and flapped to keep himself upright.

"Good boy, George!" the girl praised. She repeated the exercise again and again, rotating her wrist faster each time. When Ember got tired of holding the heavy bird, she changed arms. When both arms got tired, she had Asa hold the owl and continue the exercise. After working with George for a quarter of an hour, Ember announced, "Alright, I think he's got the flapping part. Now let's show him how powerful those wings are."

Taking the owl back on her rested arm, she rotated her wrist quickly, but as the broad wings extended, Ember tossed the owl a short distance into the air. In a panic the startled bird flapped furiously and actually flew for a few feet before tumbling into the grass.

"HE DID IT!" Asa exclaimed. "He actually flew a ways!"

"What a good boy!" Ember gushed as she hurried to the bird's side. She dropped her gloved hand, and George eagerly hopped onto it. Once again she praised the bird, and a rumbling chirp came from his chest. With her left hand Ember reached into her skirt pocket and pulled out a small piece of meat that she lifted to the owl's beak. Excitedly George snatched the morsel and gulped it down.

"Wow! Look at him!" Asa observed excitedly. "He'll do anything for you!"

"And a bite of meat," the young woman added with a smile.

"Well, they say that the way to a man's heart is through his stomach," the scout chuckled.

"Apparently, that's true for owls as well," Ember returned with a giggle. "When he finishes his snack, we'll let him try flying a few more times."

They observed with delight that, each time she tossed George into the air, he traveled further than he had previously.

By the end of a week, the young owl was launching himself into the air from the glove and flying around the meadow. Near the end of a lesson, as she watched him soaring effortlessly in the distance, Ember thought that this might be the last time she would see the great bird. But as she turned to head back toward the gates, she heard an anxious call behind her. Looking back, she was just in time to catch the owl as he dropped lightly onto her hand.

"Well, hey!" she said with a big smile. "I thought you might want to go exploring."

The bird answered with a deep rumble from his chest and rubbed his head against the girl's shoulder.

"Maybe the world's still a little too scary. That's okay. How about we go home and get some supper?"

Ember wasn't sure if he understood the word *supper* or not, but as soon as she said it, George began dancing from side to side on her hand. With a laugh she turned back to the fort where smoke from the many cooking fires drifted over the log walls.

As large as Ember's owl was getting, she realized that the huge bird was getting too big for the cage she had built for him. Since he was flying now, she didn't want to confine him anymore. She liked that he chose to be with her, but she wanted George to have the freedom to live his own life.

Ember got permission to construct a large, roofed perch for the owl beside one of the blockhouses near the gate, and with Asa's help, she was able to get it built in just a few days. The perch had walls around part of it to allow the bird to get out of the weather. To encourage George to stay in the perch rather than follow her home, she began to feed him in his new roost.

Grateful for his new-found freedom, the large owl took quickly to his home. The boys in the settlement thought it great fun to climb the ladder to the catwalk on the wall and feed George the mice they had caught. Except for his occasional loud hoots that startled the nearby guards, everyone in the fort adjusted to George's presence.

The Dancing Ghosts

Chapter Nineteen

A NEW LIFE

Susanna knelt over the pool of water at the creek, preparing to wash more clothes. She happened to spot her reflection in the water and was shocked to see a noticeable scar on the side of her face from the severe beating she had received.

"I used to be so pretty!" the young woman cried sorrowfully as she reached up and touched the scar. At that moment she began to reflect on all that had happened to her. Her parents and friends were all dead, her home was burned to the ground, her injury to her leg caused her to walk with a limp, and her broken arm was still much weaker than the other and ached on cold mornings. She realized that she was nothing more than an ugly, crippled slave. The thought broke her heart, and she burst into tears, sobbing into the clothes she was supposed to wash.

Suddenly two gentle hands grabbed her shoulders and pulled her into a hug. As she blinked the tears away, Susanna saw the medicine woman's mother holding her as she rocked back and forth muttering soothing words. The sorrowful young woman looked up and saw that Prisha also was standing beside them. She reached down a coarse, rough hand and began gently stroking the girl's hair. When the distressed slave saw the compassion in her mistress's eyes, she grabbed her hand and held it desperately to her own cheek.

"You have both been so good to me!" Susanna cried through her tears. "I've done nothing but cause you trouble! I'm a horrible person! I've hurt everybody I've ever been around! I don't deserve your kindness!"

The medicine woman didn't understand most of the sobbing girl's words, but the meaning of her heart was unmistakable. "Jesu say..." the squaw stopped and tried to think of the English words. Finally she gave up and said in Shawnee, "'Nikitakwelemele.'"

"What?" Susanna asked with a confused expression.

"Howeesa!" Prisha's smiling mother joined in. "Nikitakwelemele, Jesu!"

"What are you both saying?"

Still unable to remember the English word, Prisha tried a different tactic. After getting Susanna's attention, the squaw patted her own chest and said, "Jesu." Then she stepped close to the girl and gave her a hug, rubbing her back lovingly.

"You're saying that Jesus loves me?" the slave said as she wiped away her tears.

"Howeesa!" Presha answered with a smile as Susanna said the sought-for word. "Jesu love Su-ah-na! Jesu love Prisha! Jesu love nikya," pointing to her mother.

"But, Prisha," Susanna asked, "how could Jesus ever love me?"

"He Jesu, Son of Moneto!" came the confident answer. "If He love Prisha, He can love you! Trust Him! Make Him Chief! Life much good with Chief Jesu!"

"But how?" the young woman asked again.

"Talk to Him," Prisha returned. "Jesu good! Ask Him be you chief."

Tears again began to flow down the young woman's cheeks as she, for the first time in her life, voluntarily stepped into the presence of the Lord of the universe. "Jesus," she began, "I must be the last person in the world who should be talking to You, but Prisha insists that You love me and want to hear from me.

"I've lost everything, Jesus! I've lost my parents, my home, my friends, my sister...That was my fault, Lord. I betrayed Becca and Ember to save myself...I've lost my freedom, and my health. I have lost everything...but You. When my life was at its worst, You sent these two precious servants of Yours to show me Your love. I guess the presence of Prisha and her mother in my life proves that You love me, since You could have easily let me die at the hands of my wicked mistress.

"I've been such a terrible person, Lord. I've done so much that needs forgiving. I remember hearing on Sundays about You hanging on a cross for us, but I never paid any attention. You did that to pay for my sins, didn't You, Jesus? I know what beatings feel like, but Yours were so much worse than mine. I didn't have a choice, but You did it willingly...for me! O Jesus, is this really true? Can I really be forgiven and belong to You? I want that, Lord! I want to belong to someone who loves me even if I'm broken and ugly!

"I guess the fact that I'm talking to You shows that I believe in You, Jesus. I don't know how that happened, but I like it. I think I'm ready. I want You to be my Chief or King or Lord or whatever...just as long as You are mine and I am Yours!

"Thank You, Jesus! Thank You for sending Prisha and her mother to me! Thank You for coming to me and forgiving me and letting me be Yours! I love You too...Oh, uh...amen."

Susanna looked up and saw Prisha and her mother smiling at her.

"Jesu you Chief?" the medicine woman asked expectantly.

Susanna's tear-stained face spread into a beautiful smile. "YES!" she exclaimed with joy, "Jesus is my Chief!"

Six weeks after Will, Dirt, Asa, and Ember arrived back at the fort with Grey Fox, the sentinels guarding the front gates of Larkinboro saw a party of twenty men appear out of the forest, marching in pairs toward the settlement. They halted about fifty yards from the wall, and the leader called out. "HALLOO THE FORT!"

"HOWDY BACK!" one of the guards shouted in return. "WHO ARE YOU, AND WHAT'S YER BUSINESS?"

"CAPTAIN PARKS WITH THE COLONIAL MILITIA!" came the answer, not bothering to give any more information.

Quickly the gates were opened, and the captain led his men inside.

"Welcome, Cap'n," Jack Cobb said warmly as he extended his hand to the officer.

Parks returned the greeting as well as those of the other men of the fort who had quickly assembled at the news of his arrival.

"We'll set your men up with families where they'll get a hot meal and warm bed for as long as you're staying with us," said John Hackett, Will's father and one of the leading men of the settlement.

"Thank you," Parks returned gratefully. "We'll take advantage of your hospitality tonight, but we have to leave first thing in the morning. That's really why I'm here. Gather your men, and I'll tell you what's going on."

In thirty minutes, except for those on guard duty, every man in the fort had assembled in the meeting house and was listening to the captain's report.

"So General Clark's army has come at last!" Mr. Spebbington exclaimed. "HALLELUJAH!"

"Well, at least part of his army has come," Parks corrected. "The messenger he sent to us said that the general had gathered several hundred men at Fort Henry in Wheeling, Virginia, waiting for more men. Colonel Lochry of Pennsylvania was supposed to be collecting another three or four hundred men, but weeks went by, and he still hadn't shown up. Finally General Clark decided that he couldn't wait any longer. The general ordered his men into their boats, and they started down the Ohio River. He left boats and provisions behind at the fort for Colonel Lochry, as well as a message that they were to follow as soon as practical.

"I received word from the general yesterday that he and his men had landed their boats on the Kentucky side of the river and were waiting for their reinforcements."

"They're campin' on the Ohio?" Dirt Gurley asked with concern. "That's purdy far north. Lots of Injuns up there."

"Yes, that's true," Parks answered, "but the general believes that he has enough troops to defend himself."

"Maybe not," Jack Cobb said ominously. Quickly Captain Parks was informed of the Ghost Warriors' attempts to unify the hostile tribes for the purpose of destroying everyone—British, French, and American, and establishing an empire of united tribes.

"You *sure* about this?" Parks asked in dismay.

"There's no doubt, Captain!" William said confidently. "We saw it with our own eyes."

"An' their stinkin' plan is workin' too!" Dirt added. "Shawnee, Cherokee, Iroquois...ancient enemies, are all comin' together to form an alliance with the Ghost Warriors as their leaders."

"WHAT?" Parks exclaimed. "The tribes have never done that before...EVER!"

"I know!" Dirt commiserated. "It's the beatin'est thing! Why, it's enough to make a man lose faith in Injuns...uh...present company excluded." Dirt quickly added as he saw Grey Fox giving him a hard look.

"Well, this changes everything!" the captain said with concern. "I'll need to send most of my men to warn the general while I take several others with me and your scouts to find those Ghost Warriors and figure out their plans before they can bring about a disaster."

"What are your orders, Captain?" Jack Cobb asked.

"The men are tired, but we can't wait. If you can supply us with food, I will send Lieutenant Fremont with men to General Clark this evening. It'll take them several days to reach him, but if we delay, a large, organized army of Indians could annihilate his command."

"I will begin gathering the provisions," Mr. Spebbington announced and quickly left the room.

"I'll need some of your scouts to help me find those Ghost Warriors as fast as we can."

"Will Hackett," Jack said, locking eyes with the young scout, "you and Dirt will need to take the captain and his men back to where you last saw those Indians."

"Grey Fox go too," the Miami announced as he stepped forward.

"Have you recovered enough?" William asked with concern.

"Humph!" Gray Fox gave an annoyed snort at the question.

"It ain't his wound I'm a'worried about," Dirt Gurley said skeptically. "It's his belly! He's been eatin' so many cakes an' pies that he's fatter'n a toad eatin' mayflies!"

The Dancing Ghosts

Chapter Twenty

FINDING THE ENEMIES

It was a clear night. An hour before, the sun had set, and the stars were shining brightly. Captain Parks assembled his men at the gate.

All of the commotion seemed to greatly interest the resident owl. He paced back and forth on his perch as he, with his one good eye, watched with fascination the movements of the small crowd of men below him.

Jack Cobb, Will Hackett, Dirt Gurley, and Grey Fox were there. Parks spent several minutes giving his men instructions, going over in detail where they would find General Clark.

"Lieutenant, you don't have time to get bogged down in an Indian fight," Parks charged him. "If they get after you, you're just gonna have to run for it. If the Indians force you to stand and fight, the general and his men will most likely be ambushed and slaughtered. You have to get to him and warn them about the Indian army that's coming! Do you understand?"

"Hoo hoo HOO hoo hoo!" called the huge bird from just over their heads, causing all of the men to jump.

"Yes, sir!" Fremont answered, giving a salute as he nervously glanced up at the large owl staring at him from above. "We'll get to him, sir."

"As soon as we find out what the Ghost Warriors and their forces are going to do," Parks continued, "I will get word to the general. Now off with you, Lieutenant. You have a long way to go and not much time to get there."

Glancing at the sky, the lieutenant identified the North Star. "Follow me, men!" Fremont called back to small troop. "Double time!" The lieutenant turned and dashed out of the gate opening as George Washington gave them a parting *hoot.* When the troops cleared the north corner of the palisade, Fremont led his men across the star-lit plain toward the dark woods.

As soon as the column of soldiers was gone, Jack Cobb turned to Will, Dirt, and Grey Fox. "Take Captain Parks and his three men to the spot where you last saw the Ghost Warriors," Jack said to his friends. "If they ain't there, you're gonna have to track 'em down. Somehow you need to figure out what their plans are in time to get word to General Clark. You're going into an extremely dangerous situation with no one to help you, so whatever else you do...be careful! You hear?" Jack looked each of them in the eye as he said these last words, and they could hear the concern in the older scout's voice.

"Don't worry about a thing, Jack!" Dirt announced confidently. "They got me with 'em!"

"Humph!" Grey Fox snorted.

"Now what is *that* supposed to mean?" Dirt growled back.

"LET'S MOVE!" ordered Captain Parks.

With Dirt still growling at the smiling Miami, Will led them out of the gate at a rapid pace as the large owl hooted goodbye to them as well.

William had made this trip multiple times in the last two months, so he knew where he was going. The young scout had to slow down when they entered the dark forest, but within an hour a three-quarter moon had risen high enough to provide some light, and they increased their pace once more. After traveling for nearly six hours, they stopped for a rest.

"Soldiers having trouble keeping up," Grey Fox said quietly so that only Will and Dirt could hear.

"The captain did say that they were all pretty tired when they got to the fort," Dirt brought up.

"The moon has moved across the sky and ain't givin' as much light now, so we'd be travelin' much slower anyway. It might help us in the long run if we rest here till daylight."

"We make better time if they rest," Grey Fox agreed.

"I think you're both right," Will agreed. "I figure that dawn is about four hours away, but even a short break will help them."

"Captain Parks," Will called, "the moon's going down, and it's getting hard to see the trail. The sun should be up in about four hours. Let's rest here till it's light enough to see. My friends and I will take turns on watch so you and your men can get some sleep."

Seeing the logic in what he said and grateful to get off their feet, Parks instructed his men to bed down. All of them dropped where they stood and were snoring within minutes.

William slept for a few hours before a light touch on his shoulder woke him. His hands immediately went to his weapons. Recognizing Grey Fox kneeling over him, Will sat up.

"Sun coming up," the Miami announced.

"Okay," the young scout returned, shaking his head to clear his thoughts. "Let's get them up and moving again."

Within five minutes the column was racing along the trail, each one chewing on a piece of jerky for his breakfast.

For two more days they sped for the village where the strange Indians had been. When they got close, the column halted while William and Grey Fox scouted ahead.

"Where'd they go?" Parks asked in frustration when the scouts returned and reported the village gone.

"They go north," Grey Fox answered. "Been gone several weeks."

"Well, let's go find them!" the captain ordered.

Fortunately the signs of an entire village being moved left a clear trail for them to follow. They tracked them until midafternoon on the second day when suddenly Grey Fox, who was in the lead, stopped and ducked behind a large tree. Instantly everyone halted and locked eyes on the Miami, who made urgent signs to his friends.

"Injuns is comin'!" Dirt hissed just loud enough for the others to hear.

"Take cover and don't make a sound!" William ordered and immediately crept silently into the brush. Parks and his rangers knew exactly what to do and also disappeared into the surrounding woods. Immediately a hunting party of ten Shawnee warriors filed out of the woods, moving quickly along the trail. They were even with the hidden militia when one Indian in the middle of the group suddenly stopped, causing the ones behind him to bump into each other. Angry words were spoken by the warriors behind, but the standing Indian held up his hand to silence them. He began to sniff the air as he turned and stared into the surrounding woods.

"He's caught a scent of us," Dirt hissed in William's ear as they lay hidden in the brush nearby.

For several long, tense moments, the Shawnee continued searching the area until the warrior directly behind him shoved him hard in the back and shouted angrily. With an intimidated look, the standing warrior turned and trotted after their comrades.

"That close," Grey Fox said after the Shawnee were gone.

"You're tellin' me!" Dirt Gurley agreed.

"Chief Jesus looking out for us," the Miami said confidently.

"Well," Dirt answered, "the Good Lord did say, *Lo, I am with you always,* an' we was laying mighty low!"

A groan escaped the Miami's lips.

"*Hee, hee, hee,*" Dirt chuckled. "*Low* I am with you! Even you have to admit that was funny!"

"What funny is that, whenever Dirt Gurley tell joke," Grey Fox returned, "he is only one who laughs."

"Oh, is that so?" the older scout shot back. "Well, maybe that jus' proves that I'm surrounded by stale people who ain't got no sense of humor!"

"Hmm," the Indian answered with a slight smile. "Could also mean Dirt Gurley can't tell joke."

The red-faced older scout was about to respond when he was cut off. "We got to be close to their camp!" Parks hissed as he joined the scouts. "We better get off this trail!"

"Move your men into the woods to the west, Captain," Will directed. "Keep still and make no noise while my friends and I scout ahead."

As Parks and his three men found places of concealment, William, Dirt, and the Miami moved cautiously forward. They traveled parallel to the trail they had been following but remained almost a stone's throw to the west. Making no sound as they went, the three scouts eventually crossed a shallow creek and came to a small clearing with a log cabin. Communicating with Indian sign language, they decided to sneak around the cabin and keep traveling north.

Will had just begun to move when Grey Fox quickly grabbed his arm. As they looked, a small band of Indians strode deliberately out of the woods from the north and headed straight to the cabin.

"Chiefs!" Grey Fox whispered to his companions.

"An' bless my bunions if it ain't some of them Ghost Warriors with 'em!" Dirt hissed.

"That tall one is the shaman," Will whispered back.

The friends watched from their hiding place as the party of Indians marched to within ten yards of the cabin before they stopped. One of the Shawnee chiefs gave a shout, and a few moments later the door jerked open, and a large trapper with a thick black beard walked out.

All three of the observing scouts gave a start when they saw the large man. "Hey!" Dirt gasped in a low voice. "Ain't that..."

"That him," Grey Fox answered the unfinished question.

"Yeah," Will agreed grimly. "That's Rayford!"

"But he's supposed to be dead!" Dirt shot back.

"Humph," Grey Fox snorted. "Him not look so dead."

"That's because he *ain't* dead," an annoyed Dirt Gurley hissed back. "He's just *supposed* to be! How in the name of Dub Tatum did he survive falling into them rapids when we had that fight at the waterfall last year? That snake almost killed me!"

"He almost killed Ember too," Will returned, remembering the deadly battle.

"Him tough man," Grey Fox said. "Not easy to kill."

"He's a dangerous man too," Dirt added as he rubbed the top of his head, having not forgotten being lifted into the air by his hair. "We don't need to be messin' with him if'n we can avoid it."

As they watched, a very tense discussion took place between the Indians and the trapper. Part of the debate was in Shawnee, and the other half was in Indian sign language for the benefit of the Ghost Warriors, who apparently didn't speak Shawnee.

"There's a tree in my way," Dirt whispered, "an' I'm only getting' some of the signs. What's goin' on?"

"The chiefs are telling the Ghost Warriors that Rayford is part of their tribe and that he fights with them," Will, who had a better view, explained. "But the shaman's not buying it. Because Rayford's not Indian, the shaman wants to kill him."

"Is that right?" Dirt said with a grin. "Well, one thing I can say about that painted wizard is that he's a good judge of character."

"The chiefs are defending Rayford," Will added, "but the white ones don't look convinced.

Their warriors are surrounding the trapper with their spears."

"Well, there you have it," Dirt whispered confidently. "*Be sure your sins will find you out!* That's biblical, ya know."

Nothing else was reported for several long moments. Dirt craned his neck to get a better view. "What's happenin'?" Dirt asked. "How come the pokin' party ain't started yet?"

"Rayford sign to them," Grey Fox explained. "He say they need him. He say he know the American army's plan, and he can help Ghost Warriors defeat them."

"He's such a snake!" Dirt hissed. "That rascal is gonna sacrifice the general and all his troops jus' to save his own scalp."

"Dirt," Will spoke, "go back and let Captain Parks know what's going on here. Keep him and his men quiet and still until we return. Grey Fox and I will stay and see what else we can learn. As soon as we have more information, one or both of us will join you.

Chapter Twenty-One

WALNUT

"What's wrong, Prisha?" Susanna asked when she saw her mistress rush into their hut with a look of concern on her face.

"It bad," the medicine woman said, more to herself than in answer to the question. "Much bad!"

"What is it?" Susanna asked again.

Apparently Prisha's mother asked the same question, because in response to the older squaw's words, Prisha began a rapid and animated discourse. Finally the younger squaw turned to Susanna. "It bad, Su-ah-na!" she began. "Much Indian come village...much bad Indian!"

"More Shawnee have come?" the slave asked.

"Some Shawnee," Prisha explained, "also Cherokee, Iroquois, Osage, Kickapoo...much Indian!"

"And you said this is bad, right?" Susanna asked somewhat confused.

"INDIAN BAD!" the squaw snapped. "It good if come for peace, but Indian come for fight! Make war on your people! And now painted shaman come!"

"Who is that?" the young woman asked with concern.

"He bad!" Prisha said firmly. "He much bad! He come to village painted all white...he and his followers...all white."

"Why do they paint themselves? What does it mean?"

"Paint all white so people fear," Prisha answered. As she said this, she raised her hands above her head and made a scary face at Susanna. *"Hmmph!"* the squaw snorted in disgust as she dropped her hands. "Look like dead fish," she muttered with contempt.

"Why are they here?" Susanna asked again, irritated at not understanding what it meant.

"White shaman, he work magic...say have much power." At this statement the medicine woman turned and spit on the ground. "Shaman, he no power. Chief Jesu, He power...much power!"

"But the bad Indians *think* the shaman has power, is that what you mean?" the girl asked, trying to piece it together.

On hearing this Prisha made a face and waved a dismissing hand toward the hut entrance. "They foolish and full of hate. Want kill all who not Indian. They not follow Chief Jesu. They follow Watch-a-ne-toc."

"Watch-a-ne-toc?"

"Bad one," Prisha explained. "Hate Jesu! Watch-a-ne-toc!"

"Oh," the girl said as realization struck her. "You mean the devil."

"Seela," Prisha answered, nodding her head. "De-vil...Watch-a-ne-toc. He much bad. He hate...he kill. Bad Indians like Watch-a-ne-toc. Hate much...kill much!"

At this point Prisha's mother walked over and wrapped her arms around Susanna and began speaking to her daughter. Another animated discussion took place between the two. The more they talked, the tighter the mother held onto the captive young woman. Finally the medicine woman turned to Susanna.

"Nikya say Chief Jesu no want us let bad Indian kill you, so we hide you!"

"How can you hide me?" the young said fearfully. "We live in the middle of the village. People come in here to see you, Prisha, all the time. As soon as anyone sees me, they'll know I'm not Shawnee! I don't look anything like the rest of you! Some of your people have already seen me."

Prisha explained all of this to her mother, who just started laughing as she spoke her response. With a smile the medicine woman turned back to the girl. "Nikya say when she finish with you, everybody think you Shawnee...even you."

The older squaw spent several minutes telling her plan to Prisha, who immediately grabbed a basket and left. Still giggling and carrying on a one-sided conversation with Susanna, the squaw stirred the fire and put a large bowl of water on the coals.

The pot was starting to steam as Prisha returned. When she set her basket down, Susanna saw that it contained close to twenty walnuts. They were older nuts that had fallen weeks before, and their normally green husks were now black and soft.

The older squaw waved Susanna over, and all three of them began to pull off the mushy black husks from the nuts and drop the sticky mess into a separate bowl. When all of the husk material had been collected, the older squaw said something, and both Prisha and her mother grabbed a fistful of the black goop from the bowl and began rubbing it into Susanna's hair.

The startled girl squealed and tried to pull away, but Prisha held her. "Sorry, Su-ah-na, but this only way make you look Shawnee. We make you yellow hair pretty and black."

The slave girl was completely disgusted by the whole process, but she knew they were trying to save her life. It took nearly half an hour for the two squaws to be completely satisfied that they had covered all of the girl's blond hair with the black, pasty, husk material. Susanna felt nasty with the smelly mess plastering her head.

"When can I wash my hair?" she asked anxiously.

"Nikya say not till tomorrow," Prisha translated. "Must leave stain on hair for whole day."

"A WHOLE DAY!" the miserable young exclaimed. "But it stinks! I smell like a walnut!"

"Mmm, yes," Prisha returned with a laugh. "Very tasty."

Just then Prisha's mother gave more instructions, and they began scrapping the remaining husk material into the steaming bowl of water.

"We aren't going to eat this stuff, are we?" Susanna asked in disgust as she saw what they were doing.

"Nikya not done yet," Prisha answered, still smiling. "She have more plan for you."

"Great," the girl said sarcastically and rolled her eyes.

The older squaw kept moving the pot so that it stayed hot but never came to a boil, stirring it the whole time. After an hour she began dipping small pieces of tanned buckskin into the pot and studying the results. Finally she gave a nod and pulled the pot off the fire to cool. Over the next quarter of an hour, the squaw continued to dip her finger into the water, testing the temperature. When she was satisfied that it had cooled enough, the old squaw set the bowl beside Susanna and said something.

"Take off you clothes and bath all over in this," Prisha directed.

"What?" the stunned girl asked as she looked at the repulsive mixture. "Why would I do that?"

"Nikya say you skin too white," the medicine woman answered. "This make you look Shawnee."

In a panic the desperate young woman looked imploringly at Prisha's mother, who only smiled and nodded excitedly at her.

"Best way to stay alive," Prisha said encouragingly.

Finally, with a deep sigh, Susanna pulled off her work dress and began to rub the black liquid on her arms and legs.

"Bah!" the older squaw growled when she saw the girl's reluctance. She jumped up, and soon she and Prisha were each scooping up a double handful of the dark stain and rubbing it vigorously all over the squealing girl.

The two squaws stopped and appraised their work. The older woman looked into Susanna's face and spoke to her daughter.

"Nikya say you hair and skin be dark like Shawnee, but not you eyes. She say you have robin egg eyes."

"People have told me that my blue eyes are beautiful," the girl returned.

"If warriors see them," Prisha shot back, "they get you killed. Nikya say you never look at faces. Always look at feet. Don't let anyone see you eyes."

Between the stickiness of her hair and the irritation of the stain on her skin, the miserable girl got little sleep that night. The next day was no better, because Prisha and her mother felt that it would be safer to wait until dark for Susanna to go to the creek to bathe. When the sun finally went down, Prisha wrapped a blanket around the young woman and went with her to the water. "Wash hair and skin," the medicine woman advised. "Don't scrub with sand."

"I just want to get the sticky chunks out of my hair," Susanna answered as she eagerly crawled into the creek. "I don't think I will ever get rid of this smell."

After nearly twenty minutes Prisha called for her to get out. The reluctant girl gave her hair one last rinse and stood up. She wrapped the blanket around her to dry off, and the two began walking back to the hut. As they strolled, a light breeze blew past the washed slave. Prisha sniffed the air as it went by. "Seela," she said with a nod. "Smell still there."

"I'll never get rid of it!" Susanna groaned.

"Su-ah-na," Prisha began, "since you look like Shawnee, you need Shawnee name."

"Oh, that would be fun," the young woman answered with a smile. "I would love to have an Indian name!"

"I think we call you Puckanie."

"Puckanie," Susanna repeated. "Okay, I think I like that. I'll be Puckanie. What does it mean?"

"It mean *walnut.*"

Chapter Twenty-Two

HIT AND RUN

"Of course Rayford knows the general's plans," Captain Parks groaned in frustration after he heard the report William brought back. "I'm the meathead that told him what they were! In my defense, I had no idea at the time we had the conversation that he was a renegade. The skunk insisted that he was loyal to the American cause."

"Don't beat yourself up over it, Captain," Will Hackett said. "You couldn't have known."

"Where's the Miami?" Dirt Gurley asked when he noticed that William had come back alone.

"When Rayford told them that he knew General Clark's plan, the shaman ordered him to be brought back to the Shawnee village. Grey Fox plans to disguise himself as a Shawnee and try to slip in and find out what they're going to do. We both figured that he had a better chance of looking like a Shawnee than I did."

"Well, I've seen you in a' Injun suit before," Dirt returned, "an' while I'll have to admit you made a tolerable lookin' heathern, ol' Grey Fox, bein' a' actual Injun an' all, would be a bit more convincin'."

"Get your men ready, Captain," Will directed. "Since we're going to have to hurry to get to the general once Grey Fox returns with the information, I told him to meet us in the woods on the northwest side of the village. That's where we need to go."

With William in front and Dirt Gurley guarding the rear, the young frontiersman led the small column very cautiously in a wide circle around the west side of the Shawnee encampment. At one point they could hear dogs from the village barking. Will didn't think that they were barking at them because they had made almost no noise and were traveling downwind from the village. Even so, he called a halt and had everyone wait quietly for almost a quarter of an hour before he started again.

When they arrived at a spot that Will judged to be directly northwest of the Shawnee village, he halted. "We'll wait here for Grey Fox to return," he said to the others. "Keep your weapons close. We will need to leave immediately when he joins us.

I'm going to slip closer to watch for my friend so that I can guide him here." Without waiting for a response, Hackett turned and disappeared soundlessly into the woods.

He crept close enough to clearly see the entire west side of the village. Motionlessly he watched for almost two hours, then he noticed an older-looking Indian hobbling along with the use of a stick, coming in his direction. Just as the crippled warrior got to the last hut, he suddenly whipped around behind it with his back to the wall. Will watched as the Indian took secretive glances around the edge of the hut. When he was sure that he was not being watched, he tossed away his stick and raced for the woods.

William could tell that it was the Miami by the way he ran. He was sprinting to enter the woods fifty yards to William's right. Without hesitation Hackett ran to join him.

When the young frontiersman got close, he saw Grey Fox throw his powder horn and shot pouch around his neck and grab the rifle that he had left hidden against the back of a large tree. The Miami welcomed his friend with a nod, and without speaking, William turned and led them at a run to meet the others.

"To save his hair, Rayford tell everything he know," Grey Fox began when they had joined their friends. "He describe place on Ohio River where another large creek come in. He say that where gen'ral will be."

Everyone turned and looked questioningly at Captain Parks. "Unfortunately, that's exactly where the general and his men are at this moment."

"Well, we should have time to warn them," Dirt spoke up. "The Shawnee may spend two or three days dancin' an' workin' theirselves up into a fightin' frenzie 'afore they actually leave to attack."

"That what they usually do," Grey Fox shot back, "but this different! White shaman say 'No war dance.' Ghost Warriors do their dance to call on spirits to fight for them. He say, when they finish dance, all warriors—Shawnee, Iroquois, Osage, and Cherokee—are to 'be ready to leave to kill gen'ral and his army.'"

"GREAT HONK!" Dirt gasped. "If that's the same dance we saw 'em do when we was scoutin' 'em, it don't last long. They'll likely be leavin' in less than an hour!"

"How many warriors do they have?" Parks asked with concern.

"Five hundred...maybe more," the Miami answered. "They have great Iroquois war chief, who shaman say will lead them to defeat gen'ral's army."

"Do you know who he is?" William asked.

"They call him *Thayendanegea*."

"Wait!" Parks interrupted. "I've heard of him. He went to British schools and has been a real thorn in the side of the colonial troops. His English name is Joseph Brant. He's one tough Indian! This is really bad!"

"We've got to leave now if we're gonna have a chance to warn General Clark and his men!" Parks exclaimed. "They're in worse danger than we thought!"

"Captain Parks," Will said firmly, "take your men and get to the general as quickly as possible. Let him know what's coming. My friends and I will do all we can to slow the Indians down and give General Clark time to prepare!"

Parks quickly described to the scouts the area on the Ohio River where Clark had made his camp. Giving rapid orders to his men, the captain led them in a long distance run to the northwest.

"So how in the name of common sense do you expect the three of us to stop a whole army of Injuns?" Dirt asked incredulously.

"I don't expect us to stop them," Will returned. "We just need to slow them down."

"Oh, is that all?" Dirt shot back sarcastically. "You had me worried for a minute."

"Come on!" William announced. "Let's head northwest and see if we can find some good spots for an ambush."

They raced through the woods for the next thirty minutes. Twice they noticed signs of Captain Parks and his men having passed ahead of them. They came to a small, open grassy field, and William sped across, the others following in single file.

As soon as they reached the woods on the meadow's other side, the young frontiersman halted. "Spread out a little," Will announced. "We'll fire at them from here."

"I don't know, Will," Dirt said as he appraised their surroundings. "I wouldn't call this a great ambush spot."

"It's not, but it will have to do for now. We'll slow the Indian army down more if we ambush them multiple times rather than try to find the perfect spot."

"Sort of like hit an' run tactics," Dirt said, giving an understanding nod.

"Right!" William agreed. "When they get here, try to shoot them in the legs or the hip. That way they're burdened with wounded comrades. Now spread out about a stone's throw from each other so we can spot them if they try to flank us. If they do, give a meadowlark call, and we'll all immediately run to the northwest."

"Better make it a crow caw," Grey Fox added. "Dirt Gurley's meadowlark call sound like dying blackbird."

"Why, you ornery rascal," Dirt shot back. "I'll have you know that, when I give my meadowlark call, all the female birds just flock to me."

"That because they all coming to funeral."

"HEY..."

"Okay," Will said, cutting off the red-faced, older scout, "make it a crow caw. Now spread out before they get here...and make every shot count!"

They didn't have to wait long before two Iroquois warriors trotted into the clearing. When Will saw that they were alone, he quickly waved to his two companions to get their attention and signed his intentions. Both waved back their understanding.

The three friends watched the two lead scouts move across the open ground almost a stone's throw apart. The Indians searched the area for signs of enemies. Will noticed that their adversaries seemed relaxed, indicating that they weren't expecting trouble so close to their village.

The ambushers held perfectly still even as the two warriors entered the woods in front of them. Just as one of the Iroquois walked past the large tree where William was hiding, the butt of the young frontiersman's rifle landed solidly against the side of the Indian's head. With a loud groan the unconscious victim dropped to the ground.

The second warrior heard the noise and turned to see what had happened to his friend. When he did so, the butt of Grey Fox's rifle took care of him as well.

William and the Miami removed the knives and tomahawks from their unconscious victims and threw them as far as they could into the woods. The Indians' powder horns and ammunition pouches were hung around their own necks, and the extra two rifles were propped against the trees they were hiding behind.

Within five minutes the first of the Indian army burst from the woods and into the clearing. Immediately the rifles of the scouts spit fire, and three of the first warriors dropped, screaming in pain as they grabbed their legs. Will and Grey Fox quickly grabbed the extra rifles and fired again. Another of the army cried out as one of the rifle balls found its mark.

Fierce yells of anger erupted from the distant woods as the forest shadows were lit up by the muzzle blasts of many rifles. Hiding behind their tree trunks, the three friends quickly loaded their weapons.

The Indians disappeared in the thick woods. Only an occasional rifle blast gave away a position. After firing and reloading two more times, William signed to his friends. They signaled back their understanding, and William saw Dirt drop low to the ground and slip noiselessly into the woods. Will fired the captured Indian rifle and broke the hammer off with his tomahawk; then he too retired from the fight, leaving the broken weapon behind. Half a minute later he heard one of Grey Fox's rifles go off, and William knew that the Miami would rapidly join them.

When the young frontiersman and Dirt Gurley found each other, they only had to wait a few moments before Grey Fox arrived. William gave a nod to his companions and raced away to the northwest.

The Dancing Ghosts

Chapter Twenty-Three

FIGHTING SMARTER

"So is what we jus' did purdy much the plan for slowin' down that army of cutthroats?" Dirt called from behind William as they ran through the woods.

"The way I see it," Hackett returned, "setting ambushes is all we've got."

"You know we cain't keep pullin' the same type of thing on them rascals. They'll jus' send out flankin' parties to hit us from the sides when we try to attack 'em."

"I figure they're doing that right now," the young frontiersman called back. "We need to come up with something they aren't expecting. Have either of you got any ideas?"

"The only thing my brain is tellin' me is to keep puttin' the next foot in front of the other," Dirt huffed as he ran.

"Dirt Gurley need new brain," they both heard the Miami call from behind.

"Oh, is that so?" the older scout snapped back. "An' I suppose *you*, O Wise One, know exactly what we need to do!"

"Set traps."

"TRAPS!" Will shouted back. "Grey Fox, that's brilliant!"

"If you'd a gimme a minute, I'd a thought of that," Dirt grumbled.

"Grey Fox," Will said as he suddenly came to a stop, "watch our back trail. Let us know when you see or hear them coming.

"Dirt, we need four sticks, each of them one or two feet long and sharpened to a point. Hurry!"

As his two companions rushed to their assignments, Will Hackett whipped out his tomahawk and cut off lengths of small vines running up into some of the trees. With these he grabbed a large sapling growing beside the deer trail they were following. He pulled the stiff, young tree around the trunk of the hickory growing beside it so that the sapling was drawn as tight as a spring. Just as Will completed tying the bent tree in place, Dirt arrived with the sharpened stakes. Will grabbed one and tied it to the top of the sapling.

"You see what I'm doing?" Will said as he worked. "Leave me one more of those stakes, and you take some of these vines and go set two more of these on the other side of the trail. We'll place the triggers along the path so the Indians set them off when they run by."

They were just finishing when Grey Fox ran up. "They come!" he announced. "Must go now!"

Will and Dirt grabbed their rifles and sprinted along the trail after the Miami. After running for two minutes, they heard agonizing screams behind them, followed by a chorus of furious war cries.

"Sounds like some of traps worked," Grey Fox called back to the others.

"We set the traps low so that when the saplin's shot around, the stakes would hit 'em in the thighs or hips," Dirt called back. "The brilliant part is that they don't know how many traps we set. They'll have to slow down to watch for 'em."

"And while they're doing that," William added, "we'll run a ways further along the trail. When they start thinking that we didn't set any more traps, we'll spring the next ones."

They pressed on for nearly an hour when suddenly William, who was leading, stepped in a hole and fell hard on his face. Dirt and Grey Fox were quickly at his side to help him up.

"You okay?" Dirt asked with concern.

"Yeah, I'm fine," the young scout said sheepishly. "I skinned my chin and my hands, but that's all. I never saw that hole. It was covered over with leaves."

"Hmmph," Grey Fox snorted. "Instead of *Walks Without Sound,* maybe we should change your name to *Stumbling Ox.*"

"Alright, make fun of me," Will shot back, "but it could have happened to anyone. That hole was completely covered with leaves."

"Could it happen to one of them rascals behind us?" Dirt asked with a devious smile.

"Yes, it could!" William answered enthusiastically. "Dirt, cut and sharpen more stakes, but sharpen them on both ends this time.

"Grey Fox, gather some twigs and leaves to cover the pit. I'll make it a little bigger."

The Miami found what he needed quickly and went to help Dirt sharpen stakes. When they both returned to William, he was finishing his project of widening the hole to have a better chance of one of the warriors stepping in it.

"It was where a small tree died, rotted and fell over, leaving this hole where the root was," the young frontiersman explained. "Hand me those stakes."

Leaning down into the hole, William shoved the sticks firmly into the ground at the bottom of the pit. "Now, cover the pit with your litter, Grey Fox, and let's go."

Just then two shots rang out. With a grunt of pain, Will dropped hard to the ground. Grey Fox, who was already kneeling beside the pit, was beside his friend in an instant. There was a red crease along the young scout's left temple. "Kajika! You okay?" the Miami asked anxiously.

Just then Dirt's rifle fired.

William blinked his eyes hard, trying to focus his vision. "I...I think so," he stammered.

"Then get up!" Grey Fox ordered as he stood and shouldered his rifle.

"They sent runners to chase us down!" Dirt exclaimed as he rapidly loaded his rifle. "I dropped one of 'em, but there's at least four more! We really need to get goin', fellers!"

Grey Fox fired his rifle at the small war party and tossed the weapon to William, who was just standing up. The Miami then snatched Will's rifle and took another shot.

"Load later!" Grey Fox ordered. "Run now!"

They each grabbed one of William's arms to support him and raced through the woods. After running twenty strides, they heard a scream of pain behind them.

"Pit work," the Miami huffed.

After several more minutes of hard running, they came to a place in the woods that was more open. Without slowing their pace, they continued toward the thicker woods ahead. As they neared the heavy brush, Grey Fox called to Dirt Gurley. "Can you see Shawnee runners?"

The older scout craned his neck around to take a quick glance at their back trail. "There's two of 'em still after us!" Dirt reported, "an' they's a' comin' fast!"

"You loaded?" Grey Fox asked.

"Yep," Dirt answered.

"Then drop closest one," the Miami ordered. "I take other."

As soon as Grey Fox said the words, they stopped quickly, and as Dirt took aim at one of the two rapidly approaching warriors, Grey Fox quickly began loading his rifle. Dirt's weapon barked, and one of the pursuing Shawnee grabbed his thigh and dropped to the ground.

Rather than stop to help his companion, the second warrior continued sprinting toward the three scouts.

"Uh oh!" Dirt called as he scrambled for his powder horn. "You better hurry! The second one didn't stop!"

After pouring some black powder down the barrel and a small amount in the pan, Dirt snapped the frizzen shut. As he grabbed for a patch and ball, he stole a look at the rapidly approaching enemy. "He's gettin' closer!" the older scout cried as Grey

Fox was still loading. Pressing the ball and patch into the mouth of the barrel, the older scout was just grabbing his ram rod when he looked up again. "HE'S HERE!" Dirt screamed as he dropped his not-yet-loaded rifle and grabbed for his knife. Just as the determined warrior was in the act of leaping for them, the Miami's rifle went off. At the same moment the attacking Indian landed on Dirt Gurley and drove him to the ground.

Grey Fox quickly grabbed the warrior and tossed him off the older scout. The Miami also stepped on the Shawnee's wrist that held his tomahawk and yanked away the weapon. Groaning in pain, the warrior used his free hand to grab the wound in his hip that Grey Fox's rifle ball had caused.

"You okay?" the Miami asked while reaching down to help the older scout.

"Well, you took your own sweet time!" Dirt Gurley snapped as he climbed to his feet.

"It work out," Grey Fox answered as he walked over to support William, who was still dizzy from his injury. "No harm done."

"NO HARM DONE?" the older scout shouted in response. "Why, that murderin' cutthroat almost took my head clean off!"

"That okay," the Miami answered offhandedly. "If Dirt Gurley lose head, he have no need for hat."

"Have mercy!" Dirt exclaimed, shaking his head, "You're about the coldheartedest Injun I ever met!"

"Enough gum-flapping," Grey Fox ordered as he tried to steady William. "Help with Kajika. We need go."

Chapter Twenty-Four

FAILURE

Running through the forest caused Will Hackett's head to ache more, but he noticed that his dizziness lessened over time. With Grey Fox and Dirt Gurley taking turns running beside the injured scout to keep him from stumbling, they were able to keep up a good pace. After thirty minutes they came to a deep creek that crossed their path. "Shawnee army must cross creek to get to gen'ral," Grey Fox reasoned, "so we cross here."

The three lifted their rifles and powder horns over their heads and stepped into the creek. Discovering that the cold water was only chest deep in the middle, the three friends reached the other side without incident. The Miami led them just inside the woods on the opposite bank and then stopped.

"We rest here," Grey Fox announced. "Dirt, you bandage Kajika's head. I watch for enemies."

"Well, it's nice to know you're worried about *somebody's* head," Dirt snapped irritably as he began to tend to William's injury.

"They coming!" the Miami called after a few moments. "Better hurry!" It wasn't long before Grey Fox spotted movement in the woods in several places on the other side of the creek.

"They here!" he announced and took aim.

The older scout was just tying off the ends of Will's bandage when Grey Fox's rifle blasted. The other two quickly snatched up their weapons and joined in the attack.

"We can't stay here!" William directed as they each finished reloading. "They've probably already sent groups of warriors across the creek above and below us. We need to go now!"

"Can you run?" Grey Fox asked.

"I've got a big headache," Will admitted, "but I'm not dizzy anymore."

"They'll try to cut us off!" Dirt said what they were all thinking.

"We must run fast!" the Miami answered and immediately sprinted through the woods to the northwest.

After twenty minutes Dirt called from the rear. "I jus' heard something' off to our left."

"I heard it too," Will agreed.

"Enemy warriors trying to get ahead of us," Grey Fox added.

"How'd they catch up to us so fast?" Dirt wanted to know.

"They sent their fastest runners in front of the others," answered Will.

"Any guesses as to how many there are?" Dirt asked again.

"Three...maybe four," the Miami answered.

"The three of us could probably take 'em," Dirt reasoned, "but if'n we stop runnin' to fight 'em, the rest of that pack of rattlesnakes will catch up to us. So what do we do?"

"Dirt, you keep running," Will called as they raced along, "and make as much noise as you can.

"While he's doing that, Grey Fox, you and I will drop back and get behind them."

"Good plan," Dirt agreed. "When I hear the fight start, I'll hurry back to help, but we got's to finish 'em fast!"

As Will and the Miami slowed down, the older scout snatched up a stick and began whacking it into the brush and tree trunks as he ran past. He also kept up a loud recitation of his skills as an Indian fighter.

The young frontiersman and his companion angled to their left in the direction they anticipated to intercept the Shawnee or Iroquois runners. Though they moved faster than a normal walk, neither of them made a sound as they passed through the brush.

Before long, Will raised his hand, and they froze. They heard quick footfalls coming from the left. Easing his head above the branches of the bush that he was hiding behind, Will took a glance at the oncoming warriors. Motioning to his companion, he and Grey Fox eased closer to where the Indians would pass. The young scout raised four fingers to indicate to the Miami how many enemy fighters he had seen.

Will and Grey Fox determined to take the last two runners first. Hackett had picked his spot well. As the first pair of warriors passed, the ambushers could have touched them. When the next ones arrived, two gun barrels suddenly protruded from the brush, tripping the sprinting Indians. Both fell face first onto the hard ground and, before they could regain their feet, were clubbed unconscious by the butts of the two rifles.

The yells of the fallen warriors alerted their friends, who quickly turned to face the attackers. With fierce war cries, the two startled Shawnee raised their rifles to fire. A shot rang out from the forest behind them, and with a grunt of pain, one of the two Shawnee fell. Realizing he was surrounded, the last warrior spun to face the new threat but was quickly dropped by Grey Fox, who put a rifle ball in his leg.

"Should we take their weapons?" Dirt asked as he came trotting up, kicking one of the dropped rifles out of reach of its owner.

"No time!" Grey Fox exclaimed. "Army come!"

"They're too close!" Will called from behind. "I can hear them rushing to the sound of the fight. Run hard! We've got to put some distance between us!"

They hadn't made five strides when William heard a war cry behind them. He jerked his head around in time to see one of the enemy's advance scouts raising his rifle to fire at them.

"TAKE COVER!" he warned the others and quickly jumped behind a tree just as the gun went off. William immediately poked his rifle around the trunk and dropped the scout as more screaming warriors burst through the brush.

"THEY'RE ON US, FELLERS!" Dirt cried. "WE AIN'T OUTRUNNIN' 'EM THIS TIME!"

"HURRY!" they heard Grey Fox call as he raced deeper into the woods. "THIS WAY!"

Weaving their way through the thick forest, they chased after their friend. The angry chorus of war cries was echoing from the woods close behind them when they reached him. He had come to the edge of another creek, and they saw the Miami drop off the bank and land with a splash in the water below. As they rushed to follow him, they saw their friend throw two large rocks at the bank on the opposite side. These two stones caused a mini dirt slide that made the ground looked disturbed.

"Get down!" Grey Fox ordered when the two had joined him. "We hide under bank!"

The three sat in the creek with their backs against the overhanging bank.

"Grab the log!" William hissed urgently, and all three of them gripped the rotted log lying in the water just in front of them, and tugged it back against their chests.

Immediately a multitude of moccasined feet leapt over the bank, splashed into the water, and surged up the other side. The three friends ducked their heads behind the log to escape detection.

Several long minutes passed before they risked stealing a look. "Whew!" Dirt breathed a sigh of relief. "I thought sure we had done lost our hair that time!"

"That was smart of you to throw those rocks, Grey Fox," William said in a low voice. "It made the ground look like we had climbed up the other side."

"Old Indian trick," the Miami answered.

"I'm just glad there weren't any old Indians among them," Will said in relief.

"Fellers, we done messed up," Dirt whispered urgently. "We let 'em get by us! "

"Couldn't be helped," Grey Fox hissed back.

"The general an' his army are in deep muck now!" Dirt shot back. "What are we gonna do?"

"Maybe if we swing to the east, we could get in front of them again."

"Will," Dirt snapped, "you saw how fast them varmints is travelin'. You know as well as I do that there ain't gonna be no getting' in front of 'em again!"

"Hopefully we bought the general and his men enough time to get away," William returned, but he didn't sound confident.

"I don't know, Will," Dirt answered, shaking his head. "If Parks cain't get General Clark an' his army movin' fast enough and far enough to keep this mass of bloodthirsty heatherns from catchin' 'em, they're done for! That's a fact, an' you know it! The truth be told, we didn't slow 'em down much...not much at all, an' I feels terrible about it!" He paused for a moment and then added, "I don't know what we could have done different, but it weren't enough...not by a long shot!"

The three sat in sad silence as they waited until they felt it was safe to emerge from their hiding place.

"Only one thing to do now," Grey Fox finally said, breaking the quietness.

"What's that?" the older scout asked gravely.

"Pray for gen'ral an' his army. Chief Jesus his only hope."

Chapter Twenty-Five

A DEADLY CHANGE IN PLANS

"I was still hoping we could get around them when they stopped to rest," Will Hackett said to his friends as they chased after the Indian army, "but they haven't stopped except to drink at some of the creeks they cross."

"That painted shaman is drivin' 'em like a crazy man!" Dirt called back.

"Since we tried to stop him," Will answered, "he knows his plans have been discovered. He probably thinks we're still ahead of him, and he's pushing his warriors to get to the general and his men before we can warn him."

They trailed the Indian army until it got dark. The moonbeams filtering down through the branches above were the only light the scouts had to view their way. In the darkness the three friends tried to stay close to the rear of the Indians.

"Can you still hear 'em, Grey Fox?" Dirt Gurley asked when they had stopped during a particularly dark part of the night.

After a long pause the Miami answered, "No...they too far ahead."

"So do you want to wait until it's light enough to see their trail?" Dirt asked as he turned to Hackett.

"No," Will returned. "We know where they're headed. We'll just keep going northwest until we hit the Ohio River. When we get to General Clark's camp, we'll find the Indians."

With the moon having set, they had to watch for clearings in the woods where the stars could be seen to confirm their direction. Their progress was slow until the first hint of dawn. As the eastern glow began to light up the world, they were able to travel with more speed.

The sun was high in the sky when the weary scouts reached the banks of the river the Indians called *Beautiful.* The majestic Ohio River bordered the northern edge of the Kentucky Territory, and it impressed William every time he saw it.

"Many Indian pass here," Grey Fox announced as he pointed to the moccasin prints in the damp ground.

"According to Captain Parks, the general's camp was upriver from here," Will added.

"White shaman's army headed that way," the Miami returned.

"I sure do hope Parks got 'em out of there!" Dirt spoke anxiously.

They decided to take a few minutes to rest before starting after the painted shaman's army. Suddenly the quiet was disturbed by the sound of multiple booms in the distance.

"What in tarnation was *that?*" Dirt exclaimed, rising to his feet.

"It came from upriver!" Grey Fox declared.

"The general didn't get away," William said sadly. "That was cannon fire."

"Cannon fire?" Dirt asked in surprise. "Well, if'n General Clark's got cannon, then maybe things ain't quite so bad!"

"Maybe," Will admitted. "Let's go see. By the sound of it, we still have a ways to travel."

They started another long distance run northeast along the bank. It was well into the afternoon when they heard rifle blasts. Cautiously the three slowed their advance.

"We ver' close," Grey Fox said in a low voice as he stopped and faced the others. "You two stay here," he hissed. "Grey Fox go closer and find out what happening."

William saw the wisdom in letting the Miami scout the Indians' position. If he were spotted, it was likely that, as an Indian himself, Grey Fox would just be taken for another member of their diverse army.

The sun had set and darkness had fallen before the Miami suddenly appeared beside them. The abrupt and silent return of their friend caused Dirt to jump.

"GREAT GRANNY'S GARTERS!" the older scout hissed angrily. "Cain't you step on a twig or make some sound to let folks know when you're comin'? My heart stops every time you do that!"

"What'd you find out?" Will asked. "Where are General Clark and his men?"

"General in camp on other side of Indians, but they ready for big fight," the Miami answered. "Gen'ral have four small cannon."

"That's enough to make them painted heatherns think twice before they try to rush in there an' take their scalps," Dirt said with a nod.

"Were you able to figure out what the white shaman is planning?" William asked again.

"He big mad," Grey Fox returned. "He screaming that spirits will fight for them if they just attack. But Iroquois war chief won't lead them. He say many braves die if they attack. Gen'ral too strong, he say, because they have much men and big guns."

"So what are the Indians going to do?" William asked.

Grey Fox shrugged. "Don't know. War chief and painted shaman still arguing. Iroquois war chief strong man. He speak his mind and not fear Ghost Warriors."

"Until we know their plans, we can't do much to help the general and his men," William concluded.

"Right," the Miami agreed. "Grey Fox go back and see what they do." The Indian turned and moved quietly back into the shadows.

"An' don't scare the liver outta folks when you come back, you ornery rascal!" Dirt hissed after him.

Three more hours had passed before Grey Fox appeared again, but this time he had a look of urgency. Dirt, who was on watch, placed his hand on Will Hackett's shoulder to wake him.

"Big changes!" the Miami whispered when Hackett had joined them. "Short time ago Iroquois scout arrive from upriver. He say more soldiers come in boats. The Iroquois captured some who had been sent ahead with a letter to gen'ral. Letter say American officer an' one hundred and twenty men coming to join gen'ral, but they have no food and no ammunition. They several miles upriver and ask gen'ral for help."

"That's terrible..." Dirt said, but then caught himself. "Hey, wait! Them cutthroats can read?"

"Gray Fox not only Indian who learn to read," the Miami returned with a snort.

"So which one of 'em read the letter?" Dirt asked again.

"The Iroquois war chief, Thayendanegea."

"That's right," Will remembered. "Captain Parks said he went to British schools and that his English name is Joseph Brant."

"I reckon them reinforcements comin' down the river are in a heap o' trouble," Dirt speculated.

"More than you know," Grey Fox agreed. "The war chief tell painted shaman he can do what he want, but Thayendanegea taking Iroquois warriors with him to attack the soldiers upriver. He leaving now. Plan is to ambush soldiers at dawn."

"Are all the Indians going with him?" Will asked.

"Yes," the Miami answered. "Angry shaman signed to his followers that the spirits want Shawnee and Cherokee to fight with the Iroquois to kill the soldiers upriver, then they come back and kill the gen'ral an' his men."

"We won't be able to help those poor souls upriver," Will said, expressing his thoughts, "but maybe we can get the general and his men away from here. Okay, so we need to get word to the general about all this, and we need to keep an eye on the Indian army.

"Here's what we'll do," Will Hackett said decisively. "Grey Fox, you trail the Indians. We need to know if and when they're coming back. While you're doing that, Dirt and I will go to the general's camp and let them know what's happening. We'll have the soldiers get in their boats and head downriver as fast as they can go.

"No boats!" the Miami announced. "Painted shaman burned them to trap soldiers."

"There ain't no place around here they can run to!" Dirt expressed with concern. "Harrodsburg is the closest, an' it's still quite a ways off. The way that white shaman drives them warriors, there's a good chance the Injuns'll catch the soldiers before they could get to the fort."

"You're probably right," Will agreed, "but Harrodsburg is still their best chance. Grey Fox, try to catch up to us when you know what the Indians are going to do."

When General George Rogers Clark decided to camp on the banks of the Ohio River, he had not known how long he and his men would have to wait for Colonel Lockry and his men to join him. Lockry had failed to show up at Wheeling, Virginia, at the appointed time. Clark had known that recruiting enough men was going to be difficult for the colonel, so he had waited another ten days. When his men had begun to get restless, Clark had left boats, some provisions, and a message for Lockry to follow him down the river, then he had set off. Clark and his men had floated along with the current for over two weeks with no signs of hostiles. They had halted their journey once and made camp on the banks of the river, but after several days and still no Lockry, he had left a note for the colonel hanging from a pole and decided to move again.

Clark and his men had passed the mouth of the Miami River and floated for several more miles. Traveling slowly, they had hoped that the reinforcements would catch up to them. Now they were deep into Indian territory, and Clark had decided that he could go no further without Lockry and his men. Ordering his men to pull the boats up onto the south bank of the river, they had constructed a rough breastwork of logs they found or felled and made their camp there.

When Captain Parks and his men arrived with the news of the approaching Indian army, General Clark realized that his men had a better chance defending themselves than trying to run. At Clark's insistence, they had brought four six-pound howitzers in the boats, along with powder and ammunition. Clark ordered the cannons brought from the boats and set up behind the logs. As soon as the army of Indians had arrived, Clark quickly stopped the initial charge by using his six-pounders. At this point War Chief Brant had begun to question the wisdom of attacking the Americans.

In the middle of the night one of Clark's soldiers guarding the southern breastwork heard a voice on the other side of the logs. "Don't shoot!" the voice hissed just loud enough for the guard to hear. "We're friends!"

The startled guard quickly summoned others to join him. "Who's there?" he called as they all raised their rifles.

"We're friends!" the voice answered.

"Well, maybe you is, an' maybe you ain't," the suspicious guard returned, "but none of my friends is on dat side of the logs. Stand up and let's get a look at you!"

"We're not going to stand up 'cause we don't want to get shot. My name is Will Hackett, and Dirt Gurley is with me. We're scouts who were with Captain Parks. Call him...he knows us."

A couple of minutes later, Captain Parks was led to the spot. "He says his name is Will Hackett," one of the guards informed him.

"Hackett, is that you?" Parks called over the wall of logs.

"Yes, it's me and Dirt."

"Let them in, boys!" Parks ordered. "I know 'em."

The two scouts were quickly led to the general, and William informed him of the Indians' plans. When Clark heard that Brant was going to ambush the soldiers coming down the river at dawn, he looked at the dark eastern sky.

"How far away is this happening?" the general asked urgently.

"My friend who brought us this report said that the ambush was to take place a number of miles north of here. You can't get there in time, General, and with all the Indians together, you don't have enough men to beat them."

"Poor Colonel Lockry," the general sighed sorrowfully. "May God have mercy on him and his men."

Chapter Twenty-Six

MUCH NEEDED HELP

"We cain't do nothin' for Colonel Lockry, General," Dirt Gurley spoke up. "He's in the hands of the Almighty. But we *can* do somethin' for you an' your men, an' that is to get your army as far away from here as possible afor' them cutthroats get back...an' mark my words, them rascals is a'comin' back!"

"You said they burned the boats?" General Clark asked, turning to Will Hackett.

"Yes, sir," the young scout returned. "The White Shaman wanted to keep you where he can get to you."

The general whipped out a hand drawn map. "Captain Parks, would you say that we are about here?"

Parks looked carefully at the location of the general's finger. "Yes, that's about right, sir."

"That means that the closest fort is down here at Harrodsburg," General Clark concluded. "That's a long way...and with our wounded, I don't think we could make it before the Indians catch us."

"There is another option, sir," Parks said, still studying the map. "Silas Harlan has recently finished work on a stockade between here and Harrodsburg. He calls it *Harlan's Station.* I've been there, sir. It's got strong, high walls and a couple of small cannon guarding the gate."

"I know Major Harlan!" the general acknowledged. "He's about the bravest man I've ever been in battle with. How close is his station?"

"It's still going to be several days of hard marching, sir," Parks answered, "but we have a much better chance of getting there than to Harrodsburg."

"Does anyone know of any better options?" the general asked, looking intently at every face at the meeting. No one responded. "Alright then...ARTILLERY OFFICERS! SPIKE THE CANNON!" roared General Clark across the camp.

"Major Miller, get them ready to move out! Have every man fill their powder horns from the stores, then destroy the rest of the powder. Assign two men to assist each of the wounded who can walk.”

“What about Dunham, sir?” the major asked. “He’s wounded too badly.”

“I’ll not leave him behind,” the general ordered. “Make a litter and put a man on each corner. If they start slowing down, we’ll change out the men. If we have to, we’ll put two men on each corner. Now hurry! We’re leaving *now!*”

The pink glow of coming sunrise lit the eastern horizon as Captain Parks led the caravan south into the woods. They moved as quickly as they could. Major Miller was charged with keeping an eye on the rear of the column to make sure there were no stragglers. Dirt Gurley scouted ahead, and Will Hackett dropped behind to watch for pursuit by the enemy.

It was the middle of the afternoon when William, still scouting the rear of the column, detected the approach of someone moving rapidly through the forest. As the newcomer drew near, the young frontiersman sprang from behind a large tree, rifle at the ready. He found himself face to face with Grey Fox, whose rifle was pointed at Will’s chest.

“Glad you made it back,” Will said with feeling as he lowered his weapon.

"Ambush over," the Miami reported. "Soldiers have no chance. Many dead, the rest prisoners. Indian army now come for gen'ral."

"Come on," Will said. "Let's get you to General Clark so you can tell him what you know."

"How many were killed?" the general asked the Miami reluctantly.

"American colonel had one hundred twenty soldiers. When fight over, Grey Fox count forty-one dead. One was the colonel. The rest taken prisoner."

"Grey Fox told me," Hackett added, "that Chief Brant took the prisoners and his Iroquois warriors and went north."

"He's taking them to Detroit," Clark said confidently. "The British reward the Indians for each prisoner they bring in.

"So the Iroquois are gone," Clark continued. "What about the rest?"

"The painted shaman still mad that Brant and Iroquois not attack you," Grey Fox answered. "When Grey Fox left, he and other Ghost Warriors were doing a war dance to get rest of warriors excited to return and kill all of gen'ral's soldiers."

"We've seen his war dances, General Clark," Will spoke up, "and they don't last long."

"Major Miller! Captain Buckner!" the general ordered. "Get 'em up an' moving! We've rested enough!

"Captain Parks, I know we have wounded men with us, but I need you to pick up the pace!"

"Yes, sir," Parks returned with a salute.

"And speaking of our wounded," General Clark said, still addressing Parks, "is there a doctor at Harlan's Station?"

"No, sir," came the answer, "an' there's not one at Harrodsburg either."

"Dunham may die without one," the general said with concern.

"We have a healer at Larkinboro," Will Hackett volunteered.

"Hmmm," Grey Fox agreed, "she good healer. Good with bullet wounds." As he said this, he reached up and touched his healed shoulder.

"We're going to need her!" the general said urgently.

"I'll leave for Larkinboro to get her now, sir," Will answered.

"Get some men from there to come with you," the general ordered, "and Hackett, when you return and get close to Harlan's Station, be careful! The Indians will most likely already be there, and we can't let anything happen to that woman!"

"I understand, sir."

General Clark then turned to the Miami. "Grey Fox, I need you to scout our back trail. Try to give us as much warning as you can before the Indians catch up to us."

"Grey Fox will let you know, Gen'ral sir!" the Miami answered while giving an awkward salute.

"You can count on Grey Fox, General," Will said as he looked at his friend. "He's the best scout I know...except for me, of course," he added with a smile and a sideways look at the Miami.

Grey Fox snorted at William and said, "Try not to get lost this time."

Two days later Remember Warren walked out of the Middlebrooks' house wearing her buckskins. The young healer had been busy all day gathering herbs and packing her medicine bag. She had checked all of her medical supplies and equipment as well as filled her pouch full of smooth rocks and clay bullets. One more mission remained.

She walked briskly to the gate but could not find the person she was looking for. After making some inquiries, she traveled purposefully to another house and knocked on the door. When it opened, Ember said, "Hello, Mrs. Whitlock. May I speak with Asa?"

"I'm here, Ember," a familiar voice sounded from just inside the cabin. "Come on in. Mother will sit with us."

When Ember stepped into the living area of the Whitlock home, she saw Asa sitting by the hearth with leather pieces and his mother's sewing basket all around him. "I didn't realize you were so domestic," Ember said with a smile.

"Oh, if that were only true," Mrs. Whitlock added with a laugh as Asa's cheeks turned bright red.

"I'm just trying to fix the strap on my powder horn," the young scout said defensively.

"Well, you better get it fixed," the healer returned, "because you're going to need it."

Asa's eyes quickly fixed on the young woman's face. "Did you get another message from the Lord?"

"Yes," she answered. "He told me that He has work for me to do, and, Asa, He said that you need to go with me."

"Where are we going?"

"I don't know," Ember replied. "Just get ready, and He'll show us the rest when it's time."

An hour later a call rang out from one of the guards on the wall. "RUNNER COMIN' IN!" When the runner was close enough to recognize, the voice called out again. "IT'S WILL HACKETT!"

The gates were swung open, and the young frontiersman ran through the opening and straight to the water barrel by the well.

"What's the news, Will?" Jack Cobb asked as he watched the young scout swallow his third dipper of water.

Still breathing hard and interspersed with drinks of two more gourds of water, Will Hackett related all he knew of the Indian attack on the American troops. "His wounded men need a healer," he said as he finished, "and I've come back to get Ember Warren."

"You can't take her into that nest of villains by yourself," Jack said firmly.

"You're right," Will returned. "I'll need some volunteers to go with us."

"Count me in," Asa announced as he and Ember walked up, ready to travel.

Thirty minutes later, after he had rested, replenished his supplies, eaten a meal, and drunk three more dippers of water, William, Ember, Asa, Jack Cobb, and a group of seven men gathered just inside the front gate of the fort. The owl, George Washington, had saluted them with several loud hoots, but when he noticed Ember was with them, he got very agitated and began dancing along the edge of his platform. The young woman called to her feathered friend, trying to assure him that everything was all right, but the bird only got more nervous.

Once everyone was assembled, Jack gave the command, and Will led them in a long distance run out of the gates and north into the woods. Seeing Ember leave with them, George squawked with concern and leaped into the air, frantically flying after them.

For the next two days, Will led them toward the place where Captain Parks had said Silas Harlan had built his stockade. They only stopped for short breaks to rest, but whenever they did, Ember noticed the owl perch on a limb above her. She knew that trying to send him away was useless. As long as there was moon or starlight enough to see, they kept moving. Only during the darkest parts of the night would William stop for a few hours' sleep.

The young frontiersman kept a close eye on Ember. He knew she was a strong woman and that she knew how to survive in the woods, but he was also aware that her abilities were being tested to their limits with this hard march. Whenever it looked to him like she might be slowing down or struggling to get her breath, he stopped for a short rest and a bite to eat.

On the second day, Ember, concerned that George needed to eat soon, tried to interest him in a piece of jerky, but the strange-looking substance couldn't entice him. In the afternoon of the same day, she had not seen the owl for a couple of hours and thought that maybe he had gotten hungry and returned home. When the next rest was called, Ember had just sat down with her back against a tree when she heard a heavy thump on a limb above her. Looking up, she saw George busily consuming a fat mouse.

"I don't know how you caught it with just one eye, George," she called up to the large, ravenous bird, "but I guess if you're hungry enough, you can push yourself to do anything."

On the third day they came down out of the forested hills and into the lowlands. The ground became wetter, and occasionally they had to skirt marshy bogs. Once while doing that, Ember stumbled over a dead limb and fell headlong into the mud. Jim Hart, who was running just behind her, quickly helped her up as George hooted with anxious concern overhead.

"You okay, Miss Ember?" the woodsman asked urgently.

"I'm not hurt, if that's what you mean," she answered irritably, frustrated at her clumsiness.

When Asa came running up, he was quickly at her side asking the same question.

"Well, I've never been quite this filthy before," she huffed, shaking clumps of mud from her fingers. "William," she called to their leader when she saw him coming to check on her, "there's a creek over there. Can I clean myself up a little before we continue?"

"Of course," the young frontiersman answered. "We'll rest here for a few minutes while you wash up."

"I need to try to wash some of the mud out of my clothes," she explained, "so I'm going to wade up the creek a ways for some privacy."

"I can appreciate that, Ember," Jack Cobb spoke up, "but we're getting closer to enemies. Someone needs to go with you."

"I'll go!" Asa volunteered enthusiastically.

"Now, just cool yer forge, Asa," Harvey O'Doul, a father of six, spoke up. "She don't need the likes of you pesterin' her to death with yer *moony eyes*. You stay here an' park yer carcass. I'll look after her."

A red-faced Asa sat down on a log as Harvey and George followed Ember up the creek. When Ember thought she was far enough away from the rest of the party, she called back to Harvey, "Okay, Mr. O'Doul. I'll clean up here."

"Alright, lass," Harvey called back. "I'll just set myself down on this log with my back to you.

Let me know when yer ready to return to the others."

"Will do," Ember returned as she quickly began scrubbing the muck from her clothes and body.

The splashing went on for several minutes. Finally it stopped, and Harvey figured Ember was getting dressed. Several more minutes passed. Unexpectedly, O'Doul heard a loud shrieking hoot and an intense cry of pain. Jerking around, he saw Ember standing on the opposite bank, held firmly by two Shawnee, one with the talons of a huge owl tearing at his face. A third warrior stood beside them with his rifle pointed in Harvey's direction. He seemed unsure as to whether to shoot at O'Doul or to help his companion who was being attacked by the owl.

Jack Cobb had started to be concerned at how long it was taking Ember to clean up. He was just asking Jim Hart to go check on the girl and her guard when the quietness was broken by a rifle shot.

Chapter Twenty-Seven

RETURN TO SLAVERY

With their weapons at the ready, Will and Jack charged up the creek with the others close behind. They found Harvey lying on the left bank, struggling to lift himself up.

"O'Doul!" Jack cried as he knelt quickly beside his friend. Harvey had a wound through both cheeks, and he was spitting out pieces of broken teeth.

"Jack?" O'Doul asked as he blinked to clear his vision.

"What happened?" Jack asked.

"WHERE'S EMBER?" Asa cried in a panic.

"They took her," Harvey answered weakly.

"Who took her?" Jack pressed.

"Shawnee," O'Doul responded. "Two of 'em grabbed her, and a third got the drop on me. I thought I was gone beaver for sure, but that big owl of hers flew into one of 'ems' face. I tried to bring my rifle up while they was distracted, but the Indian was faster. I reckon I'm fortunate the rifle ball went through my cheeks rather than through my skull."

"A little bit lower, and it would have shattered your jaw," Jack said as he studied his friend's wounds, "an' a little higher, an' you'd a been talkin' with the Lord instead of me right now."

"He probably looks a lot better'n you do," Harvey returned with a poor attempt at a smile.

"We've got to go after Ember!" Asa announced.

"We will, Whit," Will said, placing his hand on his friend's shoulder.

"Okay," Jack announced, taking charge. "Things have changed, so we need a new plan. I'll take two with me and go after the girl. Will, you get poor O'Doul here to help. Harrodsburg is the closest to us."

"Ember was my responsibility," William declared, "and I'm going with you to get her back!"

"I'm coming too," Asa added determinedly.

When Jack saw the resolve in the young men's eyes, he changed his orders. "Alright, I'll take Will and Asa with me.

"Jim Hart, you know these parts as well as anyone. Take the rest of the men with you and get Harvey to Harrodsburg. Once you're there, gather as many men as you can and reinforce General Clark at...where was it, Will?"

"Harlan's Station," the young frontiersman answered. "I'll tell Jim what Captain Parks told me about its location, but I'm sure the folks at Harrodsburg know where it's at."

"Well, get it done!" Jack Cobb shot back. "We need to go!"

For the second time in her young life, Ember Warren found herself a captive of the Shawnee. She was rushed through the forest at a rapid pace. Her attempt to cry for help was quickly ended when a large knife flashed in front of her face. After a couple of hundred yards, the leader slowed their speed only slightly.

The Shawnee who was attacked by George gripped Ember's arm with one hand as they ran. Fresh, deep scratches furrowed his face. After he had knocked the ferocious owl away from him, Ember saw the great bird fly off, disappearing into the thick forest.

As they raced through the trees, the young woman glanced around looking for signs of George. She hoped that he was not injured and that he wouldn't try anything like that again.

Ember's legs were wobbly and her chest was heaving when they entered a clearing and joined a party of fifteen warriors. Remembering the

Shawnee words she had learned during her last captivity, she understood that these Indians were a part of the group who had come to attack General Clark's men. Two guards, each with a tight grip on her arms, kept the young woman from trying to escape while their leader explained to the others the circumstance of her capture.

"OH, YES!" a gruff voice called with fiendish pleasure from the other side of the party of warriors. Fear and dread gripped Ember's heart as she saw the monster Rayford pushing eagerly through the group of Indians. "I told you that you belonged to me! And after all the pain an' trouble you've caused, I'm gonna hang yer head from my cabin door!"

Just as Rayford drew near to the girl, the warrior who was the leader of the party that had captured Ember stepped between them with his tomahawk in his hand.

"Get outta my way, Yellow Bear!" the big trapper growled in Shawnee. "I got no fight with you. This woman was my slave, an' I'm takin' her back!"

"Maybe she *was* Rayford's slave," the warrior growled back, "but she escape! She Rayford's slave no longer! She Yellow Bear's slave now!"

As Ember listened to the argument, she took the time to study the Indian opposing the trapper. He wasn't as muscular as Rayford, but he was every bit as tall, and by his threatening stance and words, it was clear he felt he could defend his claim. *Maybe he could, at that,* Ember thought to herself.

She could also see that the veins in Rayford's neck were protruding, and his face was red. She wondered if he would risk upsetting the other warriors by attacking Yellow Bear. Even as she had these thoughts, Ember noticed the angry trapper clenching and unclenching his fists.

Finally Rayford gave a loud snort and said, "I ain't gonna fight you right now, Yellow Bear...not while them white painted demons is here." He glanced over at the other warriors as he spoke.

When Ember followed his gaze, she saw one of the lance-carrying Ghost Warriors standing with the others. By his expression she could tell that he could not understand what was being said, but the concern and suspicion on his face was easy to see.

"You keep her for now," Rayford said, addressing Ember's defender, "but when we gets back to the village, I'm comin' after what's mine!"

Dropping his eyes to look in Ember's, he added, "And when I do..." The fierce trapper did not finish the sentence. Instead, he smiled and drew his finger across his throat.

Yellow Bear pushed past Rayford and signed to the Ghost Warrior his intention to take his slave back their village and that he would return to help with the fight. Without waiting for a reply, Yellow

Bear turned and ordered the unwounded Indian holding Ember to bring her as he left the clearing and headed south.

The last thing the stumbling young woman heard was Rayford calling after her. "I'LL BE A'COMIN' FOR YOU, GIRLIE! YOU CAN COUNT ON THAT!"

At that moment, Ember called to God in her heart. "Lord, this evil man wants to kill me. He's already tried once. But Lord I know that my life is in Your hands, not his, and I will trust in You."

It was well over an hour later when Will, Jack, and Asa stepped into the clearing. Jack and Asa stood on the edge of the woods as they allowed William time to study the foot prints on the ground. He took some time as he circled the clearing repeatedly, examining the signs. Finally he returned to his friends.

"They brought her here," he announced. "There were close to twenty braves waiting on them. Most of them left and went northeast."

"Did they take Ember with them?" Asa asked anxiously.

"No, they didn't," the young frontiersman returned. "It looks like two of them took her in tow and went south."

"Are you sure, Will?" Jack asked.

"Yeah," Hackett replied confidently. "Ember dragged her feet a couple of times as they left the clearing and gave us several clear footprints."

"That's my girl!" Asa exclaimed proudly.

William glanced at Jack Cobb who, in answer to the unasked question, gave the young scout an affirmative nod, and Will immediately turned and entered the woods to the south.

Yellow Bear had seen the angry look in the White Warrior's face when he signed that he was leaving with his prisoner. He knew he was going to be in trouble if he didn't return quickly, so he kept them moving. He stopped only when he felt that his captive was about to drop.

Ember, for her part, tried to drag her feet and slow their pace, but the captor beside her figured out what she was doing and began pricking her in the hip with his knife when she did it. Once she thought she heard rustling in the tree branches above them, but if it was George, she never saw him.

They traveled day and night, eating pemmican and only stopping when she couldn't go on. Ember was exhausted when they finally reached the village. Yellow Bear dragged the fatigued young woman into his hut and dropped her in front of the cooking fire. He explained to his squaw that the girl was their slave, and she could do what she wanted to with her. He then demanded some food and said that he must go back to the war.

Wearily Ember pushed herself up from the dirt floor and looked around.

"Is that you, Turtle Girl?" a young voice called to her from a pile of furs on the other side of the hut. Looking at the slave was a plump Shawnee girl eating a piece of flat bread.

"Waxing Moon!" Ember said with surprise. "Is this where you live?"

"Auntie Prisha always say you too slow," the girl returned. "Tapakikisafeewee knew she see you again. You too slow to escape."

Chapter Twenty-Eight

TEARFUL REUNION

"EMBA!" Prisha exclaimed when she saw the young woman walk into her hut with Moon Beam and Waxing Moon. Ember rushed to her former mistress and gave her a long hug.

Finally the Shawnee medicine woman pushed away from the girl's embrace and asked in Shawnee, "What are you doing here?"

"Yellow Bear captured her and brought her home as a slave," Prisha's sister answered. "I recognized her at once and knew you would want to see her."

"I am sorry that you are a slave, Emba," Prisha said with feeling, "but my heart is so happy to see you again!"

At that moment Ember happened to notice Prisha's mother beside the cooking fire, and next to her was dark-haired young woman backing slowly away and looking fearfully at Ember.

"There is no need for fear," Ember said in Shawnee to the scared woman.

"Emba," Prisha explained, "this is Su-ah-na."

Still confused, Ember looked hard at the girl and saw her blue eyes. "Susanna?"

Suddenly the trembling girl fell to the ground in front of Ember and began sobbing. "I'm sorry, Ember! I'm so sorry for stealing your stuff and leaving you and Rebecca stranded in that cave!"

Ember was so surprised at seeing Susanna that for the moment she was at a loss for words.

"It's actually worse than what you know," Susanna continued, still crying. "After I left you, I got caught by Rayford and the Indians, and to save my life, I told them where you and Rebecca were! Ember, I've been such a horrible person...Can you ever forgive me?"

As she watched the grief-stricken young woman at her feet sobbing and begging for forgiveness, Ember's first reaction was anger at the traitor, but in that instant she heard the sweet voice of Jesus in her heart. *My friends betrayed me, too.*

And you forgave them, Ember responded in her heart, *just like you forgave me.*

I gave my life for all of you.

As Ember heard these precious words, all of the anger seemed to flow out of her and was replaced by an awareness of the deep love that Jesus felt for this broken woman at her feet.

Reaching down and grasping the arms of the crying girl, Ember gently lifted her up so she could look at her face. "I already have forgiven you, Susanna, and so has Rebecca."

At these words, Susanna threw her arms around Ember's neck and sobbed some more.

From across the room Waxing Moon stopped eating her flat bread and snorted, "Mushroom Girl and Turtle Girl...they *both* a mess."

As Prisha and her sister watched this drama play out, Moon Beam, with a confused look on her face, nodded toward the two slave girls and asked in Shawnee, "Why are they doing this?"

With a peaceful smile Prisha answered, "A year ago when they escaped, Su-ah-na betrayed her sister and Emba."

"But they are hugging like sisters!" Moon Beam exclaimed in disbelief.

"That is because Emba has forgiven Su-ah-na."

"FORGIVEN HER?" Moon Beam gasped. "SU-AH-NA BETRAYED HER! EMBA SHOULD BE TRYING TO KILL HER!"

"Emba follows Chief Jesu," Prisha answered. "He say we are to love our enemies and forgive them. I have told you this before, Moon Beam, but you would not listen."

Prisha's sister studied Ember as she lovingly hugged the crying woman who had betrayed her. Finally she said to Prisha, "I will listen now."

"As I have told you," Prisha began, "the Great Spirit Moneto wanted to show all people what He is like, so many seasons ago He sent His Son Jesu to live among us and show us how much Moneto loves us. But like Su-ah-na did to Emba, we have all betrayed Moneto."

"I have not betrayed Moneto!" Moon Beam shot back defensively.

"Sister," Prisha returned, "Moneto made the world and all that is in it. He made me, and He made you. He made all of us. Moneto deserves to be our chief! Have you made Moneto or His Son your chief, Moon Beam?"

The squaw thought on this question before answering. "No," she said simply.

"So in spite of all that Moneto has done for you," Prisha continued, "you have rejected Him as your chief. By making decisions that please you, you have shown that you are your own chief. By doing that, you have betrayed Moneto, as all of us have. We deserve the same judgment you gave to Su-ah-na...death. But Moneto loves His children. He does not want to kill us, but He is also just and must punish our evil. So to express His justice *and*

His love, Moneto sent His Son Jesu to live with us and to receive our punishment. Jesu willingly died a terrible death to pay the price for our evil. But then to show us that He wants to give those who follow Jesu life forever with Him, Moneto raised His Son from the dead! When we make Jesu our Chief, He takes our evil on Himself and receives our punishment, and Moneto makes us His children and gives us new life.

"Emba has believed in Moneto's Son Jesu and has made Him her chief. She has a clean heart that is full of Moneto's peace. Chief Jesu now lives in her heart, so even though Su-ah-na betrayed her, Emba can forgive her. When you make Jesu your Chief, He comes to live inside you, and He will give you love even for your enemies."

"This has happened to you?" Moon Beam asked her sister.

"Yes, it has."

Again the squaw turned to look at Ember and Susanna, who were now laughing and talking with each other through their tears.

"I would like Chief Jesu to live in me like that," she said as a tear rolled down her cheek as well.

"Come," Prisha said with a smile. "We will go back to your hut and talk to Moneto."

The next morning Prisha, Moon Beam, their elderly mother, Waxing Moon, Susanna, and Ember took baskets and walked out of the village and into the surrounding woods.

"What are we doing?" Susanna asked as she walked beside Ember.

"Moon Beam told me that we are going hunting for mushrooms," Ember returned.

"That should be easy for you, Mushroom Girl," Waxing Moon called over her shoulder from just in front of them.

They were just outside the village when they heard thrashing in the limbs over their heads. Suddenly the squaws were startled as a very large great horned owl dropped from above and landed solidly on a stout limb just in front of them. A cry of alarm burst from all of them as they drew back from the bird...all of them but Ember. She smiled at the big, one-eyed bird.

Both squaws began talking so fast that Ember was unable to understand their words.

"This bad sign!" Waxing Moon exclaimed. "Ver' bad sign!"

"It's just an owl," Susanna returned.

"Owls always mean something bad is to happen!" the plump Shawnee girl explained. "An' this not jus' owl! Look how big he is! This no regular owl! He so big, he must be spirit owl! He stares at us with one eye! It bad sign!"

"Oh, it's a bad sign alright," Ember snapped. "It's a sign that Seth Middlebrook and Lij Nelson have been feeding him way too many mice!"

Pushing past the startled others, Ember walked up to the large bird. "George, you're getting as fat as a Christmas goose!" As she said this, she pulled the leather sleeve of her hunting shirt down to cover her arm and extended it toward the owl. To the shock of everyone else, the huge bird eagerly hopped onto Ember's arm and began giving a deep, contented rumble as he rubbed his head on her shoulder.

"Emba?"

Ember turned and saw the rest of her party staring at her with open mouths and wide eyes.

"Oh," the young woman said as she saw the confused and startled expressions of the others, "this is George Washington. He's a friend of mine." Ember spent the next several minutes explaining how she had rescued the owl as a baby and, because of his injured eye, had raised him.

"George and I have been through a lot together," she concluded. "He's kind of attached to me now. I believe he thinks I'm his mother."

It took some doing to convince Moon Beam and her pudgy daughter that George was not an evil spirit animal, but soon they were both gently stroking the feathers on the great bird's chest.

"It is clear that Moneto has given you the gift of healing as He has to my sister, Prisha," Moon Beam said. "Moneto even brings His creatures for you to heal."

They each took turns petting the owl, amazed at his gentleness. "Emba, I like your owl," Moon Beam said again, "but you must not bring him into the village. The Shawnee people see all owls as bad, and they will not understand. They will harm you and your friend."

"I understand, Moon Beam," Ember returned. "I do not wish to do anything that might harm George or that would cause trouble for you or Prisha."

Chapter Twenty-Nine

A SIGN FROM ABOVE

With their baskets full of mushrooms, Prisha led the way back to the village. When they reached the outskirts of the Shawnee settlement, they had to stop while Ember dealt with her owl. It took some time for her to convince George to remain in the woods. Every time she turned to leave him, he would start dancing excitedly and hooting loudly. As much as she hated to do it, Ember finally had to raise her voice and speak firmly to him. Eventually George seemed to understand and hung his head as Ember and the others left him.

As they entered the village, they passed a number of inhabitants performing various chores. Susanna remembered to keep her eyes down as they walked along, and with her dyed hair and darker, stained skin, no one noticed her. Ember had no such disguise, and it seemed that everyone stared at her. It happened so frequently that it made her feel uncomfortable.

When they reached a spot in the village that was near the creek, Prisha turned to the two slaves. "Emba, you an' Su-ah-na take mushrooms to the creek an' wash them. When you finish, bring them to the hut."

Ember translated this to Susanna, and they both collected all the baskets.

"I go with them," pudgy Waxing Moon announced as she pulled another piece of flatbread from where she had stuck it in her belt. "That way they no get away." She said this in English for the benefit of the two slaves, then gave them both a suspicious look.

"Well, if you're coming with us," Ember returned in Shawnee, "make yourself useful." Ember set one of the baskets of mushrooms on the ground for the girl to pick up.

"I no slave!" the Shawnee girl shot back in a haughty tone.

"Tapakikisafeewee!" The stern call came from Moon Beam.

"Yes, Neegah," the girl returned humbly to her mother.

Moon Beam gave her a stern look and pointed toward the basket. With a faint nod

Waxing Moon picked it up and followed Ember and Susanna to the creek.

Kneeling beside the stream, the three each pulled a mushroom from their baskets, dunked it into the clear water, and rubbed it vigorously with their hands. It didn't take long before all of the edible fungus was washed and ready to be carried home. They had just started back to the huts when a shout stopped them in their tracks.

"OH NO!" Susanna hissed when she saw her former mistress leading a large number of Shawnee towards them. The fear in Susanna's stomach began to lessen when she noticed that everyone was looking at Ember. Keeping her eyes down, Susanna slipped to the side as the crowd arrived and ran as quickly as her injured leg would allow back to the hut.

"YOU NOT SHAWNEE!" the furious squaw yelled in Ember's face. Then turning to the large crowd with her, she yelled at them. "SHE NOT SHAWNEE! GREAT SHAMAN OF THE WHITE WARRIORS SAY THAT SHE MUST DIE!"

"I AM JUST A SLAVE!" Ember yelled back in Shawnee, but everyone was talking and paid no attention to her. Seeing how angry the squaw was and that she was getting everyone worked up, Ember tried to sneak off while everyone was listening to the Indian woman vent her wrath, but the squaw spotted her, grabbed her hair, and yanked her back.

After slipping away from the crowd, Susanna and Waxing Moon ran to Moon Beam's hut as fast as Susanna's injured leg would allow. Waxing Moon arrived first and began yelling and crying as she pointed back toward the creek. When Susanna arrived, Prisha and Moon Beam, who hadn't understood anything Waxing Moon had tried to say, demanded to know what had happened. Susanna's lack of knowledge of Shawnee made her attempt at an explanation just as difficult to understand. Finally Waxing Moon calmed down enough to tell them what happened, and Prisha shot out of the door.

"SHE NOT SHAWNEE!" the infuriated squaw preached to the crowd as she pulled hard at Ember's hair. "WE MUST KILL HER! THE GREAT SHAMAN SAY WE MUST KILL ALL WHO ARE NOT INDIAN!"

Fear began to grow in Ember as she understood the venomous words and saw the eager nods of agreement by the mob. Almost immediately, sticks, rocks, and a few knives and tomahawks appeared in the hands of the angry Indians.

"YOU MUST NOT DO THIS!" Ember cried through tears of pain. "IT IS WRONG!"

Once again her hair was painfully yanked as the hate-filled squaw turned to the young woman. She drew back her hand to strike Ember, but before the blow fell, a strong arm gripped her wrist, stopping her.

The raging squaw spun around to see who dared oppose her, and she found herself face-to-face with Prisha, who was screaming what sounded to Ember like a war cry.

The look of hate on the woman's face quickly turned to a look of fear when she saw her adversary so close.

"HAVE YOU LOST YOUR MIND, RED SWAN?" Prisha yelled at the woman. "DO YOU KNOW WHO YOU ARE ATTACKING? THIS IS MONETO'S OWN DAUGHTER!" When Prisha said this, the crowd gasped and lowered their weapons.

"YOU ARE GOING TO BRING THE CURSE OF THE GREAT SPIRIT DOWN UPON THE WHOLE VILLAGE IF YOU ATTACK HER! RELEASE HER HAIR!" Prisha now had everyone's attention, including Red Swan's, and the squaw let go of Ember's hair.

"How do you know she is Moneto's daughter?" Red Swan growled suspiciously.

"This woman's name is Emba," Prisha began, "and she talks with the Great Spirit, Moneto...and He hears and answers her."

"She is a Shem-a-noe," Red Swan spat back. "She is our enemy. How can she be Moneto's daughter? The white shaman said we must kill all Shem-a-noes!"

"The white shaman," Prisha said mockingly. "That white-painted stork does not get his power from Moneto but from Watch-a-ne-toc, the Evil One."

"You dare say such things about the shaman?" Red Swan gasped.

"I will prove to all of you," Prisha returned confidently, "not only that Emba talks to Moneto, but also that the shaman is evil."

"How will you do this?" one of the men in the crowd asked.

"Yes," others in the crowd agreed. "How will you do such a thing?"

After quieting the crowd, Prisha spoke again so all could hear. "Emba will ask Moneto to give us a sign to let us know what He thinks about the shaman."

At this declaration there was earnest murmuring from the crowd; then everyone, including Red Swan, nodded in agreement.

Nervously, Ember drew next to the medicine woman and whispered, "Prisha, what do I do?"

"Call out to Moneto to give us a sign to tell us what He thinks of the shaman and his white warriors!" Prisha answered loudly so all could hear. "Call out now! Speak so all can hear!"

Seeing that everyone was staring expectantly at her, Ember raised her hands to heaven and poured out her soul to God. "O Great Father in Heaven, You are wonderful and beautiful! I know you hear me, Father, but I come to you now for the Shawnee people. You know all things, and we ask You Who Knows the Hearts of All Men to show us the heart of the shaman. He has come to the village declaring great things about himself. Please reveal to us, in a way that we can understand, what You see when you look into his heart. Thank you for hearing me and answering this prayer. I ask this in the name of Your Son Jesus Christ. Amen."

"Now what?" Ember whispered to Prisha.

"Emba, we already know what the Heavenly Father thinks of the shaman," the medicine woman whispered back. "We just need to show them...so call your owl."

It took a moment for Ember to comprehend Prisha's plan, but when she did, an understanding smile began to spread across her face. Ember turned in the direction of the woods and called out in a loud voice, "GEORGE!"

As Ember continued calling, Prisha explained to the crowd that she was calling for Moneto's sign. They didn't have long to wait. With a flapping of wings, suddenly the largest great horned owl many of them had ever seen landed on the top of the hut nearest to Ember.

An audible gasp erupted from the crowd when they saw the huge bird, but Red Swan was not convinced. "How do we know Moneto sent the owl to her?" Red Swan asked accusingly.

Prisha smiled at Ember, who pulled the leather sleeve of her shirt down on her arm and called to her feathered friend again. Eagerly George dropped from the roof and glided onto Ember's offered arm. This time shouts went up from the gathered Shawnee as sticks and rocks were dropped from their hands. Even Red Swan backed away in fear.

"Now you know what Moneto thinks of the shaman and his followers. Do not fear them. Fear Moneto!"

Chapter Thirty

HARLAN'S STATION

"General Clark, the men are completely done in!" Major Miller reported with concern. "They need to rest!"

"I understand your concern, Major," the general shot back, "but if we don't keep them moving, there's a good chance we'll all be slaughtered! Push them to keep going!"

"But sir..."

"Major Miller, as I recall, this is your first time fighting Indians. There are some things you need to realize. Indians can be persistent when they are pursuing their enemies. The Shawnee are particularly relentless, and Grey Fox has confirmed that they are after us.

"These men are in no shape to fight off a major Indian attack! If we let them catch us, we are all dead! Reaching Major Harlan's fort is our only hope! Now do you understand why we have to keep them moving?"

"We'll keep going, sir," the major returned. "Do you know how much farther it is to Harlan's Station?"

"Captain Parks said that if we keep moving, we should be there before sundown."

Major Miller looked for the sun through the leafy canopy above them. "If that's true," he spoke his thoughts, "then we must be close, because it's well past noon."

"Keep them going, Major," General Clark encouraged. "They only have a little farther to go."

Less than an hour later, Dirt Gurley came trotting down the line of march looking for the general. "I spotted it, Gen'ral!" Dirt announced as he reached Clark. "Purdiest little fort you ever seen. Harlan built it beside the Salt River, an' it's only four miles ahead!"

Just then the faint sound of a rifle sounded in the distance from the way the soldiers had come.

"That cain't be good," Dirt announced at the sound. "Better push hard for that fort, Gen'ral! Them Injuns ain't far behind!"

The word was immediately sent up and down the line that their enemies were close but that the fort was only four miles ahead. Using all the strength they had left, the soldiers made themselves keep going.

It wasn't long before Grey Fox came running up the line. "They are close, Gen'ral!" the Miami huffed. "Ver' close!"

"The fort is close too!" Clark returned.

"I think you not make it before they catch you," Grey Fox answered with concern.

"Captain Parks!" General Clark shouted. The captain quickly presented himself. "Captain, you know your way around these woods. I need you to pick five good woodsmen to go with you and Grey Fox and try to slow down the Indians. You have to buy us enough time to get the men to the fort!"

"We'll do our best, General!" Parks answered with a smart salute.

In less than a minute, Parks and his men were racing back the way they had come, following Grey Fox. The Miami's senses were on high alert as he rushed toward the oncoming army of warriors. They had run for over a half a mile when Grey Fox suddenly stopped and held up his hand. "They just ahead," the Indian said in a low voice.

Parks turned to his men and spoke in a low voice. "I picked you fellas 'cause you're all hunters or trappers, an' you know how to fight. It's gonna be a hit an' run attack. Spread out, pick your targets, then change positions. We've got to slow those Indians down to give the general a chance to get the men to safety. Keep movin' back towards our friends an' don't get left behind! Now go!"

They had just gotten into position when they spotted two Shawnee scouts moving hurriedly towards them. Immediately the Miami's rifle barked, followed quickly by another off to his left. Both Shawnee dropped. Within seconds the thick forest in front of them came alive with the cries of furious enemies.

Large numbers of painted warriors began to materialize out of the forest, and when they did, the rifles of Parks' men began to do damage. After firing their rifles, each man would wait until the next person fired, then while the Indian's eyes were searching for the location of the second shooter, the first would retreat quietly behind the brush to a new spot.

The Shawnee fired at the sign of gun smoke, but then would be fired upon from multiple other locations. It took the Indians several minutes to figure out that it was only a small number of fighters shooting at them.

"THEIR FLANKIN' US, BOYS!" Parks called out when he saw warriors moving away from the main war party. "MOVE BACK!"

Bending low, Grey Fox and the men of the rear guard moved stealthily towards the fort. After covering a hundred yards, they took up new positions from which to fire. Parks had them repeat this process a number of times. Just as they were making another move, a Shawnee rifle ball tore through Parks' hip. Grey Fox heard him cry and rushed to his side. "Go on!" Parks groaned in pain. "I'm done for!"

"You not done for," the Miami shot back. "You just need help."

Grey Fox lifted his injured companion up until he was standing on his good leg. Handing Parks his rifle, the Miami then lifted the wounded captain onto his shoulder and began racing back towards the fort.

"WE NEED GO!" the Miami shouted to Parks' men.

The others could see the Shawnee warriors rushing in mass towards them and knew that further resistance was useless. With their weapons in hand, they all sprinted for the fort.

Dirt Gurley paced nervously back and forth beside the gate at Harlan's Station as the last of General Clark's men hurried through the opening to safety. His eyes were riveted on the edge of the forest across the one-hundred-yard clearing surrounding the enclosure. The hundreds of rifle blasts echoing from the woods sounded very close.

"O Lord," the concerned scout prayed, "there's a whole heap of rifle balls flying through them woods right now, an' my friend Grey Fox an' the others is out there in the middle of it. Please, Lord, give them Injuns bad aim. Send them bullets somewhere else other than into my friends, an' bring 'em all back here safe...uh, amen!"

Just as he finished his prayer, Dirt saw five men sprinting out of the woods. Not recognizing the Miami among them, the faithful scout began racing towards the woods. At that moment he saw Grey Fox running out of the forest carrying Parks. The Miami hadn't made ten strides when the first of the Shawnee warriors burst out of the woods.

"OUR PEOPLE'S A'COMIN'!" Dirt shouted up to the guards on the wall. "HELP 'EM OUT!" As soon as he said this, Dirt raised his rifle and took more careful aim than he could remember and squeezed the trigger.

The closest enemy fighter to Grey Fox was rapidly gaining on him. He had his tomahawk in his hand and was just drawing it back to strike when Dirt's ball struck him. At the same instant multiple rifle blasts sounded from the top of the wall, causing the first of the Shawnee warriors to stop and retreat, running into those coming behind. The confusion allowed all of the rear guard to make it through the open gates.

It was at that moment that the shaman and the White Warriors arrived. The tall, white-painted tyrant screamed some orders, and his ten faithful followers formed a semi-circle in front of him, leveling their spears at the rest of the Shawnee threateningly.

With exaggerated signs the fanatical leader said, "Our enemies are there in front of you...hundreds of scalps! The spirits have given them into your hands! Now go kill them! Kill them all!" As soon as he signed this, the shaman gave a ferocious war cry. This was immediately taken up by his ten guards and was reluctantly joined by the rest of the Indian army.

In the middle of all the racket, the shaman began screaming words that no one but his guards understood. The ten White Warriors yelled at the Shawnee and pointed vigorously at the fort in the distance. To make sure the army was convinced of their orders, the shaman's guards poked the nearest Shawnee with their spear points.

With this encouragement, those still smarting from the sharp lances pushed through the screaming crowd and ran for the fort. As they did so, the rest followed. The large army of screaming warriors burst from the edge of the clearing and rushed with murderous intent at the small fort.

"HERE THEY COME!" Dirt Gurley cried from his place along the catwalk.

"STEADY MEN!" General Clark called down the line of defenders on the wall, then turning toward the tall guard posts over-looking either side of the gate, he called, "WAIT FOR MY ORDER, MAJOR HARLAN!"

"YES, SIR!" Silas Harlan called back from the top of the nearest one.

"They're gettin' close, General!" Dirt felt obliged to say when he saw the massive array of killers running towards them.

"PICK YOUR TARGETS, MEN," Clark called out, "AND LET THEM HAVE IT!"

Flames erupted from over a hundred rifles at the same time, decimating the front line of charging warriors. Knowing that the defenders on the wall must reload, the Shawnee behind kept rushing toward the fort.

As Dirt Gurley feverishly reloaded his rifle, he glanced up and realized that the attacking army would be climbing up the walls before they could fire again. Suddenly he heard General Clark's voice boom over the din of battle. "HARLAN, NOW!"

"FIRE!" Dirt heard Silas Harlan cry, and two enormous booms shook the walls of the fort. The two six pounder brass cannons that Harlan had mounted on top of the guard posts sprayed hundreds of lead balls at the war-crazed warriors.

"Whoa!" Dirt said as he saw the devastating effect of the grape shot. "That stopped 'em!" he said to Grey Fox, who had just climbed onto the wall to join his friend.

"Humph!" the Miami grunted as he too watched the retreating Indian army leaving so many of their number lying on the field. "First time Grey Fox feel sorry for Shawnee."

Just as the retreating army reached the safety of the tree line, they were met by the spears of the shaman's ruthless guards. Standing on a log behind the White Warriors, the raging shaman told them that they were all cowards and that the spirits would kill all of them and their families if they didn't go back and attack the fort.

As the cheering defenders on the walls of Harlan's Station watched the fleeing Indians, Silas Harlan himself climbed up to join General Clark.

"Heh, heh," Harlan said as he viewed the field in front of the fort. "I reckon that ended the war!"

"Good job, Major!" General Clark said, clapping a hand on Silas Harlan's shoulder.

"I hates to tell you this," Dirt Gurley, who was standing nearby, said, "but he ain't gonna' let 'em quit...an' that's a fact!"

"Who?" Harlan asked.

"What are you talking about, Gurley?" the general said.

"The only reason them heatherns is fightin' us," Dirt explained, "is that tall, white-painted shaman out there yellin' at 'em right now! He's convinced 'em that he's got power over the spirits, an' he's the one who's drivin' the Injuns to fight us!"

Both General Clark and Silas Harlan stared hard at the crowd of enemy warriors in the distance. "Is that him yonder?" Harlan asked as he pointed toward the tiny white figure behind the Shawnee.

"That circle of white figures is his guards," Dirt answered. "The shaman is that taller feller furthest back. He must be standin' on somethin' 'cause he's a little above the others."

"Hmmm," Harlan mused, studying the distance. Finally he called out, "MACGREGOR!"

A large, deep-chested man with a short beard stepped out of the line of defenders and walked up to them. "Aye, Boss?"

"Can you see that tall white fellow on the far side of that herd of In'juns?" Harlan asked the marksman.

MacGregor stared hard at the crowd of enemies. "Aye, ah sees 'im."

"Snuff his candle," Harlan said with meaning.

With an understanding nod MacGregor checked the direction and speed of the wind, licked his thumb, and touched it to the sight on the end of his rifle barrel. Leaning on the top of the wall, he took careful and deliberate aim before squeezing the trigger.

The furious shaman was in the middle of signing more threats at his army when MacGregor's rifle ball ended his speech. The White Warriors heard their leader grunt and fall backwards off the log. Just as the Shawnee were realizing what had happened, Rayford's rifle went off, dropping the White Warrior in front of him.

"GET RID OF 'EM," he yelled, "AFORE THEY KILL US ALL!"

As if on que, the Shawnee attacked the rest of the White Warriors. When all of the Shaman's guards were down or had run off, the Shawnee gave a whoop of victory and left to go back to their village.

Rayford hung back, searching for his intended victim. He spotted Yellow Bear just pulling himself from off the ground where he had been in a fight with one of the White Warriors. Looking around, Rayford saw that the rest of the Shawnee were leaving and not looking his way. Like a snake striking, Rayford stepped over and swung the butt of his empty rifle hard into the side of Yellow Bear's head, dropping him to the ground. With an evil smile, the wicked trapper said to prone warrior, "I tol' you that you cain't take what's mine."

Chapter Thirty-One

RAYFORD

Several days later Prisha, Ember and Susanna were carrying firewood from the forest to the huts with the squaws and Waxing Moon.

"Do you really talk with Jesus, Ember?"

"Everyone can talk with Jesus, Susanna."

"But apparently He answers you back," Susanna returned with a sideways look.

"On a few occasions I believe I've heard Him," Ember answered. "The really wonderful experiences I've had with Jesus are the two times He took me to heaven—once when I almost died from a snake bite and once when..."

"Yeah, I know," Susanna said humbly, "when I hit you in the head with a bucket."

"I guess I really should thank you for that," Ember giggled. "I had the most amazing time with the Lord."

"What was it like?" Susanna asked.

"It was breath-takingly wonderful!"

"Is that even a word?" Susanna laughed.

"It's the only one I can think of that comes close to what I experienced," Ember smiled back. "There are sounds, smells, tastes, and colors there that you could never imagine. Everything in heaven praises and worships the Lord. The people I met were sweet and wonderful...even the animals were wonderful! But as amazing as all of that was, none of it compares to Jesus Himself!

"He has this...this...uh...sweetness and this radiant beauty and love that just seems to come out of Him and engulfs you! I guess it's what the Bible is talking about when it refers to His glory. Whatever it is, it's wonderful, and I love it!

"His voice is so genuine, caring, and compassionate! When He talks to you, you know He loves you and cares about you!"

"I've never had anyone talk to me like that," Susanna said sadly.

"One day you will, sister," Ember returned with a sweet smile.

The last few days had been peaceful and pleasant. They were not bothered by anyone in the village. Everyone seemed to have a new-found respect for Moon Beam's slave who talked to Moneto. They passed through the village with the firewood and were nearing Moon Beam's and

Prisha's huts. Prisha suddenly stopped them and yelled. "NO! NO! GO AWAY! LEAVE HERE AT ONCE!"

Looking up, Ember and Susanna were terrified to see a very red-faced Rayford, rifle in hand, staring straight at Ember. As soon as he spotted them, he began walking purposely straight for them.

Prisha turned and, with a look of panic, said to the two slave women, "Run! RUN!"

Tossing the armload of firewood aside, Ember grabbed Susanna by the arm and pulled her towards the woods as fast as Susanna's injured leg would allow.

Seeing the murderous look in her former husband's eyes, Prisha screamed angrily and ran straight for Rayford. When she got close enough, the medicine woman threw herself at the big trapper. Instantly Rayford's hand flew up and caught Prisha by the throat, lifting her off the ground with very little effort. He held her there, helplessly thrashing as he squeezed her neck.

Another scream sounded, and a thick limb came crashing down painfully on the forearm the trapper used to grip Prisha. With a powerful yell the huge man dropped the squaw and grabbed his arm. As he did so, Moon Beam hit him again in the shoulder, breaking the tree branch.

"GET AWAY FROM ME!" he yelled and powerfully swung his left hand that was holding his rifle into the squaw, stunning Moon Beam and sending her flying into the brush.

When Prisha's mother saw what the man had done to her daughters, she ran up to him and began beating his chest with her fists. Looking up from where she lay gasping on the ground, Prisha tried to yell to her mother but was unable to speak.

When the old woman hit Rayford, he grabbed her by the hair and slung her into the brush with Moon Beam. Spotting his escaping victim, Rayford growled and sprinted after the two women.

Ember and Susanna made it out of the village and were running across the open area for the woods.

"WILL! JACK! LOOK!" Asa exclaimed. He was hidden in the brush, watching the east side of the village. His two friends had stationed him there and were leaving to slip through the woods to the other side. At his words both scouts turned.

"One of those women is Ember!" Asa cried as he pointed at two figures in the distance rushing out of the village. "I'm sure of it!"

They had tracked Ember to the village and had been quietly working their way along the edge of the woods, trying to spot her and to identify which hut she was being kept in. As they observed the running women, the three scouts saw that they were over fifty yards from where the escapers were headed.

"Come on!" Will ordered and started on a track that would allow them to intercept the girls.

Jack abruptly called, "Somebody's after them!"

Will and Asa looked as they ran and saw a very large man sprinting after Ember and her companion. "That's Rayford!" Will returned anxiously.

"He's the guy that tried to kill her!" Asa said as he heard the name.

"It looks like that's what he's trying to do now!" Will answered. "Run hard!"

"It's a good thing you spotted them, Asa!" Jack huffed from behind.

Ember glanced back at the approaching killer and knew they were in trouble. "Lord Jesus, help us!" she prayed out loud.

They had only gone a short distance into the woods when suddenly Susanna jerked free from Ember's grip and came to a stop with her hands on her knees, gasping for breath. "You'll never get away dragging me," she huffed. "Run, Ember. RUN!"

"Not without you!" Ember returned anxiously and reached for her arm again.

"Gotcha!" the hate-filled voice announced. Looking up, Ember saw Rayford standing only ten paces away, his eyes cold and merciless. "I tol' you I'd come...an' I've got plans for you."

Taking a deep breath, Ember handed her fears to her Lord and looked boldly into the face of death. "Rayford, I know you've done a lot of evil things," she said in a strong, clear voice, "but God can forgive you."

"SHUT YOUR MOUTH!" the trapper roared in fury, his longtime hatred of God bursting out of him without restraint.

Tell him I love him, Ember heard in her heart. "Jesus loves you, Rayford!" she repeated her Master's words.

"STOP!" the raging trapper screamed and growled his fierce anger.

"He really does love you," she called back, "and He died on the cross for you to prove it."

This time it wasn't words that came from Rayford's mouth but a gurgling, mindless shriek. With hate-filled eyes he snapped the rifle up to his shoulder and aimed at the woman's heart. Before he could pull the trigger, a huge mass of feathers and talons slammed into the trapper's face.

"It's George!" Susanna shouted joyfully as she saw Rayford stagger backwards, flailing his arms and rifle in a desperate effort to separate himself from the attacking owl and his terrible claws.

Roaring like a man possessed, the trapper fought frantically to get the flying attacker away from him. Finally Rayford managed to grip one of the bird's wings and, with a yell of rage, hurled the creature into a thick clump of brush.

"GEORGE!" Ember cried.

At the sound of her shout, Rayford's attention was back on his longed-for victim. Locking his eyes on the girl and giving an evil grin, the killer raised his rifle again. "There's no one to save you this time!" he snarled as he took aim and squeezed the trigger.

"NO-O-O-O!" shrieked Susanna and threw her body into Ember's as the rifle went off.

"Oh no, no, no!" Ember cried in panic as she saw her friend drop beside her, groaning and gripping her chest. Ember burst into tears when she saw the fatal wound. "WHY, SUSANNA?" she cried in anguish as she cradled the dying girl's head in her lap. "WHY DID YOU DO THAT?"

"It was...my last chance...to love you."

When the murderous Rayford saw that he had failed to hit his intended target, he threw down his rifle, yanked out his knife, and stepped determinedly toward Ember.

Just then a fierce Shawnee war cry rang out, and a powerful body landed hard on Rayford's back, driving him to the ground. Furious that his plans had been interrupted again, the trapper fought this new antagonist like an enraged bear. To his surprise, the warrior on top of him fought with just as much passion. Rayford managed to send a hard elbow into his attacker's ribs and shove him off. When the furious trapper regained his feet, he found himself facing Yellow Bear.

"YOU HAD THAT COMIN' BACK AT THE FORT, YELLOW BEAR!" Rayford roared in Shawnee as he threatened the warrior with his knife. "I TOLD YOU SHE WAS MINE!"

"You tried to kill Yellow Bear," the warrior returned coldly with an angry glare. "Now you try to kill my family!" As he said this, he pointed to Prisha as she struggled to help Moon Beam and her mother. "You are no friend to the Shawnee!" the warrior announced. "You are our ENEMY!" Roaring his war cry, Yellow Bear leaped at his foe.

Rayford was ready and parried the Shawnee's knife with his own. As Yellow Bear's left hand shot for the trapper's throat, Rayford grabbed it with his left, stepped to the side, and threw the attacking Indian to the ground. As soon as he hit, Yellow Bear rolled over quickly, just in time to see the large trapper diving on top of him. When the Shawnee saw the knife coming straight for his chest, he dropped his own knife and grabbed Rayford's wrist with both hands to keep the sharp blade from stabbing him.

Frustrated again, Rayford threw his left hand on top of his right and used all of his weight to force the knife down towards his enemy's chest. Both fighters strained, using all of their might, but Rayford had the advantage, and slowly the point of the blade descended.

Just as the weakening Yellow Bear felt the first bite of the knife point, a rifle blasted, and Rayford dropped lifelessly to the side. When the Shawnee warrior looked for his rescuer, he saw three grim-looking frontiersmen standing beside Ember and Susanna.

The Dancing Ghosts

Chapter Thirty-Two

THE HOMECOMING

Smoke still curled from Jack Cobb's rifle after firing the shot that saved Yellow Bear. On one side of the older scout, Asa Whitlock knelt beside Ember. Standing on Jack's right was William Hackett. Propping his unfired weapon against his side, the young frontiersman looked at the Shawnee warrior and signed the word for friend. He then stepped over to the fallen Indian and offered his hand to help Yellow Bear to his feet.

"These are friends of mine, Yellow Bear," Ember said in Shawnee, "who have come to rescue me. When I saw that the trapper was about to kill you, I asked Jack Cobb to save you."

"Why?" the warrior asked suspiciously, as he let William help him to his feet.

"Because you fought Rayford and kept him from killing me."

Yellow Bear looked back at his family and saw Prisha supporting his wife and his mother-in-law. Moon Beam saw the look of concern in her husband's eyes and said, "We are safe."

The Shawnee warrior then turned to face the others. The Indian studied the large young man who stood before him. "Who is this?" Yellow Bear said while signing the same question.

"I am *Walks Without Sound*," William signed. "These are my companions. We do not come as enemies. We came to take back the young woman. She is our healer and is like a sister to us."

"She speaks to Moneto, Husband," Moon Beam said as the squaw stepped beside Yellow Bear. "She has told us much about the Heavenly Father and His Son, Chief Jesu."

"It is true, Yellow Bear," Prisha added.

"Husband," Moon Beam began again, "Emba is like a sister to Prisha and our mother also. She has become very dear to us. As much as we will miss her, I ask you to let her go with her friends."

"They did save your life, Yellow Bear," Prisha added encouragingly.

The Shawnee warrior thought on these words for several moments. As he did so, he reached up and touched the shallow knife wound in his chest. He then glanced down at the body of the man who almost killed him. Finally he faced the frontiersmen. "The girl is yours," he signed. He then turned to see about his wife and the others in his family.

Prisha left her wobbly mother in her sister's hands and moved quickly to Susanna's side. When she saw the location of the bullet wound, she gave a gasp. "Su-ah-na!" the medicine woman sighed as tears began to stream from her eyes.

"Prisha," the wounded young woman wheezed in a barely audible voice, "did...you see? I wasn't...selfish...First time."

"You were wonderful, Susanna!" Ember said through her tears. "When I tell Rebecca what you did, she will be so proud of you."

"Please...tell Becca...so sorry. So, so...sorry."

"I promise I will, Susanna," Ember vowed as she wiped her cheeks, "but she has already forgiven you. I heard her say it. She has forgiven you, just like Jesus has."

"Jesus," the dying woman sighed at the mention of her Lord.

I am here, my precious one.

"Oh, Ember," Susanna wheezed as her wide eyes looked past her friends and into a face appearing above them, a face that she could only describe as pure love. "He is...h...here!"

"You see Jesu?" Prisha asked in amazement as she and Ember began looking up, following Susanna's eyes. But they saw no one.

"Oh, yes!" the wounded girl was able to answer. "I...I see Him.

"Jesus...have you...come...for me?"

I have, dearest, the beautiful face answered with the sweetest smile Susanna had ever seen. *I have waited long for you, precious Susanna, and today is your celebration day. But before I take you home, I want you to tell your friends something for me.*

"H...he says...tell you both...loves y...you. He's getting...a p...place ready...for you," Susanna managed to say with the last of her energy. Then a large, beautiful smile spread across her face as she said "but He h...has c...come for ME."

As these last words left her smiling lips, Susanna saw the hand of Jesus reaching down through what appeared to be a portal of beautiful light. *Come now, Sweetheart,* Jesus said with a smile as He took her hand and lifted her up to join him. *It is time for you to leave the land of shadows. There are many here eager to celebrate your homecoming.*

Oh, my! Susanna exclaimed as she looked around at the glorious sights surrounding them. *Ember was right! Everything is absolutely amazing!*

He, he, he, Jesus chuckled, *It gets much better.*

"She is gone, Emba," Prisha announced through her tears as she watched their friend take her last breath.

"Because of her selfishness," Ember said in Shawnee, "much of Susanna's life was miserable and sad. But you and your sweet mother let Jesus love her through you. When Susanna finally saw how much Jesus loved her, she surrendered herself to our Chief. I'm sorry she didn't get to live the good life she wanted here."

"Su-ah-na okay," Prisha smiled through her tears. "She is with Chief Jesu! A good life here is nothing compared to the life she has now. But I will miss her."

When she said that, Ember threw her arms around the medicine woman's neck and held her as they both cried some more.

After several long minutes Prisha pulled away from the embrace and looked at Ember. "You go with you friends, Emba. Leave Su-ah-na with me. I will take care of her."

When Ember translated the squaw's words to the others, Jack Cobb answered, "I know you and Miss Rebecca would like to have her buried at Larkinboro, an' I'd be willin' to carry her body back there, but we have to get you to Harlan's

Station as fast as we can. There are injured soldiers waiting for you there. To tell you the truth, Miss Ember, we more'n likely won't be back to Larkinboro for a few weeks. I think it's best to leave her here and let your Shawnee friend take care of her."

On hearing the older scout's wisdom, Ember sadly nodded her head in agreement and reached down to gently stroke Susanna's hair once more.

"My sister Moon Beam will help me," Prisha said, "and we will bury Su-ah-na here and mourn for her like she was our sister."

"Thank you, Prisha!" Ember returned with feeling. "Thank you for everything! I am so glad you saved Susanna from Red Swan and brought her to live with you and your mother. She would have died miserably without ever knowing Jesus except for you."

"We just did what Chief Jesu wanted," the medicine woman answered.

"I am so glad I got to see you again, Prisha," Ember said with feeling as she gripped both of the medicine woman's shoulders. "I have been using all that you have taught me. So you see, Jesus has been using you to help people that you have never met! The reward that Jesus gives me for helping people with my medicine, He will give to you as well because you taught me."

When she heard those words, a large smile began to slowly spread across the creased features of the medicine woman. "Is it so?" the medicine woman asked with a look of wonder on her face.

"Yes, Prisha," Ember replied, hugging the squaw again, "it is so!"

"*Hmmm*," the squaw said thoughtfully, "maybe I teach others to heal and to love Chief Jesu and send them out like you. Then Prisha get *big* reward!" As the squaw said this she smiled, and for the first time Ember heard her laugh.

"Oh, Prisha, I miss you so much," Ember said again. "I know you are needed in the village, but I wish we could be together."

"Ember, here's someone who needs your help!" Asa called. He stood a short distance away and held George, the great horned owl, where he had pulled the bird out of the brush. "I think one of his wings is broken."

Ember quickly rose and hurried over to her feathered friend. Carefully examining the drooping wing, she realized that Asa's guess was correct. "Oh, my poor, brave boy!" she said soothingly as she stroked the bird's neck feathers. "Thank you, George! You saved my life when you attacked Rayford! But don't you worry, I'll get Asa to help me, and we'll reset your wing and get you bandaged up right now."

As she lifted her arm to receive the injured owl, her eyes met Asa's. She realized that she was looking at someone who cared for her enough to risk his life to rescue her. Instead of reaching for the owl, she rested her hand on Asa's arm. "Thank you for coming for me!" she said with sincerity.

"I had to, Ember," he answered tenderly. "You mean the world to me."

"You mean the world to us too, Ember," Will Hackett said with a mischievous smile, and Jack couldn't suppress a chuckle.

"Thank you *all* for coming after me," Ember quickly added as her cheeks began to glow a bright red. She turned from the others and reached into the pouch at Asa's hip to retrieve a bandage roll she knew he kept with him.

"So you think George'll be okay?" Asa asked to change the subject and rescue Ember from her embarrassment.

"Sure," the healer smiled back as she picked up a couple of sticks to use to make a splint for the broken wing. "It's nothing that a little loving care and a few fat mice won't cure."

THE END

Appendix A
Chapter Questions and Lessons

In writing entertaining bonding experience for my family, but I wanted to teach some important character and this story, I not only wanted to create a fun and spiritual lessons to my children and grandchildren as well. I have always told my children stories, especially the ones that I heard from my father, and there were occasionally some spiritual lessons stuck in them. I was impressed by the fact that those were the lessons that my children always remembered.

It struck me that one of the reasons Jesus used stories so much in His teaching was because they made the lessons so memorable. I researched and learned that, when teaching is placed within a gripping or engaging story, not only does the information reach the mind of the reader, but the teaching is also connected to the reader's emotions. Said another way, when the emotions are engaged, the lesson is remembered and the heart is taught, and that is where real life change occurs. Please understand, I do not believe that a teaching technique causes heart or life change. Only the Spirit of God at work in our hearts can do that. But when we follow Jesus's example of how to teach and combine it with fervent prayer, I believe that we are giving our children and students the best opportunity for the Holy Spirit to reach their hearts.

If it is your goal to use stories to reach the hearts of others, then I believe the most effective way to use my books is for parents to read them to their children or for teachers to read them to their classes. After completing a chapter, take time to talk about the spiritual and character lessons learned and give the listeners an opportunity to verbalize their discoveries. As a help, we have assembled this appendix with a collection of discussion questions and important lessons found in each chapter. Use any or all of these questions as a place to start, but be sensitive to the direction of the discussion, and add your own questions to accommodate what God is doing in the hearts of your listeners. Remember God's part in this whole process and always pray (if not audibly, at least to yourself) each time before reading, asking the Lord to use the story to teach His lessons to your listeners' hearts.

In His Service,

Alan W. Harris

Chapter One

Describe why you would have to be constantly alert when traveling through the wilderness.

What character qualities did Asa need to be able to find their way back home?

Describe the discipline it took for Ember to become a medicine woman.

What was Katherine's response when she saw she was being attacked by the cougar?

Character Qualities to Identify:

Ember showed **Courage** when she attacked to wounded cougar with her sling.

Courage: *the ability to show strength in the midst of pain, grief or fear.*

This in contrast to **Cowardice**: *allowing fear to prevent you from doing the right things.*

How did Jesus show Courage?

Chapter Two

What character qualities did Asa show as he prepared to defend Kate and Ember's retreat?

What attributes did Kate show when she realized that Asa was going to sacrifice himself for her?

What would it take for a person to give their life for another? (Apply this to Jesus sacrifice for us.)

Describe what it means to be observant and why that is an important quality.

Determining to scout the strange Indians showed what important character traits in the town leaders?

Character Qualities to Identify:

Taking care of the injured owl showed that Ember was **Tenderhearted.**

Tenderhearted: *Compassionate, easily moved to love, pity, or sorrow.*

This is in contrast to **Indifference:** *Lack of sensitivivity to those in need.*

How did Jesus show tenderheartedness?

Chapter Three

What character qualities are essential to be a good tracker?

Do you agree or disagree with Dirt's decision to continue tracking the Indians after they had left the area. (Explain your answer.)

Why is it important to prepare ahead of time for possible risk or danger?

What is needed to make proper preparations?

What does it mean to be deceitful and where does deceit come from?

Character Qualities to Identify:

In order for the girls to become accurate with their slings they must show **Persistence** in practice.

Persistence: *Continuing consistently in a course of action in spite of difficulty or opposition.*

This is in contrast to **Neglect:** *To disregard or give little attention to something.*

How did Jesus show persistence?

Chapter Four

What character qualities did Ember show when she attacked Rayford to save Prisha?

What bad qualities did Rayford show and what were the consequences?

What bad traits did Susanna show during the escape and what were the consequences?

How must it feel to be the betrayer?

Character Qualities to Identify:

In order for God to forgive them, Becca and Ember were required to show Susanna **Forgiveness**.

Forgiveness: *A conscious deliberate decision to release feelings of resentment or vengeance toward a person who has harmed you.*

This is in contrast to **Blame:** *To assign responsibility for a fault.*

How did Jesus show forgiveness?

Chapter Five

Describe the character of the Ghost Warriors.

What would be someone's motivation for lying to others and tricking them?

Why is it important to Satan that we believe lies?

How powerful is the truth?

Character Qualities to Identify:

Will showed **Discernment** in figuring out the Ghost Warrior's plot.

Discernment: *Noticing the details so as to be able to judge properly and to understand something.*

This is in contrast to **Heedlessness:** *Showing a reckless lack of care or attention.*

How did Jesus show discernment?

Chapter Six

What character qualities are required to successfully care for an injured animal?

What priorities must be considered in the animal's care?

What reward is there in caring for someone who cannot care for themselves?

Describe the good attributes Prisha and her mother showed Susanna.

Character Qualities to Identify:

Ember and Rebecca showed **Creativity** in inventing clay bullets.

Creativity: *The ability to come up with useful ideas in solving problems.*

This is in contrast to **uninspired:** *an unhelpful mental dullness.*

How did Jesus show creativity?

Chapter Seven

How did the four friends show thoroughness in their scouting?

In what way did Asa show lack of self-control and what was the consequence?

What valuable attributes did Will show to his friend Grey Fox?

Character Qualities to Identify:

Will showed **Cautiousness** as he led He and Asa out of the swamp to get help.

Cautiousness: *wary, prudent, careful to avoid possible danger.*

This is in contrast to **carelessness:** *reckless, foolish.*

How did Jesus show Cautiousness?

––––––––––––––––––––

Chapter Eight

What special traits would it take to find your way through the wilderness at night?

How can moon and stars be used to find direction?

How did Will and Asa show their reliance on God?

Why is it important to be faithful in the little things God gives us to do?

Character Qualities to Identify:

Ember showed **Faithfulness** in her preparations for the work she felt God was calling her to do.

Faithfulness: *Firmness in keeping a promise or in observing a duty or responsibility.*

This is in contrast to being **Unreliable:** *untrustworthy, aimless, fickle.*

How did Jesus show faithfulness?

Chapter Nine

How did Will's plan to rescue Grey Fox show wisdom?

What were Ember's responsibilities as a healer?

What is the best way to handle fearful situations? (*Psalm 56:3*)

What effect can faithful prayer have during a trial?

Character Qualities to Identify:

The three friends showed **Endurance** during the run to rescue Grey Fox.

Endurance: *The quality or ability to withstand hardship or stress.*

This is in contrast with **Indolence:** *Slothfulness, laziness.*

How did Jesus show Endurance?

Chapter Ten

How did Ember show compassion to the Shawnee warriors?

Name some of the good character traits Ember used in examining and treating Grey Fox.

How does one get good character or bad character in their life?

What are advantages of having good character?

What are consequences of having bad character?

Character Qualities to Identify:

The friends showed **Flexibility** in being willing to eat whatever they could find.

Flexibility: *Willingness to adjust ones thinking or behavior to fit changing situations.*

This is in contrast to **Intractableness:** *Ridgid, stubborn.*

How did Jesus show Flexibility?

Chapter Eleven

Describe Susanna's bad character.

What was the source of Susanna's bad attitudes?

What are the consequences of being a selfish person?

How would you describe Susanna's prayer?

How did Prisha and her mother show Jesus to Susanna?

Character Qualities to Identify:

Prisha showed **Determination** to find a way to heal Susanna's leg.

Determination: *firmness of purpose, resolve, commitment.*

This is in contrast to **Indifference:** *Apathetic, having no interest, insensible.*

How did Jesus show Determination?

Chapter Twelve

What attitude should we have as we read God's word?

Do you agree with what Grey fox said about the Kingdom?

Can you be in the Kingdom if you are not letting the King rule in your heart?

What evidence do you see in this chapter that Ember is in the Kingdom?

Character Qualities to Identify:

As soon as Ember thought she understood Jesus' will she showed **Obedience.**

Obedience: *Fully submitting to one who is in authority over you.*

This is in contrast to **Defiance:** *resistance to authority, contempt for those leading you.*

How did Jesus show Obedience?

____

Chapter Thirteen

Name some qualities that made Grey Fox and Will valuable friends to each other.

What does it cost to be a good friend?

What will good friends always do?

What will good friends never do?

Character Qualities to Identify:

William and Dirt show **Resourcefulness** in getting the enemy warriors to chase them.

Resourcefulness: *Being able to effectively use your imagination to successfully face difficult situations.*

This is in contrast to **Ineptitude:** *The physical or mental inability to do something or to manage ones affairs.*

How did Jesus show Resourcefulness?

Chapter Fourteen

What did Grey Fox mean when he said that Will, Dirt, and Jack Cobb were his tribe now?

Explain what Grey Fox meant when he said wanting respect and honor was not noble?

What were the great things Grey Fox wanted now?

What are some character qualities that would be helpful in an emergency?

Character Qualities to Identify:

Asa showed **Selflessness** in ignoring his own wound to save Ember.

Selflessness: *Ignoring your own interests or needs, and focusing on those of others.*

This is contrast to **Selfishness:** *Exclusive regard for one's own interests or happiness.*

How did Jesus show Selflessness?

Chapter Fifteen

How did Will show wisdom in stopping the pursuit of the Shawnee

What good attributes did Dirt and Will use in tracking their friends?

Describe what it takes for a person to push themselves to accomplish something they've never done.

How does one acquire wisdom? (Proverbs 7:1-4; Proverbs 9:10)

Character Qualities to Identify:

William and Dirt showed **Dependability** by rescuing their friends.

Dependability: *Being able to be relied upon, trustworthy.*

This is in contrast to **Unreliable:** *misleading, likely to fail due to poor character.*

How did Jesus show dependability?

Chapter Sixteen

How did Grey fox give glory to Jesus for their rescue?

What does it tell you about William that Grey Fox knew the young scout would warn his friends?

What are some needed qualities of a good leader?

What are needed qualities of a good follower?

Character Qualities to Identify:

When they were finally ready to head home, Grey Fox showed **Decisiveness.**

Decisiveness: *The ability to make wise, accurate and quick decisions.*

This is in contrast to **Hesitation:** *Wavering in making important choices.*

How did Jesus show decisiveness?

Chapter Seventeen

What motivated Susanna to respond to her hardships with hopelessness and depression?

Compare Susanna's response to Paul's response to his disability in II Corinthians 12:7-10

Why is self-pity so destructive?

Where does one find courage to stand against a bully?

Character Qualities to Identify:

Seeing Prisha's kindness to her moved Susanna to **Gratefulness.**

Gratefulness: *a genuine heartfelt appreciation for kindnesses received that motivates you to respond with a thankfulness.*

This is in contrast to **Scorn:** *having no respect accompanied by extreme dislike.*

How did Jesus show gratefulness?

Chapter Eighteen

What good character qualities did Rebecca show in offering to help Ember with her medical duties?

Name some other consequences of sin besides sickness and death?

How has God in His Amazing love dealt with our problem with sin and death?

Why must genuine love be a choice?

Character Qualities to Identify:

Ember showed **Patience** in teaching George to fly.

Patience: the quality of having calm endurance in accomplishing a hard task.

This is in contrast to **Frustration**: *a sense of anger and impatience at the inability to complete a task when desired.*

How did Jesus show Patience?

Chapter Nineteen

Describe what happened that finally broke Susanna's heart.

How can a broken heart have a good result in a person's life?

Describe the relationship Prisha has with Jesus.

What kind of relationship do you want with Jesus?

Describe Susanna's feelings when she said that she wanted to belong to someone who loves her.

Character Qualities to Identify:

Prisha and her mother showed **Hospitality** to Susanna**.**

Hospitality: *An attitude of generosity where one willingly receives guests or strangers and shows them kindness.*

This is in contrast to **Unfriendliness:** *an aversion or dislike for other people.*

How did Jesus show hospitality?

Chapter Twenty

What special character qualities did Lieutenant Fremont and his men need in order to reach General Clark in time?

What is a responsibility?

Describe the important responsibilities Captain Parks had to meet.

What is the hard part about having responsibilities?

Describe the kind of person you want to have the important responsibilities.

Describe someone who is irresponsible.

What are the consequences of being irresponsible?

Character Qualities to Identfy:

In order for the Lieutenant to accomplish his task he needed **Reliability.**

Reliability: *the quality of being dependable, trustworthy and someone who can be counted on to fulfil an important task.*

This is in contrast to **Careless:** *Negligent, taking insufficient care.*

How did Jesus show reliability?

Chapter Twenty-One

What attributes of Jesus are being expressed by Prisha and her mother toward Susanna?

What positive effects can loving others have on you?

Where does hatred come from?

Where does genuine love come from?

Character Qualities to Identify:

Prisha and her mother showed **Loyalty** to Susanna.

Loyalty: *consistent devotion, faithfulness in meeting the needs of someone else.*

This is in contrast to **Betrayal:** *treachery, willingly turning against someone who was counting on you.*

How did Jesus show loyalty?

———————————————

Chapter Twenty-Two

What important attributes did Grey Fox need to successfully infiltrate the enemy camp?

Describe how Will and his friends showed wisdom in dealing with the Indians.

What character qualities did the three friends show by putting themselves in danger to slow down the army of enemies?

Explain what it means to have a strong sense of duty.

Character Qualities to Identify:

Will and his friends showed **Discretion** by retreating from the attacking Indians.

Discretion: *the ability to avoid anything that results in unwanted circumstances.*

This is in contrast to **Rashness:** *careless, unwise, acting with thoughtless hast.*

How did Jesus show discretion?

Chapter Twenty-Three

Why do you think Dirt could not come up with any fresh or creative ideas at first?

What are some things that block creative problem solving?

How should one approach difficult problems?

What was the problem with constructing all the traps?

Character Qualities to Identify:

Will and his friends showed **Adaptability** by using what they found to make their traps.

Adaptability: *the ability to be flexible and change to adjust to shifting situations.*

This is in contrast to **Stubbornness:** *refusing to change or adapt from a predetermined course.*

How did Jesus show adaptability?

____

Chapter Twenty-Four

Describe the wisdom the Indians showed in sending out their fastest runners to catch up to the ones they were chasing.

What character qualities did Grey Fox show in throwing the rocks at the opposite creek bank to fool the Indians chasing them?

Why was Dirt so upset at letting the Indians get past them? What does this tell you about Dirt?

How did Grey Fox bring Jesus into their situation?

When should we bring Jesus into our problems?

Character Qualities to Identify:

Grey Fox showed **Leadership** in guiding his friends to escape the Indians.

Leadership: *the quality of being able to effectively direct a group of people to successfully achieve a common goal.*

This is in contrast to **Incapacity**: *lack of adequate strength or ability, weakness.*

How did Jesus show leadership?

Chapter Twenty-Five

When deciding whether to attack General Clark's men, how did the Indian war chief show more wisdom than the painted shaman?

Describe how valuable Grey Fox was to his friends and the soldiers.

What were some of the things General Clark did that was wise?

What poor decisions did General Clark make?

Character Qualities to Identify:

William had to use **Persuasive**ness to convince General Clark that he could not help Colonel Lockry and his men.

Persuasiveness: *the ability to use good reasoning to convince someone to take a course of action.*

This is in contrast to **Inconclusiveness**: *The inability to produce clear results, the lack of ability to resolve a question.*

How did Jesus show persuasiveness?

Chapter Twenty-Six

What kind of character did General Clark show when he refuse to leave any of the wounded men behind even though they were running for their lives?

 Do you think it was wise to bring Ember to where the Indians were attacking? Explain your answer.

What character qualities did Ember show by getting prepared beforehand for the trip she believed was coming?

What good character traits did the friends show as they made the long trip to Harland's Station?

Character Qualities to Identify:

By turning his back to Ember so she could have so privacy to get cleaned up, Harvey O'Doul showed **Virtue.**

Virtue: *Behavior that shows high moral standards.*

This is in contrast to **Impropriety:** *not being socially proper, immodest, vulgar.*

How did Jesus show Virtue?

Chapter Twenty-Seven

What does Harvey O'Doul's response to being wounded tell you about his character?

What good things can God bring out of pain, injuries, and illnesses?

Describe Rayford's bad character.

What long term effects do hatred, lust and deceit have on a person?

Character Qualities to Identify:

By trusting in God in a dangerous situation, Ember showed that she possessed **Security.**

Security: *Making decisions for my life based on what is eternal and cannot be destroyed or taken from me.*

This is in contrast to **Anxiety:** *worry, nervousness and fear about future events.*

How did Jesus show security?

Chapter Twenty-Eight

How was Ember able to forgive Susanna?

Why is it important to forgive those who have offended you?

What does continued guilt do to a person?

What happens in the guilty person's heart when they realize they are genuinely forgiven?

What did Prisha say gives us the ability to love our enemies?

Character Qualities to Identify:

Through the power of Christ in her, Ember was able to show Susanna **Forgiveness.**

Forgiveness: *feelings of resentment or vengeance toward someone who has harmed you, regardless of whether they deserve it or not.*

This is in contrast to **Vindictive:** *having a strong and unreasonable desire for revenge.*

How did Jesus show forgiveness?

Chapter Twenty- Nine

What are you discovering about Waxing Moon's character?

What are some important lessons Waxing Moon needs to learn?

What character qualities did Prisha show in coming up with a plan to save Ember?

What does it mean to know that you can pray to God anytime you wish and know that He hears you?

In what way is it good to fear God?

Character Qualities to Identify:

When Ember prayed to God she showed Him **Reverence.**

Reverence: *an attitude of deep respect and awe.*

This is in contrast to **Disdain:** *dislike, hatred, scorn.*

How did Jesus show reverence?

Chapter Thirty

What character qualities did it take for Parks and those with him to oppose an army of enemy fighters?

What important traits would it take for a leader to make life or death decisions for those under him?

How did Parks and the men with him show wisdom as they fought the Indian army?

Describe the character Grey Fox revealed in the fight.

Character Qualities to Identify:

Grey Fox showed **Attentiveness** in helping the wounded Captain Parks.

Attentiveness: *showing the worth of a person by giving them your undivided attention in meeting their needs.*

This is in contrast to **Indifference:** *lack of interest, concern, or sympathy.*

How did Jesus show attentiveness?

———————————————————

Chapter Thirty-One

How does Embers description of Jesus cause you to look at the Lord differently?

What do you think heaven will like?

What character qualities did Prisha, Moon Beam, and Prisha's mother show in confronting Rayford?

How would you describe Rayford's character in this incident?

Character Qualities to Identify:

Susanna showed **Love** to Ember when she offered her life for her friend's.

Love: *willingness to sacrificially meet the needs of others with no thought for your own benefit.*

This is in contrast to **Selfishness:** *excessive concern for yourself with no regard for others.*

How did Jesus show love?

Chapter Thirty-Two

Even though he is an unbeliever, what good character traits to you see in Yellow Bear?

How did Moon Beam and Prisha make a wise appeal?

If you realized that you were about to die, what would you want to say to your family and friends?

How would you describe Susanna's death?

What does it mean to leave a legacy and how does one leave a good one?

Character Qualities to Identify:

When Yellow Bear decided to give Ember her freedom he showed himself to be **Honorable.**

Honorable: *knowing and doing what is morally right.*

This is in contrast to **Reprehensible:** *choosing shameful, disgraceful, or despicable behaviors.*

How did Jesus show that He was honorable?

———————————————————

The Dancing Ghosts

About the Author

 Alan Harris is a retired veterinarian who has recently moved to Luray, Virginia, where he and Valerie, his wife of over forty years, make their home. They have six children whom they homeschooled for twenty-seven years, a growing host of beautiful grandchildren, whom they adore...and a pug.

Alan was motivated to write when he desired to share an exciting story with his children. He did not want to just entertain them, but to also teach them important character and spiritual lessons. It became clear that the tale needed to be very suspenseful, and the characters had to be engaging and fun, in order to keep his children interested. The results were *The Tales of Larkin* series, which has five books. You can find out more about them as well as how to use them to teach at **StoriesChangeHearts.com**.

In searching for other subjects about which to write, Alan came up with *The Flintlock Sagas* series. The Dancing Ghosts is the third book in that new series and is a story dedicated to everyone who loves God and an exciting story. Just as he did in all his previous stories, Harris included plenty of adventure, laugh-out loud humor, and abundant opportunities to learn character and spiritual lessons.

It is Alan's prayer that his new series, *The Flintlock Sagas*, and this third book in that series, The Dancing Ghosts, will not only entertain his readers, but also help them grow in godly character and draw them closer to God the Father and His Son, King Jesus.

The Dancing Ghosts

Unknown to them is a diabolical plot to destroy them both and forever change the Larkin's future.

Book 5 **Fiery Trials** - This picks up the continuing story of Hawthorn and his friends. Two years have passed since the end of book three and the jealous Shaman have an opportunity to finally destroy the followers of Jehesus. Devastating disease and an unimaginable disaster must be faced if the King's followers are to survive.

The Flintlock Sagas

Book 1 **The Young Frontiersman** - Young William Hackett is a part of a group of pioneers starting a new life in the wilderness of Kentucky in the 1770's. They share constant peril, as well as facing the threat of attack by savages stirred up by British agents. Set during the Revolutionary War the exciting story demonstrates God's faithfulness to us, whether the battles we face are against physical enemies or spiritual ones.

Book 2 **The Maker's Medicine Girl** - No one knew the dangers of the Kentucky wilderness better than sixteen year old Remember Warren. Her village burned and her family and friends violently murdered by Indians, the girl found herself a slave of a renegade trapper and his Shawnee squaw. Though she doesn't believe it, God has not forsaken her. Will she look beyond the hardship and listen to God's higher purpose for all her suffering? The story reaches its climax as Ember is forced to make a desperate run for her life that will put her new faith to the extreme test.

Keep up with Alan Harris, his short stories about the life of Jesus taken from the Gospel of John, *The Flintlock Sagas*, and his first series, *The Tales of Larkin* at **www.StoriesChangeHearts.com**.

If you wish to contact Alan you can e-mail him at **StoriesChangeHearts@gmail.com**.